Abraham the Anchor Baby Terrorist

Sean Boling

Published by Sean Boling, 2012.

ABRAHAM THE ANCHOR BABY TERRORIST

First edition. March 17, 2012.

Copyright © 2012 Sean Boling.

ISBN: 979-8224749423

Written by Sean Boling.

Chapter One: In The Dorm Room

The cause no longer inspired him. Nobody else in the movement knew that yet. They all assumed he was going to college to become a more valuable member, an insider who would be able to help them hollow out their target while others attacked it from the perimeter. But Khalil had fallen back in love with the world he inhabited. He had come to realize that he didn't hate society; he had just hated being a teenager. And now that he wasn't one, now that he could feel himself reaching a point where he may have something to offer the world, he could not sustain the required level of anger. He no longer saw his surroundings as being filled with people trying to screw him over. Most people seemed as though they were trying to help him: some effectively, some poorly, many taking approaches that he didn't necessarily agree with, but attempting to help nonetheless. Anger no longer struck him as an emotion; it seemed instead to be a hole into which all other emotions fell, and pulling them out was exhausting. The websites filled with prayers and videos of roadside explosions and music that can only stimulate the truly devoted didn't appear to him much different than any other ardent website of any other cause, be it jihad or buying locally grown food. He frankly found the site explaining why *Star Wars: The Phantom Menace* was such a horrible movie to be more convincing than his old haunts that used to convince him that America was such a horrible society.

He liked to laugh at many of the things that used to enrage him. He frequented websites that linked to the most extreme examples of hatred in the interest of making fun of them, and he shared that interest. It was therapeutic. He wasn't just laughing at those who still thrived on fulmination, he was laughing at himself. The day his roommate came home early and caught him slapping his own ass in time to the beat of "The Humpty Dance" was revelatory: after the first few seconds of trying to come up with an elaborate story, he decided to simply beat his roommate to the laughter as a matter of gamesmanship. Only later did he realize how good it felt. All those hours, months, years of willingly seeking out people who would scream at him about how righteous he was, and how irredeemable others were, made him cringe at the recollection. The plight of all those with whom he communicated who actually lived in war zones increased his shame. What did he have to be angry about? And how would his dreams of turning his own home into a war zone help their suffering? He began to think that even their submission to the cause was also a way to provide them comfort. He had a hard time believing that they really wanted the world promoted by the talking points. He had an easier time believing that what they really wanted was what he had, and all of his classmates had. But until that happened, or more than likely if that was not possible, they would meanwhile give themselves a chance to commiserate, find purpose, establish membership, and feel exceptional.

This latest video he pulled up online was so preposterous as to be familiar. The conspiracy theories entertained by his comrades were being yanked through the looking glass by a former congresswoman who was now apparently supporting herself by appearing on half of a split screen on various cable news programs encouraging people to fear all things unfamiliar. She was gravely wedding terrorism with illegal immigration by weaving a story of pregnant Islamic terrorists flying into Mexico and crossing the border to give birth to anchor babies who would then be Terrorist-Americans whose American Dream included the white picket fence, but with the decapitated heads of their neighbors stuck on top of each picket.

Ah, just like him: a Terrorist-American. His parents were citizens, though. Khalil was not an anchor baby. Sometimes as he watched these clips or read those articles or tuned in to those broadcasts he imagined that he could maybe parlay his recent past into a career pushing those same buttons. But he had not really done anything to generate interest from those who would appreciate a turncoat to co-sign their hatred and fear. Just doing what he had been doing the past few years could be enough though: the extremist website visits, international minutes on his phone to extremist area codes, services at extremist mosques. He was probably on the no-fly list. He hadn't tried to board a plane since he was associated with the cause. His parents were funneling enough money for his schooling to prevent any family vacations for a while, and school was within driving distance of home. He could try to board a plane and be taken into custody. That would bolster his credentials, look good on the job application for split screen personality. Ultimately, however, he liked to flatter himself into thinking that he was not capable of working that hard at deceiving people.

But he was in fact deceiving the members of his brotherhood whom he no longer considered brothers, and had been deceiving his family for years before that. The family was easy to misdirect. At this point in this life they were primarily voices on a phone, with relatively rare visits in person. His putative brothers-in-arms, however, were a fairly constant presence. He may have been the only member on campus, as far as he knew, but invitations to meetings and prayer and study groups flowed constantly into his phone and onto his computer. They were a small group, so there was no blending in; the same few guys, each extending several queries per week. The places were always the same, too. There was the back room of the bakery run by a Syrian ex-pat who renounced his love for his new country after his other two bakeries shut down. There was the back room at the Halal slaughterhouse at which one of them worked. There was the back room of the indoor go-cart track which one of them was supposed to be guarding at night. The only time they didn't find themselves in a back room is when they met at the loft apartment rented by one of them in a gentrified part of the city filled with renovated old industrial buildings that now housed tech companies and night clubs. When they met there at night, they could feel and hear the bass line from the dance music pulsating through the floor and walls, which may be why they didn't meet there more often. The vibrations taunted them as they pressed their heads to the floor in prayer.

And it was during prayer that he felt most guilty, for the great irony of the movement for him was how it deflated his faith. He had grown up rather devout, his religion being the most adhesive element for a family being pulled in different directions due to the standard generational conflicts made more strenuous by the added layer of heritage. However in his family, rather than young rebelling against old, he was the one insisting on revering the homeland while his parents revered assimilation. His parents had arrived with their families when they were children, and had found that fitting in was the surest path to comfort. They were good at it. They were naturally charming in any language, in any part of the world. Khalil, conversely, seemed destined to misfire with each attempt at fitting in, sometimes spectacularly so, and needed something to make him feel special if he could not be liked. His ethnic background provided that sense of uniqueness in the absence of being accepted.

"There are plenty of people in the old country," his mother would tease him. "Why do you have to pretend to be there?"

"Somebody in this family has to," he would self-righteously proclaim.

And his father would end the conversation: "Nations come and go. Borders expand and contract. Only God is constant."

On that they could all agree. His parents did not pray five times a day, their mosque attendance was a bit inconsistent (as was their fasting during Ramadan); but they were good people, and believed in God, and did so through the religion they had grown up with. They had even traveled to Mecca when they were younger, when the pull of the homeland still had a slight hold on them and they had yet to establish a full slate of responsibilities in America. He loved to hear that story: the people on the airplane in small groups at a time converging on the restrooms in their modern clothes and emerging in their white robes as they drew closer to their destination, like a league of superheroes preparing to arrive at their Hall of Justice; their numbers growing as they drew closer to the site, groups merging into clusters and the clusters merging into a galaxy of the devoted, circling peacefully, appearing from above like some celestial body captured by the lens of the Hubble Telescope.

He felt closest to his parents when thinking about this story. He often felt that if he had known his parents when they were his age, they probably would not have hung out with him. But Mecca solved that problem. It was an experience they had that he could emulate; the awkward and the confident walking the same circle.

And now his affiliation with the movement was ruining his religion for him. At first it made sense: exploiting something he was good at, playing to his strengths, taking something his loved ones appreciated and become even better at it than they were. And his strength in this field would allow him to feel above the people he didn't love, the people at school and in the community who shunned him. But spending time with his newfound associates eventually allowed him to understand how people must have felt about him when he was at his most frustrated. He saw himself through the eyes of those others when he looked at his colleagues in the cause. No wonder most people had not wanted to spend time with him, while the only people who did were an agitated bunch. And this was an atmosphere supposedly fostered by his beloved faith?

He did not want to pray with them anymore. He wanted to re-evaluate his perception of God on his own, and with those who were less prone to anger. But he was stuck with them. For while their faith, their version of it, was strong, they did not seem capable of accomplishing much related to a fatwa. They had attracted no financial backing thanks to a lack of ingenuity when it came to mapping out any sort of plan; they had established no firm goals, much less a strategy to achieve them, which only added to their torment. And it was this fecklessness which scared him into staying, as he had the distinct impression that they would try to make up for their inability to achieve anything on a grand scale by taking out their frustrations on anyone within their trembling small scale who betrayed them. They would enthusiastically fill their empty posturing about the West with the destruction of one of their own, up close and personal, all of their rage against abstractions made concrete, hands-on, face-to-face.

So he stayed, and he stalled, and when he prayed with them he counted the threads in the rug and traced its patterns as he lowered his forehead to the floor. And when he wasn't around them, he did not pray; he spent most of his time on campus: studying, indulging his curiosity, putting the most embarrassing parts of his past behind him, imaging how he would be able to contribute something of value to the world, exchanging ideas with classmates, growing. He cultivated a habit of pressing the back end of his pen into his forehead as hard as he could stand while he studied, so that the light bruising it left would serve as proof to the members that he had been praying. He felt guilty at maintaining such a façade; for he still loved God, but the rituals had left him cold lately thanks to sharing them with those whose faith troubled him.

The one person he had met through the cause who seemed like someone who perhaps shared his ambivalence was their overseas contact, Tariq. There was something in his voice during the conference calls, a weary tone when responding to the gang's latest cockamamie scheme, which led him to believe he may be a sympathetic ear. He had spoken to Tariq alone on the phone before, and chatted with him on the web. They were able to speak honestly about what was wrong with the group's ideas, as the rest of them would get rather defensive and not want to listen to any critiques. He of course was all too willing to allow Tariq to go off on them, naturally adding his own criticisms as well. And on those rare occasions when the group managed to devise something that actually had promise, Khalil would subtly steer their contact away from the proposal during their follow-up conversation by coming up with some ideas as to why it was ultimately just another flop.

He decided to see if he could push their relationship beyond business and get a more accurate reading on his feelings towards the cause. The video clip of the ex-congresswoman would be the perfect conduit. It made her look a lot worse than them, what with the lunacy of her terror baby hypothesis on display. And if Tariq was indeed wrestling with ambivalence, he could be an important ally in finding a way to extract himself from this mistake Khalil was living. He copied and pasted the link into an e-mail destined for Tariq and called him while he did so. As the phone service found its way to the other side of the globe, he felt the usual nerves when it came to having to speak Arabic. He never studied, just learned by ear from his parents and various family members, and he always felt like he had the articulation of about a middle-schooler. Plus it was exhausting to work out the translations in his head for everything he heard and wanted to say. He could not think in Arabic. In contrast, Tariq could read and write in English perfectly fine, but preferred not to speak it, presumably for the same reasons and to perpetuate a commanding image when addressing the troops. This would not be the conversation to try and convince him to speak it, either, as there was already some additional tension in speculating how to uncover any hidden hesitations his contact may share with him. He projected that this must be what it feels like to call a girl to subtly find out if she had any feelings for him. The connection finally went through.

"Hello, Tariq? This is Khalil."

"I know. I can tell by your lousy Arabic."

Khalil laughed perhaps a little bit too loudly. "Come now, you must have other foreign contacts. I cannot be the worst speaker."

"I do have other foreign contacts."

Khalil waited for him to say more. He did not. Finally they both laughed with a casual familiarity. Tariq picked up the conversation.

"Did you call to warn me about the next big idea from my worst group of American contacts? I still do not know how you found yourself in their company."

Khalil saw an opening, and fumbled for the right way to capitalize on it in Arabic. "I too am confused." Dammit. Not being fluent in a language makes being subtle nearly impossible.

"So why are you calling?" Tariq understandably did not see any reason to pursue that line of conversation. Khalil felt like he was fishing without any bait.

"I have a link I'm sending you," Khalil said, actually using the word 'link'. He sent the e-mail while he spoke. "Have you seen the video of the woman who says terrorists may be sending pregnant jihad women into Mexico to cross the border and have babies here?"

"Why would we do that?" Tariq said.

"I know. Can you believe it?" Khalil chuckled as if to cue Tariq to do likewise. But no chuckle came.

"Seriously; why would we do that?"

"Oh. Um, because the babies would be citizens of the United States."

"Really? Is that the law?"

"Yes. I thought you knew that."

"No..." Tariq's voice trailed off. This was not going the way Khalil was hoping it would.

"It is just a way to scare people," Khalil explained, disheartened to have to explain a joke. He scrambled for a way to at least lighten the tone. "Maybe it is because of the group I am in, but sometimes I feel that people here make us out to be more than we are."

That definitely did not come out the way he wanted to. He held his breath as Tariq maintained several more seconds of silence on the other side of the planet.

"You live close to the border, Khalil, yes?"

"The border with Mexico?"

"I do not think we would make very convincing Canadians."

"There are Muslims, Middle Eastern immigrants in Canada..." it suddenly dawned on him. "Hold on, Tariq. Do you actually think that this is a good idea?"

"You do not?"

"I...well..." He could not come up with a way to turn this conversation around, much less in a manner he could translate into Arabic.

"Why are you sending me this video?"

"I thought it was funny."

"And you thought I, too, would think it is funny?"

"Yes." This was a disaster. Khalil clenched his face tightly, then relaxed it and stared up at the ceiling.

"I do not think it is funny," Tariq said tersely.

Khalil wondered if this could possibly get any worse. "Well...you have not watched it yet."

"I think it is a brilliant idea," Tariq announced enthusiastically, as though his previous gravity was all a mere set-up for this unabashed endorsement.

So it could get worse after all; much, much worse.

"Hello? Khalil? Are you still there?"

Chapter Two: In Algiers

Finding a woman who has brought shame to her family is not easy. Tariq had been searching for several weeks. Having convinced several of his clients that the anchor baby strategy was worth a try, he had been sifting through devout communities looking for the perfect candidate to give birth to their investment. Business had been a bit stagnant lately. No investors were bailing out on him, but he definitely got the impression that they were starting to expect a bit more action for their money. That was always the hard part with his business model. More action meant more attention. And while attention was part of what characterized a movement, you had to pick your spots and plan meticulously, making sure that those who actually pulled triggers and pins and drove vehicles were ready to accept full responsibility, without dragging any of the money interests into it. The best way achieve that separation of labor and management was of course to make sure the trigger men arrived at their fevered state on their own, so that out of self-righteous pride they would not even think of naming anyone else.

That is what made the anchor baby scheme such a great pitch: it was something new, which would play out across an extended time frame, thus allowing him to generate both intrigue and cash flow over a lengthy period. He initially visited shelters for fallen women in the various cities he toured, but he quickly came to the conclusion that those who had been abandoned by their families would be unstable and not trustworthy. His best option would be a woman who was pregnant out of wedlock, and was being hidden by their family, ideally a poor family, so that they would appreciate an opportunity to distance themselves from their daughter in service to a pious cause (and a handsome payday), while the daughter would appreciate an opportunity to escape from behind the walls of the family compound.

But to find such a situation presented some logistical challenges, and in order to establish that prolonged timeline he found so potentially lucrative, he needed to get the front end of the deal going soon before it started to appear that maybe he could not implement his plan, and investor interest consequently sagged. One could not place an ad in a newspaper or online. Aside from leaving a paper trail on his end ("Seeking devout family of disgraced daughter for lucrative offer in service to God"), the family would be trying to lay low, and more than likely would not be plugged in to the world at large and its information services. He could fit his search into his schedule easily enough. He was used to mixing investor meetings with employee recruitment. His current and potential financial backers inhabited the more cosmopolitan parts of each city he visited, as there wasn't a lot of seed money to be solicited in the old neighborhoods. There was labor to be found in those neighborhoods, though; very enthusiastic and devoted employees. And so morning meetings in a shining high rise were followed by afternoon interviews in a stucco hut. Courtesy shuttles from hotels to four-star restaurants were followed by rusty cabs from tenements to teeming bazaars and dinner from a food cart. This polarized agenda played out via short hop airline shuttles across the Arabian Peninsula and Mediterranean ferry boats along the shores of North Africa. His business card heralded him as a Venture Capitalist, and he saw no irony in that whatsoever.

The first several families he had met through various contacts had not panned out. Sometimes the family members lurked in the background if it was a one-bedroom unit, other times the father was the only one present if there was enough space to allow him to hold court. Regardless of the household dynamics, he had yet to reach the point of discussing any specifics related to their daughters.

A few of them spoke local tongues that he did not understand, and he had to rely on someone in the family to translate, which was no help because the only Arabic they knew was through Quran verses they had memorized, and trying to piece together words they were used to chanting in a certain order did not lead to many coherent statements. It reminded Tariq of his conversations with Khalil, that bright kid in America who was saddled with those idiots. If this idea of Khalil's worked out, he would make sure the kid was rewarded. Perhaps a promotion; maybe Khalil could take on a similar role to his own in the states. The fact that Khalil had to strain to speak decent Arabic and still managed to convey such a potentially great idea was a tribute to his ingenuity. Besides, he got the impression that Khalil was not as committed spiritually to the movement, and would therefore make a poor foot soldier. He instead had the ability to keep the cause at arm's length and make more rational decisions, making him management material. Tariq saw a lot of himself in the kid. "The kid". He chuckled whenever he used that phrase, as he was only a few years older than him. But he was much wealthier than Khalil, and Tariq considered success to be a much more accurate measure of maturity than age.

The other few families accused him of blasphemy. He concluded the only reason they agreed to meet with him was to bellow at him about giving their faith a bad name, and all the different ways he would receive God's wrath as punishment. He had heard this speech in various forms before, so he just let them rant and thanked them for their time before excusing himself. One of the fathers, though, caught him off guard by asking him why he does what he does in the name of religion. Tariq paused a moment to prepare himself to be part of a conversation, as he had assumed he was just going to sit there and listen to the man complain.

"Did I claim to be doing it for Islam?" he replied.

"Why else would you be doing this?"

"Why do you think?"

"For power? For money?"

"Power comes with too many headaches," Tariq said nonchalantly.

The man shook his head and gave a contrived heartsick glance over at his family, who sat quietly in one corner of the room. It occurred to Tariq that they were there at the father's insistence, so that they could see him cut this blasphemer down to size. "Money; you take our faith and use it to make money."

"I believe it works both ways, sir."

Now he was genuinely riled up. "What do we get from the likes of you?"

"Recognition."

The man acted as though he had just been punched and needed a moment to recover. "The worst kind of recognition!" he spluttered.

"Wrong," Tariq countered, confidently guiding the conversation towards his standard business pitch, which he usually reserved for investors. "To those who hate you anyway, our services show them you are not a group to be trifled with. To those who do not hate you, they will tell people that our actions do not represent your entire faith. We take the hate, we take the love, and we create respect."

The man stared at him for a while. Tariq was not expecting him to be swayed. He was just curious how he would react, since Tariq had always used a more pious pitch when recruiting labor. Finally it appeared as though the man may cry. He angled his head away from his family to prevent them from seeing his face.

"Such a bright young man," he said, quietly. "Why did you use your talents for such a murderous pursuit?"

Tariq felt his own brand of self-righteousness surge. He stayed calm, as usual, but it was one of those rare moments in which he had to work a little bit harder to do so. "I could have been much worse," he said in an even tone. "In the interest of putting our society front and center, I could be a politician sending many more people to their deaths in battle; I could be the owner of a company that abuses workers and ruins the landscape in order to turn profits that will catch the attention of the developed business world; I could be a lawyer that defends such a company and use 'my talents', as you call them, to concoct elaborate excuses for why my bosses' practices have killed people. My business, however, kills relatively few people in the interest of drawing attention to a cause."

The man seemed to have regained his footing while Tariq had been defending his work. "Every example you gave," the man scolded him gently, as though he had decided Tariq was mentally unstable, "involves killing people. There are plenty of professions that are not in any way related to death."

"Of course there are," replied Tariq. "But there is no money in them."

Tariq was not sure he won the debate. But he did end the conversation.

A few days and a couple of stamps on his passport later he finally found the family he needed. The father was perfect. The hatred in the man's eyes was not directed solely at Tariq, but at the whole world. His intense devotion to God was finally going to pay off. This was not a transaction, this was a sign. Tariq loved it when people referenced his appearance as an answered prayer. It gave him the ultimate upper hand in conducting negotiations. The man brought out his daughter almost immediately and proceeded to talk about her as though she was not there, as though she was a car that they were haggling over.

"Only two months pregnant," he preened. "She confessed as soon as the first month passed, so we were able to get her out of sight before anyone else knew anything. People think she has gone away to take a job in Cairo. She is already gone to them. Actually getting her out of here would be of great help to us."

Tariq looked at the young woman as her father listed her selling points. She wore the hijab, a rather plain one; no fine material, hints of fashion sense, nor flairs of individuality; nothing that would indicate she was secretly straining to be free of it. Her eyes drifted around the room disconsolately, as though sitting in a classroom for a subject she did not enjoy. She was ordinary looking, which was another positive attribute as far as Tariq was concerned. He did not want a woman who would attract much attention. Just to make sure, he asked if he could see her without the hijab, in order to get a sense of what she would look like when posing as a Mexican. The father barely hesitated, and asked her to comply.

Her expression shifted to hatred, directed solely at her father.

He caught her gaze and shot back: "So now you decide to behave modestly?"

Without seeming to concede the point, she defiantly removed her head covering. No waves of alluring locks came tumbling down; she did not shake her head and have everything fall into place as she transformed before their eyes into a candidate for Miss Algeria; not at all. She was as plain as before, with shoulder-length hair; her most distinguishing feature was her bitterness. Tariq looked her over, nodded his approval, then turned his attention back to the father as she set about re-covering herself.

"Any emotional connections to the man she was with?" Tariq asked the father.

"No," he said. On that point father and daughter seemed to agree. Tariq could not wait to inform the investors. He was sold on her, but figured he had better include some pro-forma questions to enhance the professionalism of the mission, and maintain a strong position for the looming negotiations.

"And are you aware, sir, that once she is working for us, she will be posing as a non-Muslim for significant portions of time?"

"I am. And I hope that will help her repent. To have something as beautiful as faith and then lose it can make one appreciate it even more."

"Truly," Tariq responded solemnly, coddling the man's devotion. "And because of the sinful nature of the conception, I assume that you and your family are not interested in helping raise the child that is due to arrive?"

"You are correct."

At this point Tariq heard some soft female sobs from an adjoining room. For a moment he feared he may have jeopardized the deal, but quickly reckoned that any emotional appeals from his family would strengthen the man's resolve even more. Confident of his take on the situation, he applied more pressure.

"I also want to make sure that we are clear on how long of a time commitment this will be. I understand things are difficult between you and your daughter right now. But are you willing to part with her for such a long period of time?"

"To bring the child to term and give birth is not so long."

The daughter burst into the conversation. "I will stay in America and raise my child."

The two men, stunned, turned to stare at her. Tariq tried not to look too pleased.

"I will raise my child to be a great soldier in service to God, a greater example of faith than any of the role models I have known in my life."

Oh, what a positively wonderful development. This moment was worth all the extra trekking from city to city he had endured to find just such a candidate. The only concern Tariq had now was whether the father would let his daughter live long enough to complete the transaction. The man practically shook as he glared at her. Tariq gathered this would be a good time to bring up money.

"Well, sir, for such a dedicated long-term commitment," he interjected soothingly, "I am willing to offer an even better price than the one I was prepared to extend to you."

"And what would that be?" the man said, peeling his crazed glare from his daughter and turning back to the negotiating table. The sobs from the next room grew a bit louder.

"You name it," Tariq smiled.

As expected, the man named a price that Tariq would have found laughable if their roles were reversed. He nodded meditatively and pretended to mull over the figure before agreeing to it. Then he pulled out his phone from the inside pocket of his blazer and started swiping his finger across the screen.

"One of my business contacts owns a shipping company," he explained as he found what he was looking for on screen. "He has a ship leaving here for North America the day after tomorrow. One of the stops is in Mexico." He put the phone back in his pocket and addressed his new employee. He only glanced at the father so as not to offend him and kill the deal. "I will pick you up late tonight so no one sees you leave. You will stay at a hotel tomorrow near the port to prepare for your journey and start your training."

She nodded dutifully, as oblivious as her father to the sobbing in the background, which was now much louder and higher-pitched than before. He placed his briefcase on the table, opened it, and took out a neatly-wrapped stack of cash which he placed on the table. He closed the briefcase and stood up with it, giving them some time to stare at the brick of money.

"That is not a portion of your payment. That is a bonus. I will bring the full amount we agreed upon tonight when I return for you. Would midnight be okay?"

The two of them were in a bit of a daze as they comprehended the enormous change in their family's life that sat there on the table. They looked at each other, then back at Tariq, and simultaneously started to shrug and nod.

"It was a pleasure doing business with you," Tariq bowed slightly.

As he was letting himself out, he heard the source of the sobs shriek into the room where he had just been sitting. The voice sounded as though it was about to scream some sort of protest. But then it stopped suddenly in mid-wail. Tariq grinned to himself and wondered how long they would stare at the money before they said or did anything about it.

Chapter Three: At Sea

Najah had made the decision to remain in her quarters as much as possible within minutes of boarding the ship. If all the women in the world were forced to walk past the crew of a cargo ship at some point in their lives, she thought, then any controversy about wearing the hijab would be put to rest. They might even lobby for the burka if subjected to the same crew that surrounded her. Never considering herself a great beauty, she had always felt more alluring while veiled. She feared that once the world could see what she really looked like, the lack of mystery would result in a lack of interest. But indifference was the least of her problems while making her uncovered debut under these circumstances. Half of the men looked as though they would just as soon assault her on the spot, while the other half would just as soon watch it happen and masturbate. She had never been so grateful for the rule of law before, nor skeptical of morality as a sufficient regulator of human behavior.

In light of this, she was even grateful that Tariq was on the ship. He had made it clear what a valuable investment she was, and thus was not going to allow anything to happen to her (which is why he was escorting her to Mexico). This did not change how repulsed she was by his glib rationalizations of the damage he was doing to her faith. Not her personal faith, but the reputation of her religion in general. She would be fine. She welcomed the challenges he presented her. During her orientation at the hotel when he first insisted that she board the ship unveiled, her initial reaction was to protest, but then she saw right through what he was doing, and decided to make it work for herself. If he was going to use her faith to test her dedication to the plan, then so be it. She would use one to strengthen the other. And so far, at least, she found it easier to see the value of her religious precepts by their absence in the world at large, rather than their hypocritical adherence in her world at home.

Not all of the tests were faith-based, though. He had orchestrated a dramatic encounter just before they boarded the ship, introducing her to a hulking troll of a man whom he claimed was a hired killer that would do away with her family if she attempted to betray him or renege on their deal in any way. The killer did not say a word the whole time, and Najah suspected he was just some poor dimwit who worked on the docks whom Tariq had dressed up in a suit to play the part. Although when someone claims owners of shipping companies as colleagues and drops a couple of decades' worth of pay on your family's kitchen table, you tend to give them the benefit of the doubt when they also claim to know people who kill for a living.

What Tariq did not take into account, however, was whether or not Najah still cared enough about her family at this point for his threat to resonate.

They had organized the meeting with that man who raped her, and then took no responsibility for it. He was supposed to be a promising candidate for marriage, primarily because her father worked for him and saw a chance to rise in the social ranks. But of course father presented it to the family in entirely different terms. This man would make a good husband because he was a good Muslim, a devout man, a grieving widower. The man had insisted on a private meeting, no chaperones. And after it was done, Najah could not help but wonder how his late wife had died.

But all the blame fell onto her. She was a temptress of some sort. Father was furious. Mother allowed him to be furious. He said he should have never allowed her to go to school since all she used it for was to make up for her lack of physical gifts by confusing men's minds. At first Najah thought that he was just mad at himself and was taking it out on her, and would eventually come to grips with what had happened. As time passed, however, that did not seem to be the case. Even if it was, he buried his guilt so deeply within himself and forced everyone to bear its burden so heavily that she just had to assume his decision was final. Her mother had moments when she seemed on the verge of apologizing, but could not bring herself to do so. She stood by the one who owned the home; the one who paid for the home by working for the man who raped his daughter.

She appreciated this unexpected opportunity to sublimate her own pain as well by holing up in her quarters and practicing her Spanish. It was like being back in school again. The studying she was doing was not as demanding, though, even if the stakes were higher. There were no books, no readings, no exercises, just verbal repetition through a series of audio lessons. She understood why, even if Tariq was not forthright as to his motives. They did not want her to be literate in either Mexico or the United States. This would help them maintain control over her. As for not including English lessons in her preparation, she imagined that, too, could have something to do with control, but also simply be a matter of authenticity. If she was supposed to be playing an undocumented immigrant, then she would not know much English. She would learn it eventually, though, since her child would obviously receive instruction. The prospect of coming out of this experience knowing three languages was very exciting to her.

And she did tend to view the plan in terms of what it could do for her, since she was not certain how much she would be involved in the raising of her child. Tariq had told her during the hotel indoctrination that she would naturally be involved in making sure he was healthy (though the gender had yet to be confirmed, he always referred to the baby as a boy). Once the child was old enough to begin his lessons, though, her role was expected to diminish. She would essentially be a caregiver, with no say in how he was raised. Najah wondered if she would be able to make that transition. She was assured that if it was difficult, then she could be released from her obligation and given a severance package. This of course provided no comfort whatsoever. So she studied and tried to learn as much as she could about the new places she was about to visit, and possibly live the rest of her life, all while wondering if she had inherited the gene that allowed her parents to give her up so easily, and if she could embrace that part of her when the time came.

There was a gentle knock on her door. Tariq had been delivering her meals at pinpoint intervals since they launched a few days ago. He would say nothing beyond a quick greeting and an unnecessary reminder that she could leave her dishes outside the door. She assumed at some point he would want to review what they had discussed at the hotel, and apparently this evening was one such time. He lingered as she turned off the audio player and turned her attention from Spanish phrases to dinner.

"Have you spent any time at all outside your quarters?" he asked.

"A little bit. I walked outside after departure to see Algiers from the sea, and when we were going through the Strait of Gibraltar. Since then there has been nothing but open water. And I need to study."

"I appreciate your devotion. May I take a few moments of your time before you eat?"

"Thank you for asking. I did not think the investment had the right to respond."

Tariq acknowledged her jab with a quick grin, and then characteristically moved on to business rather succinctly. "Has your faith been shaken by recent events?"

Najah was always ready to respond when it came to her faith. "My faith has never been stronger. My problem is with my father, not with God."

"Does that mean you do not care what happens to your family?"

"I would not be a worthy servant of God if I wished them any harm, regardless of what happened between us."

He was clearly pleased. "I will leave you alone, then."

Najah did not want the conversation to end yet. As much as she had gotten used to it over the past couple of months, she was growing weary of isolation. But she was also genuinely curious: "Does faith really matter to you?"

Tariq stopped his exit and slowly turned towards her. The pause made her uncomfortable, so she filled it in. "I can understand that you would want to make sure your threat against my family carried any weight. But my sense is that you have no love for Islam, or any faith for that matter."

He actually did not seem irritated by her question once he finally found his way to respond to it. "I find it to be a valuable quality in my employees."

"And what about your investors?" she said, growing more comfortable talking to him. "Are they devout men?"

"Some of them are. All of them are wealthy and powerful."

"And that is what matters most."

Tariq nodded. "My clients tend to think that if they can prod the west into panicking and digging themselves a hole, then they can fill that hole with their capital."

"Why would anyone kill for something they already have?"

Tariq sighed. "If you have never been in their position, then I cannot give you an answer that you would understand."

He started to leave, and then hesitated. "I have told you more than I probably should have. Normally I keep employees in the dark. But you are a bright young woman, Najah. Far smarter than the idiots I usually hire to do the dirty work, so lying to you would be an insult to both of us. You have been presented with a unique opportunity. Whether you do this for your faith, or to get back at your parents, or to forge a better life for yourself, I do not care; so long as you do it. Enjoy your dinner."

Najah suspected she may never again have the chance to speak to him so sincerely. "What if it is a girl?" she blurted out before he shut the door.

Tariq stopped short of closing it. "Then she will be a very dangerous girl."

He smiled at her. And then she was left alone once again.

Chapter Four: In Ensenada

Khalil understood that there were worse phone calls one could receive: an unwanted pregnancy, a death in the family, an accident. But a phone call from the leader of a terrorist organization asking you to pick up one of his investments in Mexico and drive it across the border? His youthful rage had caught up with him in soaring fashion. As he wove his way through Tijuana traffic he lamented the fact that his teenage rebellion had involved an actual rebellion. He wished he had gravitated instead towards furious music, or cutting himself, or drugs; something safe. Nope. He had to go big. And now here he was a few years later on his way to pick up the movement's answer to the Virgin Mary.

He felt as though his California license plates were a siren song to any passing cop who felt about due for a bribe. It was the end of Finals Week for many schools, however, and there were plenty of other college students penetrating the border to celebrate, most of them packed into extreme carpools, which struck Khalil as more tempting targets. The date was no accident, either. Tariq had noted over the phone how it would provide greater camouflage in Mexico and allow Khalil some time to help the girl get situated up north. There was a mosque that would provide "child care" early in its life, and a subsequent "after school program" for when it reached school age, but Tariq was relying on Khalil to assist with many of the initial logistics involving the mother-to-be. He was to help her find a place to stay so she would not be seen at the mosque, and so the child would only have to be there during the training sessions (in the interest of blending in as much as possible throughout the rest the day). He was also supposed to assist her in finding a job, so that she could pay rent. Such a longitudinal investment had to pay for itself in some ways. This was one of the features that really appealed to the investors, Tariq had boasted. Low cost, high potential. Even the cost of the birth would be covered; Tariq had researched a hospital not far from the mosque that was subject to the laws forbidding them to refuse care to women in active labor. All Khalil had to do was get her to the hospital when that started to happen. Whether he drove her there, or made arrangements with someone who would, didn't matter to Tariq; as long as she was shuttled there in time. And once mother and child were settled in and the other members of the cause had taken over, Khalil would be released from his commitment.

All of this was communicated in a single, brief phone conversation that concluded with Tariq telling him to meet them down in Ensenada at the appointed date and time, and for Khalil to find a specific meeting place which he would then text them with on his way down. He wasn't sure why Tariq would assume he would know where to meet in Ensenada. The college connection, he supposed. After all, when Khalil asked his roommate for a suggestion, he was able to rattle off several spots based on past road trips.

Khalil had asked Tariq how he knew it was the end of his school year, since Tariq was not familiar with the American college system. "I can read a calendar on a university website," he had replied. "And even if I couldn't, when the squares go from having words in bold font one week to little pictures of sunshine and umbrellas the next week, I can make an educated guess." This was the kind of dry condescension to an admittedly stupid question that Khalil had mistaken for college-aged sarcasm. It reminded him of the connection he had once felt with Tariq when they were just words on a screen to each other or voices on a phone. The prospect of actually meeting him now was terrifying.

He had strongly considered calling back Tariq and confessing how uninterested in the cause he truly was, and how the whole thing was a misguided dabbling in finding his identity which had spun terribly out of control. But that sounded so pathetic. And if there was one item from his recent frustrating past that still lingered, it was fear of coming across as weak. He thought maybe he was still not far enough removed from that phase of his life to rise above it, but it also struck him that this fear of perceived weakness, or more to the point fear of honesty, may simply be inherently male.

Then there were those "other members of the cause" Tariq had referenced who would be running the long-term legs of the operation. He imagined they would be just as dedicated as his angry little circle, only much more competent since they had earned Tariq's trust. They clearly would not appreciate being trifled with, and would see through any of the stall tactics that worked on his former cohorts.

At least he could now call those cohorts "former", those members of his original cell. Tariq released him from that obligation. He told the gang that Khalil had a special role to play in a confidential mission, and told Khalil that he was far too clever to be hanging around such a band of dolts. He had asked Tariq what his plans were for the old gang. "A group like them comes in handy for when the investors get restless and need to see some action," he said, "or when we need a diversion to allow a more promising plan to flourish."

And it was this casual dismissal of his former colleagues' lives, as creepy as they may be, that Khalil kept returning to as he worked his way through the squalor of Tijuana, and then sought refuge from as he drove along the coast, hoping some picturesque views of the Pacific would take his mind off of how deeply immersed he now found himself in a culture where people you didn't want to work with anymore were blown up.

The best that the ocean scenery could inspire in him, however, was some rationalizing. He was not actually killing anyone, he excused himself. He may not even indirectly kill anyone if the plan fell apart after his phase was completed. A lot could go wrong before the kid reached its teens, or whenever they decided to release their little Kraken. His hands would be clean.

And what really kept him driving was the prospect of spending some time with a young woman; taking a road trip together, seeking employment, looking for a place to rent, assisting in the delivery of her baby. He had never really even gone out on a date before, and now here was an opportunity to rehearse such key moments in a relationship before he was involved in one. Thoughts of gaining such valuable knowledge are what finally calmed him down a bit, more so than any visuals that the coast highway could provide. What an incredible learning experience this could be. Hopefully there would be no death toll attached to it.

***

Tariq tried not to look too disappointed when he saw Khalil approaching. There were two groups of college kids in town it seemed: those who strutted and those who shuffled, and Khalil was a shuffler. To be fair, Tariq had told him to blend in with his fellow collegians, and being in the less confident group would probably help in that regard. It would put Najah at ease, too. So with these advantages in mind, he tried hard to look past this initial in-person impression, and recall what had impressed him about their overseas correspondence:

Discovering Khalil in that idiotic cell had reminded Tariq of the groups of young men he would see lurking together in a shopping mall or marketplace, laughing at their own terrible jokes and trying to look imposing in spite of all their juvenile nervous tics. Occasionally there would be that one kid who seemed to be fully aware of how moronic his companions were, but would dutifully laugh and linger for the sake of being a part of something, even if that something was a fraud. The pull of membership was just too strong. With this recollection in mind, Tariq became even more convinced of what a great idea it was to cut Khalil loose from that low altitude orbit and allow him to feel as though the something he was a part of had profound implications. The next several months would provide an ideal assessment of his value.

While he was congratulating himself for discovering this potentially great talent, Tariq finally had to acknowledge that it was taking Khalil a long time to spot them. They were standing near the door of the bar and grill Khalil had suggested for their exchange and the foot traffic was heavy, but he and Najah seemed to be the only people not wearing t-shirts that brandished the name of their school on it. And that was far from the only feature that distinguished their style of dress from the rest. Even though he was around the same age as some of them, Tariq felt thirty years older than the students just by virtue of wearing a casual suit and carrying the modest business-class suitcase he had bought for Najah upon arrival on the east coast of Mexico. She had left home with only the clothes she was wearing, so they filled it with a couple more outfits, some shampoo, a toothbrush, and a hair brush. He could only imagine how out of place Najah must have felt. She wore what had seemed to be a youthful, floral print summer dress when they bought it, but it now looked downright parochial in this environment.

At last Khalil snapped into recognition and approached them. "Tariq?" he offered cautiously.

"Need you ask?" Tariq replied, gesturing towards himself and Najah, and then out towards the throng of student tourists.

"I know, sorry," Khalil shook his head sheepishly. "I asked my roommate for a recommendation. I should have known it would not be an appropriate place to meet."

"No worse than anyplace else around here, I imagine." He noticed that Khalil had yet to make eye contact with the young woman. "May I introduce you to Najah."

Khalil bashfully gave her a head nod. Najah did likewise. They then proceeded to ignore each other again.

Tariq continued: "Besides, there is not much to say. You already know what your role is, and I need to head back east. When you seek employment for her, I would prefer work that is paid off the books, or how do they say it in America again?"

"Under the table?"

"Yes; under the table. But if you do find that you need documents for her, the people at the mosque can put you in contact with someone who can help. And speaking of documents..."

Tariq pulled out a small red booklet with gold lettering from inside his jacket. "Here is an Oman passport for her. Use it if you need some sort of identification at the border. Tell them she is your cousin who wanted to shop in Tijuana while she was visiting you in America."

Khalil took the passport and studied it. "I have never met anyone from Oman before."

"She is from Algeria."

"Then why is her passport not from Algeria?"

Tariq sighed. "Because Algeria sounds like Al Jazeera."

"I see. So why Oman?"

"Tell me everything you know about Oman."

"Um..." Khalil tried to think of something.

"That is why Oman," Tariq said. "And please destroy it after you reach America."

He then took an envelope from inside his jacket. "Here is more than enough money for the first month rent and security deposit. According to my research, that is the standard procedure, yes?"

"Yes," said Khalil, a bit suspiciously.

"Whatever is left over, you can keep," said Tariq, assuming that Khalil's apprehension had to do with receiving payment for his efforts so far. He lumped together the two funds by design so that Khalil would be inspired to find the cheapest place possible.

Khalil took the envelope but now looked even more bewildered. "Are we going inside?" he asked, "My treat. Are you two hungry?"

"There is a ship leaving late tomorrow from Tampico, and I want to catch it. I have been gone too long already. It was worth the trip, though." He turned toward Najah and nearly smiled. "She is a valuable investment." He then handed the suitcase to Khalil and looked him in the eye: "Very valuable."

"So this is it?" Khalil said, apparently too panicked about being left alone with Najah to understand that the look Tariq was giving him was intended to be threatening.

"The less you know, the better," Tariq tried a more soothing tone. "It is not a matter of trust. It is simply company policy. If the plan fails, you can honestly tell the authorities you know nothing."

This apparently did not put Khalil at ease. As Tariq walked away, he started to think of excuses he could make to investors once this kid screwed up everything before it even started.

"Does she know any English?" he heard Khalil call after him.

"Ask her," Tariq called back over his shoulder, catching a glimpse of Najah shaking her head as Khalil looked over at her.

"How is her Spanish?" Khalil tried again to pull him back. Good Lord, he was like a child afraid of being left at school on the first day. Tariq stopped and turned around slowly like an irked parent.

"Getting better, as far as I know," he said in a tone that matched his body language.

Khalil then paused for a moment. "Well, if she seems to be struggling with it," he said thoughtfully, "we can claim that she is from Belize, and came through Mexico on her way to America. Apparently not as much Spanish is spoken there. And I think they look a little more Arabic than Mexicans do."

Tariq could not help but grin. His faith in Khalil was instantly restored.

"Take care, my friend," he said with a hearty wave in their direction. "If this works, it could be the start of a very lucrative business."

Khalil waved back hesitantly. Najah, meanwhile, had looked angry, sad, and pensive during the previous few weeks, but this was the first time Tariq had seen her look unsure. The two of them looked rather forlorn standing in the midst of all those carefree students. Tariq was grateful for this last desperate image of them as he walked away. Desperation leads to dependence, and dependence is what keeps people attached to a cause. He was certain he would not need to make any excuses for Khalil after all.

***

Najah had really enjoyed the drive from the east coast of Mexico to the west. The most horrifying ramification of her family's plan to keep her cloistered was the thought of not being able to learn much more than she already knew; to perpetually remain the same age mentally, and perhaps even regress emotionally due to frustration. The drive across the country packed a couple of months' worth of education into an exhilarating couple of days, watching the maps she had studied on the ship come to life before her eyes, relentlessly listening to and reciting her Spanish lessons, and then putting them into practice while checking into a hotel or ordering a meal. The towns carved into the foothills of mountain jungles were a refreshing dip after so much time spent in a city built on a desert. After a life so arid, everything here seemed to be heaving with existence. For someone who had loved school, as she had, who loved to study and to speculate on where it could take her, this was a pacifying antidote to the pain of having it taken away from her. Those two days were the satisfying effort of education, and the future that such effort promised her, all in one.

Which made her all the more disgusted as she surveyed the bar while she and Khalil waited for their food. After being rescued from her fear of being mentally and emotionally stunted, here she found herself surrounded by people for whom that seemed to be their primary goal. Were these people really students? She understood the need to relax after a stretch of hard work, but there was such dullness in their eyes. They seemed to be relying on the world to entertain them, absent the ability to generate any curiosity of their own. And the ones who seemed most bored were the ones attracting the most attention, as if all anyone wanted in a boyfriend or girlfriend was someone who looked good, kept their mouth shut, and gawked at them admiringly while they talked about themselves. Heretofore ambivalent about the aim of her mission, if not downright opposed to it at times, she suddenly felt as though shattering the society these people inhabited would be doing them a favor, and force them to appreciate the opportunities they so smugly took for granted. Success was theirs to lose, and they were allowing the score to remain awfully close.

But then she realized if the poverty that lived in the town could not compete with the carnal attractions to get these degenerates' attention, how could anything that her benefactors plan succeed any better? These children stuffed into the bodies of young adults would probably just see themselves as the victims, and call anything that stood in the way of themselves and their complacency as evil. The child who gets something taken away for bad behavior often does not regret the bad behavior, just the loss of that which was taken away.

While he likewise remained quiet throughout her silent diatribe, Khalil was starting to offer Najah hope that there were more appealing versions of Americans over the border. She appreciated that he was neither smooth (like Tariq) nor frightening (like just about all the other new men she had encountered over the last few weeks). She decided to focus on him and his apparent goodness, or at least his awkwardness, to take her away from anger. These qualities of his did not seem to lend themselves to a career in terror. She decided it was time to say something beyond accepting his invitation to eat and ordering food.

"How did you get involved in this business?" she broke the silence.

As she expected, Khalil wasn't quite sure what to say, and not just because his stilted Arabic made it difficult to express how he wanted to say it. "I met Tariq through a group I used to spend time with," he finally said.

"But why did you get involved with such a group?" she pressed, suspecting that he was not entirely comfortable with his role. He was not ready to admit it yet, apparently, as he came back with a standard company line about spreading Islam for the greater good. She nodded, making it clear she was not convinced, as their food arrived. She thanked the man in Spanish and was then rather proud of herself for recognizing and responding to the questions he rattled back at her. Her response to his last question was "Belize."

The man nodded knowingly and bid them enjoy their meal. Najah looked over at Khalil, who broke into a large smile.

"Impressive," he said.

"Gracias," she replied, then in Arabic kiddingly told him that means 'thank you' in Spanish.

"Not all of us college students are stupid," he slyly noted. This caught her by surprise.

"Was it that obvious?" she said.

"You looked around the room as though you had discovered something on the bottom of your shoe."

They shared a laugh. "I am so sorry. I should know that this group does not represent all of you."

Now the pretense was truly over. "What about you?" he said. "How did Tariq decide that you were the one?"

"I imagine he knew the man my father worked for, or one of that man's colleagues."

"Was it hard to leave your family?"

Najah involuntarily laughed, and felt a bit embarrassed. She compensated by quickly settling herself down and fixing him with a very sincere reply: "It was the best thing that ever happened to me."

She could tell that he was recalibrating the direction of the conversation, having now ruled questions about her family off-limits. She was very grateful that her American chaperone turned out to be so considerate, and felt guilty for making him feel uncomfortable.

"I may not have been blessed in some ways," she said, trying to put him at ease. "But I have been blessed with this new adventure. God is great."

"So I take it you are rather devout?"

Now she had him. "I thought we were in this together?"

"Yes. Of course we are."

"And that you were spreading Islam for the greater good..."

Poor Khalil actually looked frightened for a moment, as though she may tattle on him, but then obviously realized "tattle to whom?" and appeared eager to unburden himself. He sighed and took a sip of water before doing so.

"My family was fine," he said, trying to tether each other's motives. "But I had no friends. I had no interests or talents, until I came to faith. It was actually quite strong then. It would not bring me peace, however. The friends were not coming, the circle was not forming. My mistake was asking God to bring me friends, when I should have been asking God to give me strength of character to attract friends. Then I made an even bigger mistake."

He shivered at the recollection and decided to eat for a while. She did likewise before picking up the thread.

"Tariq appreciates a lack of faith in those he considers potential administrators," she teased.

He chuckled ruefully. "I know, I know. Dear God I know. But I certainly did not develop my doubts to impress Tariq."

"Why, then?"

"If you met the members of my cell, you would understand."

"I would never understand abandoning God."

Khalil bristled. "So God is a better excuse for murder than money?"

"I said nothing about murder."

"It is the reason you are coming to America."

"With you as my guide."

He stared at her deeply. Without exchanging another word on the subject, they agreed that passing judgment on each other would never again enter their conversations.

As the party raged on around them, they continued their silence while they finished their lunch. Najah's banter with the server became fairly subdued as well. She was not angry with Khalil, nor did she get the sense he was angry at her. It was anger that led each of them to Ensenada. No sense in spending any more of it on one another.

They walked out of the restaurant and stood on the threshold for a few moments. Khalil put the suitcase down as they regarded the unhinged bustle of poverty and privilege that passed before them. Najah felt as though they were waiting for an opening in the stream of humanity flowing by, looking for a chance to jump in and start their journey. She felt his hand reach out for hers. She let him hold it. They intertwined their fingers as Khalil picked up the suitcase and they waded into the current.

Surrounded by all of that heartbreak and all of those dreadful people who pretended not to see it, Najah took the most delightful walk of her life.

Chapter Five: In America

The line at the border crossing was predictably long. They had been idling for about half an hour when Najah fell asleep. Khalil changed the station from the Spanish talk radio she had been practicing with and found some San Diego easy listening instead. Normally he would have blown right past such a mellow selection, but he was experiencing the "peaceful, easy feeling" that those bygone rockers were singing about, and wanted to revel in it some more.

He looked over at her. She was slightly reclined in the passenger seat with her head resting against the bottom of the window. He had never felt so much like an adult, being so responsible for her safety and comfortable in her presence. Khalil wondered if he would be more nervous if she were more beautiful. Probably. He was trying to be honest about his shortcomings ever since his lack of introspection backed him into the cause. Looking over and studying her more closely, though, now that she was asleep, he certainly found her more beautiful than when he first met her earlier in the day. He gave himself that much credit.

They were just a couple of cars away from the inspection area. He reached over and quietly opened the glove compartment to retrieve his passport. Glancing at her forged one, he decided to leave it in there and hope he wouldn't need it.

The agent approached as the car pulled up to the last spot before the crossing. Khalil handed over his passport. The man glanced at it and handed it back. He then noticed Najah in the passenger seat. Khalil looked over as well and saw her stir for a moment, then settle into a slightly different position to continue sleeping. He looked back at the agent, who silently gestured them through with a tilt of his head toward America.

Khalil drove under the overhang and felt like waking her up just to kid her about sleeping through her big entrance, but reckoned he could just as well do that when she woke up on her own. In the meantime he sent a brief text to Tariq with the news.

His reply: "good".

He liked Tariq so much better before he had started working more closely with him.

The man did have an eye for talent, though. Perhaps the most surprising feature of his interactions with Najah so far had been how easy it was to think of things to talk about once he knew exactly what he couldn't talk about. Her family, the father of her child, the future of her child...they were such obvious items of discussion that to eliminate them was to dance right into conversations that remained light, practical, and if sometimes heavy, never painful. Anything with some weight remained in the abstract: a brief discussion about American values (not his) or Algerian values (not hers); a fleeting tangent about violence in general (not their role in contributing to it); whether those college students turning the beach into an extension of the bar and grill would find a valuable purpose in life (not whether they themselves would). And then things would immediately bounce back into bounciness.

While they had strolled along the walkway fronting the shore, they joked about trying to take a walk on the beach, as the clichés dictate couples holding hands must do, amongst all the boozy co-ed touch football games and wrestling matches they saw. Coming up with a Mexican name for her was also a reliable thread. He assumed Tariq had assigned her one, but no, the boss said she could call herself whatever she pleased, as long as it fit the profile. So they of course tossed around names which got progressively more old-lady sounding or prostitute-sounding. They spoke of what subjects they liked and disliked in school, but while they did so he saw it become a painful topic for her right before his eyes, as it appeared to dawn on her that she would never be able to attend school again. He told himself to add it to the off-limits list, and changed the subject by promising to take her to a more secluded beach for a cliché-worthy walk once they were far enough north to be able to find such a place.

Najah stayed asleep as the car maintained a steady pace for a couple of hours, but upon reaching the Los Angeles area and having to slow to a crawl thanks to traffic, she awoke.

"Welcome to America," Khalil said.

She yawned and stretched. "How long was I asleep?"

"A few hours."

"And that is the best you could come up with?"

He smiled at her and watched her take in the surroundings. It was a particularly unattractive area, one of the parts responsible for keeping the city running, filled with rail yards and power plants and vast industrial buildings surrounded by loading docks clogged with trucks.

"I was hoping to get you to that beach before you woke up," Khalil said, feeling genuinely sheepish about her first view of his country.

"No, no. This is lovely," she assured him, not trying to sound the least bit sincere.

He shook his head and let her laugh at her own joke. Her natural curiosity supplanted her sarcasm rather quickly, however. Barely a mile passed without a question from her about a certain building, billboard, or vehicle.

"You should really be practicing your Spanish," he would say every fifth question or so, which would elicit a playful "shut up" from her and at times a slap on his arm. As they finally broke free of the city and its traffic and reached the shore once again as the sun was starting to set, she became very quiet and just looked past him out the window as they hugged the edge of the continent.

"Beautiful," she said at one point, almost to herself.

"No questions, then? Do I need to explain how the sun sets?"

He could feel her smile as he kept his eyes on the road.

"You should teach me English," she said. "If I am not going to school again, I want to become even more brilliant than if I had gone."

"I am very sorry," he said.

"You will not teach me?"

"No," he corrected. "I would love to, but about school. I should not have talked about that while we were walking together. It made you sad."

"Not to worry," she assured him. "Yes, it breaks my heart. But I can still learn. I still have some control over that situation, at least."

Khalil saw an opportunity to then steer the discussion towards her family, or the father of her baby, but let it pass. He maintained course.

"You may as well be attending college with me," he said. "I will tell you everything about what I am learning. Not just English."

And whether it was because of his offer of a makeshift correspondence course, or because he did not try to open the trap door on her past when she had placed herself so squarely on top of it, Khalil could not be sure. But for whatever reason, she leaned over and gave him a kiss on the cheek. It was humbling, and an honor. He had never felt better about himself.

They were running out of sunlight, so they pulled over at the next exit that posted beach access. They could not have planned it better. The beach was about a half mile down a jaggedly-paved road that switched back a few times as it descended below the highway, and was obscured from the travelers above by a thicket of flora created by a freshwater inlet trickling towards the sea. There were but a few vehicles in the parking lot, and they could not see any of their owners anywhere as they got out of the car. They clasped hands and walked towards the ocean. The sun was low enough on the horizon that you could essentially see it setting if you stayed fixated on it, as they did. Khalil thought of those stories of near-death experiences and how the people described seeing a light and being drawn towards it, and how peaceful and loving it felt to float in its direction. He and Najah were far from floating, but even their trudging through soft sand felt about as peaceful and loving as he could imagine.

The closer they got to the sea, the more the shoreline on each side of them opened up and revealed more of itself: sand-colored cliffs with greenery clinging to it, rocks along the shore catapulting the incoming surf into the air, and not a building in sight. They slowly took it all in, revolving ponderously. Eventually, though, Khalil just found himself looking at Najah's reactions.

"I have never seen anything so beautiful," she said. "Every beach I have been to was filled with people or lined with industry, or both."

She finally noticed him looking at her. She appeared uncomfortable only for a moment, and then seemed grateful for the attention before completing her thought. "It is like seeing the earth before there were people on it."

Khalil pointed out at the horizon, which had bypassed all but a sliver of the sun. "If we keep an eye on the sun, we can watch it disappear."

They focused their attention out beyond the sea. Just before the sun's last vestige plunked below the surface, Najah announced that she had decided on a Spanish name.

"Marisol."

"Very pretty," Khalil said, both of them still staring straight ahead.

"It means 'sea and sun'."

Khalil looked over and was going to sarcastically ask her how on earth she came up with that, but saw the satisfaction in her eyes as they caught the leftover sunlight, and resisted. She really brought out the best in him.

He opened the door for her when they had made it back to the car. He went around to his side and let himself in, and found her holding up the red passport from Oman.

"We are supposed to destroy this, no?" she said.

"Oh, yes. I had forgotten about that. Thank you for reminding me. I will take care of it when we stop for the night."

Najah kept on staring at it as he started the car.

Marisol kept on staring at it as he started the car.

He figured he had better get used to calling her Marisol. He did not want to compromise her identity.

Now that it was dark, Khalil kept his focus more intently on the road as they reached the highway and started north once again. Once they reached cruising speed, he was startled by the sound of ripping paper. He looked over and saw her by the light of the dashboard tearing the passport to shreds. She then rolled down the window and started tossing the pieces out into the darkness. He glanced in the rear view mirror and saw a few of the remains swirl in the red glow of the taillights before being drafted into the night. Within several seconds she was left with nothing.

His discomfort with not knowing how to handle any of the more severe pain she may be feeling got him to thinking about where they would spend the night. He had a few more days before he had to clear out of his dorm room, but that place was not an option: too small, too many people still lurking around, and too far from where Marisol was supposed to relocate. A hotel it was, then. But he was tense just thinking about it. Obviously they would get a room with twin beds. Sleeping together, even in the literal sense of the term, was out of the question. There was her faith, her mental anguish, her pregnancy, the mission. But he really liked her, and the thought of spending the night in the same room had him assuming that sleep would be impossible, and dreading how wired and tired he would be the next day. He would check the stack of money in the envelope and either reserve two rooms, or just one for her and sleep in the car.

Chapter Six: In The Salinas Valley

Marisol had not seen her new home yet. They had driven through the valley and to the hotel in darkness, so she knew it had to be a rural area. She lied in her motel bed and noted the morning sunlight lining the perimeter of the drapes in the window. Her room was on the second floor on the opposite side of the building from the parking lot and the frontage road, she recalled, facing away from civilization it seemed, as last night before she closed the drapes she looked out into an invisible section of earth topped with stars, so what was behind those curtains now would give her a fair representation of what the area looked like. She rose for the unveiling.

What would strike most as uninspiring seemed to her spectacular. It wasn't the ocean, to be sure, but it was still something immense and unfamiliar. Miles of farmland filled her perspective, extending beyond her vision in both directions, and disappearing at the feet of the mountains in the distance before her. It was at once desolate and civilized, with its expanses marked by squares and rectangles, most filled with light green or dark green lines, others entirely black coffee brown, occasional patches of deep red rows were scattered throughout, and the fallow sections ranged from bright yellow to faded gold. A line of trees occasionally separated one frame from another, and a random house or small cluster of buildings staked their claim within some of the other territories. A tractor caught her eye in one of the fields, in the process of turning it from gold to brown as it carved into the earth below the weeds, and she wished that she could apply to drive one, too.

She cleaned up and put on one of her other outfits from the suitcase, a modest pant and shirt combination suitable for seeking work, a place to rent, and meeting the regional managers of a terrorist organization. Once outside on the balcony corridor, she leaned on the railing and tried to get a sense of the valley's smell. It was a little disappointing, but did coincide with the view, she realized, as a combination of natural and manufactured. There was soil and pesticide, crops and crates, water and fuel.

She didn't know where Khalil's room was; she had been so tired last night that she was asleep within minutes of closing the door to her room. She walked slowly along the row of doors in the morning hush, figuring he would perhaps hear the footsteps and peek out to see if it was her. But the doors remained closed as she eventually reached the front of the hotel and was overlooking the parking lot.

Khalil's car was one of just a few in the lot. She noticed that all the other cars' windows were clear except for Khalil's. His windows were heavily fogged. That struck her as curious, but she was just as curious about the view from this side of the hotel. Much of it was obscured by the buildings which rose along the other side of the frontage road and the highway beyond, which she could hear was humming with a fairly steady flow of traffic, a car every few seconds or so. The sound actually reminded her a little bit of the ocean. She couldn't see the valley floor on this side of the valley, but she could see the mountains, which were different on this side compared to the other. The mountains forming the background of her initial view through her window were more like big hills; mounds of baked bread sparsely dotted with trees. The ones on this side were definitely mountains; higher with a very rugged, steeper incline that was thick with trees. There was also a fog bank clinging along the top of it. In conjunction with the position of the sun, she concluded this was the western side of the valley, separating it from the ocean, while the softer side led further inland.

A car door opened and interrupted her geographical survey. It was Khalil, unraveling himself from the front passenger seat. Marisol looked down at him quizzically. He stretched out his arms and leaned backwards, and as he tilted his head back towards the sky, he saw her. His clenched expression then morphed into a smile.

"I have a plan," he said.

He ran upstairs and ushered her back into her room, dying to tell her what he had in mind. He was acting like one of her old friends at school who wanted to share some gossip. But she was rather excited, too, once he shared his idea. He had decided to save on a night's stay because after he checked her in, he counted the money and did some math, and realized there should be a fair amount left over to give her a tour of America, or at least of California, before she had to start work and prepare to have her baby. They would first rent a place for her to live, inform the people at the mosque and Tariq this great news, tell them they would be looking for work for the next several days, and stall as they took in as much as they could of this land they were supposed to resent.

"You would really spend all of the money Tariq gave you on me?" she said.

"What else would I spend it on?" he enthusiastically replied.

"School?"

"I have grants, scholarships, loans, my parents…I do not need it for school."

She was overcome. She put her hands up to her face and felt like she may cry, but was just too thrilled. So she sort of half-laughed, half-cried, and gave him a long, strong hug. Finally she unlocked herself from him and walked over to her suitcase. She held up her audio player.

"I will have so much time to practice my Spanish," she announced.

Khalil grinned. "Very funny; too bad Tariq was not recruiting suicide bombers."

Marisol dropped her mouth open and chased him around the room. He of course did not try very hard to get away, and seemed to enjoy sneaking another hug from her. She could tell that he was attracted to her, and she enjoyed the feeling, especially knowing that his attraction was safe, that she was free to indulge in it without fear of expectations or violence.

Over breakfast at a diner filled with shiny vinyl booths right by the highway entrance, Khalil pored over a local newspaper to look for rentals. He at first had started to use his phone to access the web, but Marisol had asked an innocent question about whether a lot of renters in this area would have computer access, which prompted him to change his strategy.

"House or apartment?" he asked her while still focusing his attention on the paper.

"House, absolutely," she replied. Then it occurred to her, "Unless that will take away too much of our touring budget."

Khalil smiled. "Some of the houses listed are the same price as apartments. We can start there, but I suspect they may be rather unappealing."

And that is exactly what he assumed about the first place they visited. He said "I told you." But Marisol loved it. The house was about a half mile east of the highway on a dirt road lined on one side with cottonwood trees that tilted several degrees from being blown by the wind for so many years. It was no more than a few hundred square feet, located on the same property as a much larger house which was equally dilapidated. The main house was surrounded by a dusty compact car and pick-up truck, and teams of small construction and farm equipment that seemed to be waiting for it to collapse so they could clean up and haul away the debris. The rental house seemed to be keeping its distance, standing on the edge of the compound, which was surrounded by fallow fields for a few hundred yards in all directions.

"Are we looking at the same place?" Khalil asked.

"My whole life has been crowded," she explained, never taking her eyes off of the house. "A small apartment, crowded with people who did not seem to take much interest in me; a crowded city; a crowded schoolroom. This is perfect."

A rustic woman who could have been anywhere from age forty to sixty, having been blustered by the wind and baked by the sun, came out of the main house to greet them in Spanish. Khalil approached her with slow, clear English, which prompted her to say she didn't speak it. Marisol understood what has happening, and stepped right in and managed to hold a discussion with her at a fairly fluent pace, using the Belize line to explain her bouts of incomprehension or incommunicability. Occasionally Marisol would update Khalil on what was happening in the conversation. The woman, whose husband was the foreman for the farm they were surrounded by, asked Marisol what language they were speaking. Marisol translated the question over to Khalil and they looked at each other expectantly for a moment.

Khalil came up with "French Cajun."

He then fed her an explanation that she fought her way through in translating from Arabic to Spanish. "Our families were part of a great migration of French settlers in Louisiana who crossed the Gulf of Mexico to Belize almost two hundred years ago."

The foreman's wife found that fascinating, and took them on a tour of the house. Marisol did not dare look at Khalil for a few minutes for fear of laughing, but then her enchantment with the house helped her overcome that impulse. The interior was as disowned as the exterior; a blank slate. Through the front door was an all-purpose main room with a salvaged table and two chairs near a kitchen sink and stove. A pair of doors off to the side led to a full-sized, fungal bathroom and a bedroom that held a rusted bedframe with a hammock-like web of springs clinging to its center. She heard Khalil mutter something about visiting a furniture store during their upcoming adventure. It was hers, though; she would not even be sharing a wall with anyone next door, much less a room with someone. She told Khalil to shut up and look on politely as she staked her claim to it and negotiated with the foreman's wife.

Marisol added fifty dollars onto the rent each month in exchange for not having to pay any other fees up front. The foreman's wife jumped at the deal. Marisol understood she was losing money on this deal over the course of the year, but she wanted to save as much of Khalil's stack of cash as possible. She communicated the terms to Khalil, and he complied by handing over the first month's rent. They then requested some sort of receipt and proof of residence. She escorted them over to the main house and she used a blank payroll receipt from a booklet her husband had on their kitchen counter that was part of a pile of paper detritus. She then pulled a contract from the pile for Marisol to sign that appeared to be homemade. Marisol was free to move in any time this month. Everyone shook hands.

Before leaving, Marisol thought to ask her about employment in the area, since she and her husband seemed so well-connected. The foreman's wife was flattered, and said that she was sure they could find something for her. Marisol added that it should be something suitable for a woman in her condition, patting her stomach and announcing that she should be showing in about a month. The foreman's wife squealed with delight, as if Marisol was her own daughter expecting her grandchild. She hugged her and said it was going to be so nice having a baby on the farm once again, what with hers all grown up now.

As she escorted Marisol and Khalil to their car, she asked them how to say "welcome" in French. Fortunately Marisol knew the word from seeing it emblazoned on some of the ferries that pulled into the Algerian harbors from across the Mediterranean, and the lingering use of French from the days of the occupation.

"Bienvenue!" the foreman's wife merrily repeated to Marisol as she and Khalil walked back to his car.

"Merci!" The couple called back in unison as they climbed in.

They managed to wait until they passed her and were on their way back to the highway on the dirt road before they started to laugh. They asked each other how they knew that word; Marisol relayed her history with the language, and found out Khalil had taken some French in middle school.

As they waited at the intersection of the dirt road and the highway, Khalil let out an exaggerated sigh and said, "Good thing you have me to help you with all of this."

"Well, you did read the advertisement in the newspaper," she offered.

He smiled and took his focus off the highway and onto her. "You are incredible. I may as well have just dropped you off at the hotel."

She appreciated the sincerity of his compliment, but she kept things light. "Nonsense; then I would have to take a bus everywhere."

Khalil saw a long enough break in the traffic to enter. Once they were comfortably merged, he asked her, "Did she ask about our relationship?"

"Yes," she replied. "I stayed with Tariq's idea: cousins."

He nodded and kept his eyes on the road. She really would have liked to pretend to be his wife. But then her new landlords would wonder why her husband was hardly around, and after the baby was born, why he was ignoring his child. Being together was impossible even as a fantasy.

The mosque was about a twenty minute drive from her new home. It was ensconced in the middle of a parking lot towards the end of a three-block business district in a small town located almost entirely on one side of the highway. The mosque looked as though it was built in a matter of days out of cinder blocks and corrugated metal. Two women behind a counter in the office reception area greeted them and provided a courteous orientation of how the process would be handled. Marisol and Khalil may as well have been ordering take-out food or renting a car from them. Everything was clinical and professional on purpose, Marisol presumed. She would not be a member of the mosque, was not even supposed to be seen near it after today; someone would be picking up her child for daycare. She speculated they were probably being paid based on how well the project was progressing. Perhaps they were being monitored, though she wasn't sure exactly how.

As Marisol was telling them about the house she rented and her job prospects, making sure to give Khalil all the credit for leading her to these opportunities, a man emerged from a door behind the two women. He seemed to be made entirely of hatred. Marisol would not have been surprised to discover that there were several quivering torture victims in the room he just exited. The ladies did not look back at him, but knew he was there. Marisol and Khalil did not look at him, either. At least she assumed Khalil was not looking at him, because she could not imagine anyone being able to do so for more than a second after first making eye contact.

The ladies continued their spiel in a slightly less comfortable fashion. They handed her some brochures from a few of the free clinics in the area and encouraged her to seek some prenatal care, made sure that she and Khalil had a plan for getting her to the hospital during labor, and if they had a back-up plan as well.

When they reached the end of their pitch, they paused anxiously, apparently waiting to see if the man still looming behind them had anything to add. He did not. He simply continued to stare, with the perceived ability to stare at everyone at the same time since few dared stare back. The ladies then asked Marisol and Khalil if they had any questions. Marisol snuck one more glance at the man, and she skipped a breath as he looked right at her when she did. For the first time since she accepted the job, the part that death played in it was made clear. His eyes were a body count. She looked away.

"No," she heard Khalil say. "No questions."

The man submerged back through the door. Everyone tried not to exhale too loudly with relief.

"Though we will not be seeing much of you," one of the ladies said. "We look forward to working with you."

"And we certainly look forward to getting to know your child," said the other.

Marisol and Khalil thanked them, and left. Neither of them said anything about the meeting. After an extended moment of silence, they instead started planning their vacation.

Chapter Seven: Around The Pacific Time Zone

Khalil needed to stop by campus and clear out a few things from his dorm room. He offered to drop off Marisol at a nearby coffee house so she would not have to be surrounded by an unrequited dream. She really wanted to see the school, though; insisted upon it. And once they were there, he was glad she did. Marisol positively floated around the facilities. She was like an art student at The Louvre, a devout Muslim at Mecca.

"Are the universities in Algiers really so bad?" he asked her as they rested on the grass near the student center.

"They are fine," she said. "But this is something more. Many of us spoke of trying to attend college in the United States."

She looked around wistfully, as though it was dawning on her that she could only look and not touch.

"I knew it," he noticed. "We should go."

"I am glad we came," she insisted. "This memory will be very valuable to me; always. Perhaps I will be able to attend later on in life."

Given the circumstances of her entrance into the country, Khalil could not imagine even such a remarkable person as her being able to pull that one off. It was once again time to run interference.

"The tour," he announced. "I have the perfect place for our next stop."

"What about your things?" she said. "You should bring them to your house."

"I can keep them in my trunk. I was going to call my parents and tell them I was taking a trip with friends to celebrate the end of the school year and I would see them in a few weeks."

"You do not want to see them? I can stay at a hotel while you visit. I understand they should not see me."

"They are quite happy with each other. I feel like a bit of an intruder these days when I visit."

Marisol apologized if she was bringing up a sensitive subject. He assured her it was not. He was happy that his parents did not live through him. "If they did," he said. "I would no doubt disappoint them. Better not to have such expectations placed on you."

She threw her head back and laughed, half sincerely, half for effect. "You have given me words to live by."

Khalil wasn't sure whether she was thinking of herself or her baby. It was so hard not to say something that somehow related to her struggles. The fact that he loved being around her in spite of these challenges provided more evidence of how much he cared about her.

"If you really want to see where I grew up," he said. "We can stop by when I know they will not be home."

"I would like that," she said. He had never been so excited about going home before.

They drove slowly down his block upon arrival. The houses weren't very interesting; the neighborhood was about two parts modest, one part upscale. He supplied some narration about some of the people who lived in the houses now and in the past. But when he heard himself tell the stories, he realized the people inside weren't very interesting either. He fashioned the only reason Marisol seemed to find the artifacts inside his old home intriguing is because of the personal connection vested in them. His old room was slowly giving way to being a guest quarters, with the few surviving remnants of him coming in the form of stickers he had plastered on the back of the door and the sides of the dresser. They weren't even accurate representations of him, either, as they were decals of sports teams and pop stars he had not really followed; he had just received the stickers free in bags of party favors or packs of candy and had thoughtlessly stuck them thus. Now here they were forming a last stand for proof he had lived there.

Marisol seemed to be enjoying the experience enough, though. She mentioned that once you were this far outside of a city in her part of the world, the conditions started to get rather bleak. He was grateful for the reminder of how good he had it growing up, and vowed to stop his interior grumbling. He was inspired to take her around to some of the parks he played at, the schools he attended, and hang-outs he frequented. He didn't tell her how often he was by himself when he troubled these places. That had already come up in one of their first conversations, anyway, and in light of her comparison to the suburbs of Algeria, at least he had not been starving or frequently ill while trying to overcome his childhood solitude. If only there had been someone like her at some point in his history with this place. Maybe there had been and he was too angry to notice.

It dawned on Khalil that he could still incorporate the grand entrance to the tour he had planned before the hometown detour made its way onto the itinerary. He turned into the shopping center with a Costco lording over it.

"Let's pick up a few supplies for our trip," he said slyly.

"Okay," she agreed innocuously.

Khalil grabbed a cart and grandly rolled it towards the gaping entrance, looking back at her and feeling a bit like Willy Wonka letting the golden ticket holders into his chocolate factory. She was taking it all in very much in stride, however. He kept on expecting the glow of wonder to finally kick in after each turn of the corner and new aisle three stories' high worth of goods. But aside from an occasional squint or contemplative stare at a specific item, her countenance was that of any other shopper. She noticed him looking at her eagerly.

"Are we going to buy anything?" she asked.

"Um...yes. Of course."

"You seem unsure. I thought we were here for supplies."

"Well..."

And then a glow finally shone on her face, but it was of recognition, not amazement.

"Ohhhh," she said. "I understand now. This was supposed to be the big 'Welcome to America' moment."

"Yes," he admitted. "It always seemed to work on my mother's family from Jordan."

"And in the movies," she piled on, "and typical immigrant stories."

"Yes, those too," he said, starting to see the humor in his gaffe.

She stood right in front of him and took his hands. "If you want to show me America, Khalil, show me the best it has to offer. Show me what is beautiful about it, what makes it unique. As for places like this, we can treat them like everyone else does: a part of everyday life; normal, everyday life."

He picked up her hands, put one on top of the other, and kissed the stack. They walked through the store getting what they needed, sharing free samples of food at the promotional stands, marveling at how anyone could possibly need such a big box of Cheez-Its, and doing what people do when they go to Costco together.

Having basked in the beauty of the everyday, they started to invest their money in the extraordinary with a trip to San Francisco for dinner and an overnight stay. En route, Khalil received a text from Tariq. Since he was driving, and he assumed Tariq would be writing in his usual sparse manner when composing English, he turned on the feature that would read it aloud for him. A robotically pleasant female voice spoke on his behalf.

"The people at the mosque said you checked in. Good."

The two of them laughed at such an incongruous voice playing the role of Tariq. Khalil translated for Marisol. They decided it would be a good idea to reply. Together they came up with something that Khalil then spoke slowly and clearly in the direction of the phone as Marisol held it aloft for him: "Yes. Was going to tell you. Busy considering different jobs being offered."

Apparently Tariq had some time on his hands. He replied back quickly. "What did you think of the people there?" his female avatar asked.

Without even bringing him up, they decided to ignore the man who had hovered in the background and focus on the two women at the counter. "The ladies were very pleasant and helpful."

Another quick reply: "What about Mohammed?"

Khalil didn't need to translate that one. So that was his name. They drove in silence for several moments before Khalil responded, "He did not talk to us."

The mechanical voice by now had seemed to adopt Tariq's personality and sounded rather steely. "Talking is not what he does." They could practically hear him laughing as he sent the text.

Upon receiving Khalil's translation, Marisol decided to change the subject and end the conversation at the same time. She suggested and Khalil said aloud: "We will keep you informed of the job search."

"Good luck," Tariq replied. And they were ostensibly free to enjoy the rest of their evening.

And truly they did, as the pall cast by those they worked for was sublimated by the beauty they surrounded themselves with, not just on their trip to San Francisco, but everywhere they went for those two weeks.

That first evening they dined while overlooking the city towards the bay, able to take in both the Golden Gate and Bay Bridge. As they walked along the waterfront after dinner, they encountered some teenagers on their senior prom celebrating their last days at the top of their sequestered heap, the teens' youthful exuberance at temporary independence made that much more lively by how overdressed they were. There was no sleeping in the car for Khalil, as price and location prohibited. They opted for twin beds, and Khalil actually found it was quite easy to fall asleep in her presence, his feelings for her making him feel contented and grateful, rather than the least bit agitated. They adopted this policy each night of their journey, and each day made it a policy to encounter majesty. They headed northward over the Oregon border to see Crater Lake, something Khalil had always wanted to do but had yet to, which allowed him to experience it as innocently as Marisol was. This allowed him to see Mount Shasta for the first time, too, both on the way there and back, and again share her wonder. But he found even as they made their way through places he had been before that he remained impressed, perhaps even more so than when he had seen them as a child. The Sierra Nevada Mountains, Lake Tahoe, Yosemite Valley...they read like a favorite book or movie, in which you find things you had not noticed before due to age and experience. Mono Lake almost had them convinced that they were on another planet, so they figured it was time to do something very Earth-like; off to Hollywood they went. Throughout their journey they texted Tariq on occasion, concocting job opportunities they were supposedly looking into but finding inappropriate for Marisol. They took a bit of delight in being the manipulators for the time being, even if they knew that time was limited. From Hollywood they traced a route back to the Salinas Valley that served as a fitting finale to their date with America: up from the underbelly of the entertainment industry into the mountains hosting the Los Padres National Forest, down into the San Joaquin Valley and its field crops and orchards, veering west through the oil fields and derricks surrounding Taft, then catching a tight road that switched back and forth up through the mountains into the vineyards and cattle ranches of San Luis Obispo County, all in a span of three hours.

Khalil mentioned the drive was like a real live version of "It's a Small World". Marisol wasn't familiar with that term, and as soon as Khalil mentioned that it was a ride at Disneyland, he realized that they had not gone there and started apologizing. Marisol waved him off. "Another standard immigrant myth," she assured him.

As they drew closer to her new home, they remembered that there was no mattress on the bedframe. They would buy one tomorrow, and spend tonight in the same motel they had utilized for Marisol's American debut. This time Khalil did not sleep in the car, in light of their twin beds' routine.

They watched a baseball game on television while lying on their respective beds, and Khalil tried to explain the rules to her. What excited her most, however, was when they would fade in from a commercial break with various shots of San Francisco, where the game was being played. She delighted in the recognition that she had been there, was a part of the landscape, if only for one day. Eventually they grew silent and just stared at the screen without reacting to anything on it, both becoming lost in their summaries of the past couple of weeks, growing tired at the thought of everyday life reasserting itself tomorrow, even if their everyday lives were now forever altered. As he hovered between sleep and consciousness, Khalil started to feel as though their beds were drifting apart, floating away from each other. The weightless sensation suddenly gave way and his bed seemed to plummet. He convulsed and awoke.

He looked over at her bed and by the light of the television could see that she was asleep. He reached for the remote and turned the TV off. When his eyes adjusted to the darkness, he looked over at her again, and found that he could still see her from the streetlights filtering through the drapes from the parking lot. He watched her with as much intensity as he had watched some of the most beautiful places on earth they had visited. She breathed deeply, stirred, and rolled over onto her side. Once she settled into her rhythm again,

Khalil rose from his bed and softly made his way over to hers. He lay himself down by her side, behind her, and waited. Then he wrapped his arms around her, and waited. He realized he was holding his breath, and tried to regain it as quietly as he could. But then he felt her adjust into a more comfortable position and he clenched up again. After a few breathless moments, she tucked her arms around his and hugged them against her. He exhaled slowly. The replenishing breath that followed was the most life-affirming he had ever experienced.

Chapter Eight: In The Routine

The job was making bouquets for a wholesaler in a warehouse just outside of Salinas, making it convenient for trucks to pick them up for distribution to various grocery stores. It was convenient for Marisol, too, as the foreman and his wife arranged for a friend of theirs who also worked for the wholesaler to stop by the house in the morning and include her in a carpool full of fellow bouquet makers. It definitely beat working in the fields, especially for someone in her second trimester, but had little else going for it. The warehouse remained cold and damp due to the early morning hours of operation; such conditions were good for the flowers, and the batches had to be completed by the early afternoon pick up. All the ladies wore rubber gloves since they had to constantly reach into piles of wet flowers to gather the pieces for their creations, which may have kept their hands dry, but did nothing to keep them warm. And the creations were not really theirs; rather they were predesigned by the stores requesting them, so all the ladies did was put them together as they might assemble a circuit board or an automobile. The wholesaler constantly skulked around and looked over their shoulders, which she could understand in terms of maintaining quality control, but he did it with a cup of hot coffee he was perpetually freshening up in one hand and a rotating array of delicious-smelling bakery items in the other hand, none of which was ever offered to his employees. Her co-workers were pleasant enough, but had no interest in widening their circle of friends. They had mostly come from the same area of Mexico, many were related, and Marisol could tell they enjoyed feeling as though there was someone beneath them. Each reminded her of her mother in their own distinct ways: their passive aggressive inquiries into whose husband was the bigger bastard, their braggadocio concerning what they had done to spruce up their measly homes, their padding of their children's biographies, and their fear of aging. Marisol's world was starting to feel small and cruel again.

She still had weekends with Khalil. Every few weeks he would bring her to the clinic for a check up to make sure her pregnancy was going smoothly. They still had to maintain the ruse of being cousins in order to avoid any uncomfortable questions from those on duty, but when they were out having lunch, running errands, or seeing a movie, they enjoyed fielding the smiles from those who would look at her swollen belly and see the two of them holding hands. Some would even congratulate them and ask when she was due and if they knew if it was a boy or girl, to which they could honestly say they did not know. The prenatal care she was receiving was bare minimum and ultrasound tended not to be included, which was fine with her because she really didn't want to know anyway.

Tariq would call Khalil every so often during his visits. She was intrigued that he was calling instead of texting like he used to. As for Khalil, the calls made him nervous, even though the topics of conversation seemingly revolved around standard shareholder concerns such as her health, her job, and if anything out of the ordinary had transpired that may jeopardize the project. Sometimes Khalil would not answer when he saw Tariq's name flash on the screen. She asked him why he thought Tariq had switched mediums, and Khalil brushed it off as an Arabic primer, a means for Tariq to keep him connected to the native language since they were spending so much time surrounded by English and Spanish. Marisol couldn't tell if Khalil really believed that. She certainly didn't. She pressed him on it once, and he gruffly tried to convince her that speaking a language in which he wasn't articulate was exhausting, and sometimes he wasn't up for it, and she of all people should be able to relate to his discomfort. Fair enough, she decided, and let it pass. They had after all bought some books and CDs dedicated to learning

English, since she was getting plenty of Spanish on the job, and Khalil served as her tutor before school started.

It was a bit more difficult for him to make it down every weekend once school did start. He did have some great stories to tell about his classes, however, so the weekends that he did manage to make it down were all the more enjoyable. But she started to feel insecure, like she needed him too much. When she accepted her assignment to come to America, she had imagined herself as becoming fiercely independent. And now here she was pining for more time with a young man. She started to pray more, feeling as though part of the problem was that she was turning her back on God. He was the reason she was here, in every sense of the word "here", and now she was putting more faith in a person instead.

Besides, there was already another person on the way who was making her life difficult enough. The third trimester was exhausting and painful. She cramped up at work constantly, which at least garnered her some attention from the human hens. While at home she was almost always lying down, either sleeping or fretting. In prayer she could not strike the preferred position, but recalled the words of one of the imams who visited her school, who assured the girls that when the day came for them to bear children, the lack of prostrations could be forgiven if the calling was sincere.

She sometimes had doubts about how much strength her rededication was actually providing her. She felt it necessary to forge on and remain consistent, though, hoping that the repetition would finally convince her that she could handle the pain that was approaching: of childbirth, of surrendering a large portion of her parenting responsibilities, and of the inevitable severing of her relationship with Khalil.

He seemed to have become oblivious to the fact that when his obligation was up, so was their time together. He had been talking about spending time with her and the baby on weekends and during semester breaks. She would remain silent and evasive when he would talk like this, at most suggesting he should pull back on his expectations, considering how busy he would be with school and how the child's training would become progressively more involved with age.

Finally one day as Khalil was applying a fresh coat of paint to a crib they had bought at a second-hand store, he asked her if there was a problem. She reminded him of the bargain he had struck with Tariq.

"I will call him, or text," he offered simply.

"And tell him what?" she snapped, deciding it was time to stop avoiding the subject.

He seemed unsure of which direction to take: hurt or anger. He went with hurt, trying to diffuse the situation. "Tell him that I want to continue to be with you."

She would not yield. "And when he asks why, what reason will you give him?"

"That I love you."

Marisol had never heard anyone say that to her before. She felt a charge of emotion that nearly broke the surface, but calculated that she had to remain in control if she wanted to save the person who said it. She worked hard to try and regain her balance as soon as possible. Khalil apparently sensed this and tried to comfort her with a hug. It worked at first; she appreciated his touch and was about to return his declaration; but then he said that everything was going to be fine. Her balance returned.

"Do you really believe that?" she pulled back and looked at him in disbelief.

He chuckled. "I never thought of myself as a romantic before. But now..."

"Love is not going to save the day, Khalil," she interrupted him and extracted herself from his arms. "Love has no place in this business. Tariq and his board of directors see love as a threat to their investment. Love is not part of the plan."

He appeared to be reconciling himself with reality, while desperately searching for ways to stave it off. "But we could try," he said. "Tell them the situation. What could it hurt?"

"You!" she belted, teetering on the edge of her emotions again. "It could get you killed. I will not let Tariq sick that horrible man on you from the mosque."

Khalil gave up. He stared at the floor, his dreams seeping out of him. Marisol watched him come to the realization that he was going to have to search for love all over again. He looked up bravely, but then lapsed back into hopelessness upon making eye contact with her.

"Once in a while," he managed to say. "Can I visit once in a while?"

She smiled and nodded. "Once in a great while," she said, and this time she initiated the embrace.

They stood there in each other's arms for anywhere from a few minutes to the rest of the weekend, as though they could not think of anything else to do.

Chapter Nine: In Labor

Even though it was during the winter break from school, Marisol did not contact Khalil for a ride when her contractions signaled her that it was time to have this baby. She relied on the foreman and his wife instead. She was surprised at herself, how measured and calm she remained during the process of checking in and being prepped. Her Spanish comprehension was one hundred percent, and her articulation was effortless, if not fluent. Even questions from the nurse about the father's identity did not faze her.

"I was raped," she responded, as though checking a box on some paperwork.

"Do you want to offer the baby up for adoption?" the nurse then asked.

"No thank you," she said, as though declining a refill of iced tea.

Listening to herself respond, she wondered if all those who treated her pregnancy like a business transaction had influenced her more heavily than she realized. Maybe she was just returning to her familiar old self. She had been so adept at suppressing her emotions back home, and thought perhaps a new version of herself was emerging with Khalil. But apparently that was just temporary. Here she was in a new country, learning two new languages, but was not growing from the experience. Her frustration with this possibility almost made labor pains a welcome diversion from these thoughts. Almost.

Her intentions to pray more were thoroughly fulfilled during labor and delivery. Any questions about whether God is just or spiteful didn't matter, she just wanted relief, and for whom else could she scream?

And scream.

And scream.

When it was over, and she lied there deflated with not a single thought in her head, the first one that came to mind is that moving between such searing single-minded intensity and total vacancy was rather comforting. It provided such clarity. There was that thing, and there was nothing.

But then she heard the baby cry, and complexity reigned once again.

A nurse held him so she could see him. It was obvious that he was a him, but the nurse made the official announcement anyway, with all the aplomb of a voice mail recording: "It's a boy."

Marisol's practiced veneer shattered. Her sobs rolled up from within her so violently that she thought she may suffocate, each gulp of air scooping out more of her insides. The decibel level of her crying far surpassed that of the baby. One of the staff members handed her the baby, now wrapped in a rough cloth blanket, and she heard a colorless "congratulations," from someone as they started to clean up and break down the equipment. The effect was that of a talent show and her turn on stage was up. She was wheeled out of the room in favor of the next contestant.

She could barely catch her breath enough to be able to wipe away some tears so that she could see her boy for a second before more tears blurred her vision. It was hard to get a good look at him in her condition. But her emotions were not inspired by him specifically, more so simply because he was a boy. She was so happy that she had not brought a girl into this world filled with so many awful men. And she was so blue that she had brought a boy into this world who was going to be groomed explicitly to be one of those men.

Upon reaching a room for her recovery, a nurse gently told her that they would have to take the baby in for measurements and an examination. Marisol handed him right over, which surprised the nurse, who had misread the tears. The nurse shifted into a more professional tone and asked what name they should put on the birth certificate. Marisol calmed herself down but could only shrug, too exhausted from the birth and her breakdown to speak. The nurse said to think about it and she could provide a name later.

Breathing deeply and regaining some equilibrium, she took in her surroundings and saw another woman sharing the room with her. She was nursing her baby and smiling over at Marisol, who managed a wan smile in return before fixating on nothing in particular in front of her. No names were coming to mind. Her whole pregnancy had been in many ways a prolonged putting-off of having to deal with this moment. She could not go with a Muslim name, and as for Spanish names, the only male she knew was the foreman, and she couldn't use him as a namesake. That would be weird. She thought of names that appeared in both Muslim and Christian sacred texts, and decided she may as well go with the instigator of each: Abraham.

The foreman and his wife came cautiously into the room. Marisol was actually happy to see them. She greeted them with a smile and thanked them for the ride. Her warm welcome served as a starter's pistol for the wife, who hence gave herself permission to wail her congratulations and flail her arms in celebration as she came in for a hug. The foreman provided ballast in the background and asked calmly if she would need a ride home. Marisol thought of the only other person she would like to see at this moment.

"Could you call Khalil for me?" she asked him.

The wife cut in. "Is that the name of your cousin?"

"Oh…" Marisol realized that she should not have provided his Arabic name.

"Such a beautiful name," the wife continued. "It must be French."

"Yes," Marisol quietly breathed a sigh of relief. "An old family name."

The foreman took out his phone and asked for the number. He followed Marisol's directions, listened to make sure the connection went through, then handed her the phone and shuttled his wife out of the room.

"We will be back later," he said. "Congratulations."

As they exited, Marisol wished for a moment that she had named her baby after the foreman. But then she remembered her son's predestined career, and remained glad that she had not. Good men are hard to come by, she thought, as she waited for the only other one she knew to answer.

Instead she got his voice mail. She spent the duration of his greeting wondering if she should really deliver this kind of news in this manner. But who knew when she would have the chance again, since the mosque forbid her to have a phone and she had told Khalil to stay away. Then there was the mother next to her, but Marisol would be speaking Arabic in order to express herself as clearly as possible, so it was a safe bet her roommate would not be able to eavesdrop. She decided to proceed.

"Hello, Khalil..." she vowed to really think about what she was saying throughout what followed, and not fill in any blank spaces with verbal saboteurs such as "umm" and "ah". She would allow dead air to linger until the right words arrived. "I had the baby. I decided to name him Abraham. That should work out well. His daycare providers and trainers can call him 'Abra-HEEM', and everyone else can use the American pronunciation. Maybe even call him 'Abe'. I went to my landlords and asked for a ride to the hospital. I did not ask them to call you then because I really thought it would be easier this way. But I am scared now, Khalil. Seeing the baby, holding him, it showed me a future that I had avoided contemplating. I see no love in my life. I do not know where it would come from. Any good people I meet, I will have to lie to them. And aside from you, the only people who will know the truth are wretched. The only man I have ever been with raped me; and the only man who ever loved me I sent away because I could not bear to face our deadline. And now our deadline is past. Perhaps we can wait before contacting our administrators, and spend what time we have together. If you agree, please come by the house as soon as you can."

Chapter Ten: On Duty

He parked in a fallow field across the highway from the dirt road that led to her house. Parking on the highway would draw attention, perhaps even from the highway patrol, wondering if he was in distress. But in the fields, everything and everybody becomes part of the landscape to those driving by who bother to look out the window. A pickup truck is supposed to be there; the people belong there; a crop is a tractor is a worker.

Tariq didn't call him very often. He took pride in that. And when he did call, it was never to remind him of his responsibilities; it was to remind others of theirs. Such was the case with the anchor baby mama and her escort. Tariq wasn't positive, but based on phone conversations he had been having with the escort, he strongly suspected the relationship had become more than professional, and that they were holding out on the organization when it came to their investment. That baby should have been born by now.

He had scouted the residence a few days earlier, and recognized the kid's car from their visit to the mosque. The larger house had an enormous nativity scene as part of its Christmas display, so he assumed the owners would be attending church this morning. Sure enough, he saw some headlights through the fog approaching the highway. When the vehicle revealed itself just before reaching the end of the dirt road, it was indeed the pickup truck that had been in front of the main house, with an older couple in the cab. They turned onto the highway easily thanks to the light traffic flow on a Sunday morning.

The Sunday calm also made it easy for him to walk leisurely across the highway. He left his truck in the fields so that the love birds would not hear him coming. But he also genuinely enjoyed the hike up the dirt road with a purpose awaiting him in the distance.

Moments like this reminded him of being on patrol in the Arghandab Valley in Afghanistan.

He liked to keep things simple; choose a side, fight for it. He didn't care whether this mindset was due to brain chemistry or growing up in a religious household. That's just how he felt, and he couldn't remember feeling any other way. When those jets hit the towers, the choice was clear: it may have been Muslims who flew them, but he was an American Muslim, and was determined to show the world that he was on the side of good.

His two combat tours conformed to his expectations of us versus them. He feigned ignorance at knowing Arabic, because he just wanted to fight, not translate. And he was deployed to areas that were dominated by local tribal languages, anyway, so he never felt as though his fib was forsaking any additional value he may have been able to provide the United States beyond personally killing as many enemies as possible.

And kill he did. He was a lethal soldier. But even more satisfying to him was that while on patrol, every single action was either right or wrong. All was life and death. Tucking in a shirt, straying off course even a few footsteps, anything could get you killed, or even worse, get someone else killed.

Most satisfying, though, was that such high stakes led to a camaraderie in which everyone was forced to see the world just the way he liked it: in black and white. Nobody in his platoon cared that he was trying to prove a point about Islam to his fellow Americans; nobody cared that he was Muslim in the first place. All that mattered was that he knew how to watch out for his fellow good guys, and take out bad guys.

When he returned home, he was bewildered at how trite everyday life felt. He could not muster any sort of motivation for any sort of routine. Nothing was at stake. And on top of that, the solidarity he had appreciated had completely evaporated. He listened, and read, and watched, and found that those most fervent in their support for the war were most fervent in their hatred for his heritage. When he passed a vehicle wielding a bumper sticker that read "I Support Our Troops", he would look over at the driver and easily imagine him or her saying "Except you".

And so he decided that if it was a religious war they wanted, then he would give it to them, and regain his sense of purpose in the process.

He passed the main house and its sprawling nativity scene and saw that the college kid's car was still parked in front of the dowdy little rental home. There was no sign of activity through the front window. The door was locked, but the latch appeared to have been installed back when white people worked in the fields. He took out his pocket knife and let himself in.

He pulled up a chair with just enough noise to draw attention. It took a few minutes for college boy to enter from the bedroom trying hard to play the role of male protector, barefoot in jeans and t-shirt and brandishing a curtain rod. When he saw who was sitting there, he gave up the pretense and lowered his weapon.

"Don't scream. You'll wake the baby."

The kid's terrified glance toward the bedroom door confirmed it.

"When were you going to tell us, Khalil?"

College boy swallowed hard. "You speak English."

"I'm a fellow American."

"Mohammed, right?" he actually seemed to be mustering up an attempt to charm him.

"That's a nickname. Nobody knows my real name."

"Why choose the name of The Prophet?"

"Because if you take my picture or describe me to anyone, you're dead."

Khalil closed his eyes and seemed to be bracing himself with silent prayer. "Are you going to kill me?" he finally asked.

"Tariq and I agree it's not worth the effort. He seems to think he may even have some more use for you. But that's between you and him. Personally, I don't see it. You don't follow orders, and you don't stand up for yourself. What else is there?"

Khalil had moved from fear to shame. "Can I say good bye?" he asked.

"No."

"Why not?"

"I want to see if you can follow orders. Of course, you could stand up for yourself."

Mohammed stood up and walked over to the door. He held it open.

"Which is it?"

Khalil leaned the curtain rod against the wall and quietly walked past Mohammed out the door.

"That's what I thought."

Khalil walked gingerly in his bare feet over the gravel to his car. Mohammed followed. They both turned as they heard the door open behind them. Marisol was wrapped in a blanket looking confused. Then she recognized Mohammed and froze.

"What are you going to do with him?" she asked in Arabic.

Mohammed looked at her inquisitively. "Just him?" She took a step back. He adjusted his position to address them both. "Neither of you would make the news if you disappeared." He turned to Khalil, "You are the wrong sex." He turned to Marisol, "And you are not pretty enough."

Marisol and Khalil looked at each other. Khalil looked as though he was about to say something, but Marisol interrupted him in English.

"I love you," she said.

Khalil exhaled deeply, trying to register at least some bravery under the circumstances. "Now you tell me," he muttered. The two of them laughed in spite of themselves.

"Savor the memory and get in the car," said Mohammed.

Khalil obeyed. He kept his eyes on Marisol the entire time he buckled in, started the engine, and backed up. He shifted out of reverse and at last turned his gaze away from her as he moved forward. The car vanished into the fog, leaving only the tail lights visible. The tail lights soon faded, too, leaving only the sound of gravel under the tires. And then all was silent.

Mohammed turned to Marisol. "What time should they pick up the baby tomorrow?"

She stared despondently into the fog where the car was last seen. "I go to work at six."

"I'll tell them to be here at five-thirty."

The baby started crying. The wails easily breached the rotting walls of the house.

"Is it a boy?" Mohammed asked.

She nodded.

"Good," he said, and started walking back up the road.

He was beyond the main house and passing by the leafless tree line when he finally heard the door shut and the baby stop crying. The road ahead inspired him to think of the future. He looked forward to working with the boy in about five years. What an opportunity, to train someone from such a young age. What a piece of work he would be.

Chapter Eleven: On Guard

Marisol had to admit that it was nice having free daycare provided. In light of the anxiety she had produced in the organization, she imagined Tariq at some point asking the women at the mosque if they would be willing to raise the child exclusively in the interest of getting Marisol out of the picture, and the women replying, "Are you kidding? No cause is worth that." But then Marisol was shouldering a fair share of the finances associated with the parenting, so perhaps there had been no discussion of eliminating her from the process.

Many days she wished they not only discussed it, but followed through and cast her out, freeing her from motherhood. It would also free her from their violent, fanatical movement, too, of course; but most of all from motherhood. Given her upbringing, she was not at all delusional about becoming a parent; she knew it would be trying. Even the low bar she had set proved difficult to jump most days, though. And while she wasn't so self-absorbed as to think she was the only mother who experienced doubts about her parenting abilities, she was burdened with the unique frustration of knowing that no matter how well she did her job, her son was destined to be a murderous creep. His future was fixed.

Unless she could somehow intervene.

For as little Abraham started to grow, increasingly there were moments that brought her great joy. She usually arrived home from work before they would bring him back. She would sit in her empty house and listen to the afternoon wind rattle the walls and whistle through the cracks and realize how empty life would be without him. Less exhausting, to be sure, but less fulfilling. As a baby, the dispiriting cry in the night was followed by a relaxing opportunity to nurse him; as a toddler, the tedious surveillance required of his ambling around the ranch often had collateral delights: the discovery of a small frog clinging to a water spigot at the edge of the fields, his unique pronunciation of some of the flotsam they would encounter on these aimless walks, or those moments when he was safely examining the dirt he was manipulating with a stick and she would have a chance to catch her breath and stare at the mountains rimming the valley as they turned orange in the late evening light and think "This still beats Algiers with mom and dad."

She wanted to be a better parent than hers had been. The true competition, however, was between her and the organization. Allowing her son to be the tip of the spear for some megalomaniacal men who would meanwhile hide behind a shield of faith was no way to win a parenting contest against anyone. She had some time to figure out ways to rig the match in her favor, as she estimated his training with Mohammed wouldn't start until he was around five years old. At that point the intensity level would be raised, he would be involved in the ultimate after-school program from a boy's perspective, learning about fighting and weapons and surveillance, things that boys find fascinating, and it would become increasingly more difficult to assert herself as his mother. She needed to find ways to make her side look appealing as well.

Consequently in the meantime, she took what the movement was offering Abraham and used it to her advantage. Though she was not party to the daily doings at the mosque, it was obvious that the first stage was early indoctrination, which involved a lot of communication. His verbal skills were impressive. The foreman's wife marveled at how much he was talking at such an early age, and thought it was so cute that he knew what things were called not only in English and Spanish (thanks to Marisol's vigilant rival home schooling), but in "French" as well. They were clearly having him read at an early age, too, sending him home with a children's edition of the Quran one afternoon with instructions to read it to him every evening. She found it to be a rather selective edition that emphasized passages which would help radicalize him later, so when the foreman's wife and her friends took her to the Salvation Army for clothes and supplies every few weeks, she would be sure to stop by the book rack and pick up some Eric Carle and Dr. Seuss as well. The transition into reading Quran verses also alerted her that it was time to make sure that when he wanted to show off what he was learning to the folks around the ranch, he needed to stick with the things that she was teaching him at home. But her rivals at the mosque once again proved to be an unconscious ally, as Abraham informed his mom that they had already told him not to share his teachings with the outside world, as such people "were not worthy of hearing the words of the prophet, peace and blessings be upon him." And while this strategy was undeniably helpful in concealing their identity, Marisol realized upon hearing him convey it to her in such a manner that she should also incorporate some lessons designed to temper a burgeoning bloat in his self-esteem. Writing was easiest to parallel, as whatever Arabic letter he was practicing, she would encourage him to also write its English/Latin equivalent so that he could share what he was doing with his "Auntie" (as Abraham had taken to calling the foreman's wife).

Auntie really wanted to take him to church as well, which was a growing source of tension in an otherwise nurturing relationship. Marisol was actually quite curious and would not have minded attending some Catholic services for the sake of observation. Islam for her was always something practiced in daily life and in private without the presence of a significant faith community. The Friday services in Algiers had been but a half hour at most without much mingling before and after, as everyone had to get back to work, so she had never felt a lack of ritual or shared worship since her move to America, and thus was not the least bit threatened by proselytizers. But there was no way she could expose Abraham to a conflicting religion. If the mosque found out, then she was sure to get a visit from Mohammed. And even though she was confident that her son could remain mum about their Sunday deeds while in training, she did not want to burden him with having to keep secrets on both fronts. Doing so would not only put him under a lot of pressure, but lay bare the antagonism between his mother and the mosque, and prompt him to possibly choose a side. Her early struggles with parenthood prevented her from being too overconfident about her chances should he decide to favor one over the other. And if not very proud of her parenting skills, she was very proud of her education of Abraham, and was bonding tightly with her son over his intellect. She did not want to risk losing him.

So she told Auntie that she was raised Protestant, and would prefer not to go to a Catholic church. This worked at first, but then Auntie the foreman's wife tried again, reminding Marisol that her family had not exactly been supportive of her since she moved into the house. Even that cousin of hers never came around anymore. So why should she remain faithful to a religion practiced by people who abandoned her? It was easy to respond to this line of attack, as familial abandonment, missing Khalil, and questioning her faith were sore subjects for Marisol at this point in her life. She fixed Auntie with a cold stare to augment her wavering voice and asked her to please drop it. When Auntie parried by suggesting that she and her husband could just take Abraham on his own, and he could decide for himself if he liked it, Marisol threatened to move out.

The concept of moving out provided her with an epiphany. She had heard one of the ladies at the flower warehouse talk about her daughter who got a job as a live-in nanny with a wealthy family up in the San Francisco area. It didn't resonate with Marisol at the time, but now that Auntie's small-scale religious fervor was unwittingly threatening to expose Marisol's ties to some large-scale fervor, she thought that such a job may be a way to move off the ranch.

Seeking new employment, much less a new residence, was a logistical challenge, though. She was several miles outside the nearest town and she had no phone, no vehicle, and consequently very limited access to information. She did not bother to ask her co-workers if they could keep her apprised of any such opportunities, as most of them knew Auntie, and anyway would no doubt prefer to hand over any promising leads to their own daughters, granddaughters, and nieces.

Her only chance was Khalil.

He had sent her a letter in care of the landlords around the time of Abraham's first birthday, to mark the occasion, and formalize his good-bye. Marisol had explained his sudden absence to Auntie by saying that he had transferred to a university in another state, so when the letter showed up with his California return address still affixed to it, Auntie shook her head and said to her, "Mija, you are like a daughter to me. If you are having family problems, you can tell me. I am here for you."

Marisol told her it was just a misunderstanding, which was actually quite true from both her perspective and Auntie's.

"But misunderstandings can get worse, Mija, if we do not deal with them, and then we start to make up stories about the other person, and then it becomes a grudge, and then we do drastic things, and then, oh my God, there we are on our death bed full of regrets."

She thanked Auntie for the advice and the offer of more sessions, but said she had a strong feeling that this letter was going to provide some clarity about her relationship with her cousin. Marisol of course was going to confirm as much to Auntie regardless of what the contents of the letter turned out to be, in the interest of staving her off, but as she suspected, Khalil's words indeed were comforting:

My Dearest Marisol,

(And I will always think of you as Marisol thanks to our beautiful sunset on the beach your first night in America). I am writing this letter in English, as I suspect your opportunities to practice are not as frequent as Spanish. Though I also suspect that you may be teaching English to

little Abraham. Oh, who am I kidding? I am writing this in English because it is the easiest language for me to express myself in, and I want to make sure I get this right.

First of all, Happy Birthday to Abraham! (Abe? Anyone calling him that yet?). I wish so badly that I could meet him, before he grows up to kill people (Kidding! Kidding! Well, kind of). I know that he is going to be smart thanks to you. So smart that I am hoping the right people who work for the cause will recognize that he is far too valuable to function as some sort of goon.

With this in mind, I want to offer my assistance in any way possible that will not jeopardize your safety (Or mine, I'm too young to die!). I have decided to go to law school when I am done with my undergraduate studies. If I could not protect you physically, then I will work to protect you legally. The school I will attend is still close by. I have included the address below so you may contact me there once I start in a couple of years.

Yes, that's right. I have not even applied yet, and I am that confident that I will gain admission. That is because of you. Meeting you was an inspiration, my love. My life was forever changed for the better thanks to you. I will not be denied the opportunity to help you in some way, or help others like you. Perhaps it will involve cutting ties with Tariq; perhaps it will involve working from the inside. But it is my life's purpose.

Thank you for providing me with one. Thank you for being born, for enduring what you did, for being crazy enough to take that journey and come here. It may have been anger that led each of us into the circumstance of our meeting, but we are fortunate that something good came of it. To find true love is hard enough, to find it under the conditions we did seems next to impossible.

You have also helped me rediscover my faith. I had lost it working with people who use it to camouflage their worst intentions. Finding you amongst those animals has led me to believe that God is good, after all. I am being selective, I know, and ignoring the role of random chance and all the cold hard facts of science and psychology that justifiably claim the world is a neutral site for a series of ruthless competitions. But as long as we are here, and people turn to faith to help them lick their wounds after each round, I want to fight for the reputation of mine, and what I assume is still yours, and seize our great faith from the clutches of evil.

I am getting melodramatic now. Sorry. But you bring out whatever poet I may have inside me. Even if that poet is corny and not worth publishing, I am glad she is there.

On this note of embarrassment concerning my writing skills, I would ask that you destroy this letter after reading it. Not actually due to my abilities, of course, but to keep you from harm. Memorize the return address on the envelope and the address below for the law school, but leave no evidence of our correspondence. And please do not send anything to either address unless it is absolutely necessary. Our contact must be as minimal as our bond is strong. If we fall into the habit of writing, I may not be able to keep myself away from you. It has been difficult enough to hold off on writing this one letter, and insisting that you likewise resist. I may have been able to grow strong without you, but the world would be much worse off without you.

Peace and blessings be upon you, my love.

Not only did Marisol memorize the addresses, but she memorized the entire letter before ritually burning it in the field behind her house one Sunday morning while the landlords were at church and Abraham was still asleep. She would recite it to herself at night in the cadence of those who chant verses from the Quran until it moved through her lips effortlessly, sounding like a call to prayer. She kept her chant close to her heart as a source of comfort against the very tangible possibility that she may eventually lose her son in one way or another.

It had been a couple of years since his letter, so if his plans were unfolding as expected, he would be at the law school now. The pursuit of his goals could ideally assist in achieving hers as well, as she supposed a prestigious law school would be scented with connections to families who needed nannies. She wrote to him and explained the situation, asking him to put the word out and be on the lookout. Aside from telling him that she loved him and appreciated his letter (and teasing him about how reading her letter proves that his prediction about getting into his school of choice had come true), she kept her communication rather succinct, as she decided that saying too much may make it too hard to stay out of touch. She slipped the envelope into the outgoing mail pile at work.

About three months and a hundred thousand bouquets later, Marisol finally received a reply. Khalil sent it care of the landlords once again. Auntie delivered it to the house and furled her brow as she presented the letter to her at the door, and seemed surprised that Marisol was so excited to receive it.

"He is still in California, Mija, why does he not come to see you?"

"He is studying to be a lawyer. He is very busy."

Auntie was unimpressed. "Hmm. Probably thinks he is a big shot now."

Marisol laughed at her. "Would you prefer I hold a grudge?"

"It is your family," she huffed. "Do what you want."

Marisol shut the door on her and ran to the table. Abraham pranced in from the bedroom. "Was that Auntie?"

"Yes it was."

"Aw, I want to say 'hi' to her."

"Later, sweetie."

"When?"

"I don't know, after dinner."

"For dessert?"

"Maybe." She really wanted to read that letter.

"Auntie makes the best desserts."

"Yes she does."

"Do you think she made platanos?"

"I don't know. Don't you have some reading to do?"

"Which reading?"

"The Quran, or that book about airplanes I gave you, something?"

"The one in Spanish or English?"

"Either one, Abraham. Just read."

"And then we can go to Auntie's?"

"After dinner." God, did she want to read that letter.

"Aw. What are we having for dinner?"

"I haven't thought about that yet."

"Can I have mac and cheese?"

"We ran out. I have to buy some more."

"Aw. What is there, then?"

"I don't know, Abraham."

"Can you check?"

"Can you read, Abraham? Please?"

"But Mom..."

"Read! Now!"

Abraham glared at her. She stood up.

"Get in that room and read something!"

He narrowed his eyes at her and slunk back into the bedroom. Marisol exhaled slowly and sank back into the chair, as though being lowered on a hydraulic lift. The promise of the letter snapped her back into excitement, and its contents did not disappoint.

After apologizing for taking so long to reply, Khalil maintained that the delay was thanks to searching for the perfect opportunity, and was confident he had found it. A classmate's older sister and her husband had a boy around Abraham's age, and their most recent nanny had to return to Sweden when her student visa expired, which was becoming a chronic scenario. They were tiring of the revolving door of Scandinavian psychology students being foisted upon them by the service they were utilizing, and were looking for something more permanent. Khalil claimed he had met Marisol while working as an intern at the United States Citizenship and Immigration Services office in Salinas. He touted her work ethic, parenting skills, and riveting border crossing story (that he deliberately left rather vague, so that Marisol could supply them with whatever details she wanted, should she get the job). He explained her isolated circumstances as well, not only for effect, but to provide plenty of logistical leeway in setting up an interview, which Khalil had already scheduled.

The family lived in Pacific Grove on the Monterey Peninsula, just over the mountains from the Salinas Valley. All Marisol had to do was find a way to the Salinas Transit Center on the day of the interview in two weeks, and catch a bus on the 68 route to the Monterey Transit Plaza, where the mother, named Chelsea, would meet her around nine in the morning. Khalil suggested that she get a ride to the Salinas station by telling the members of her carpool that she had an appointment concerning her citizenship process with the Application Support Center at the same USCIS office where he had conducted his imaginary internship. The flower commuters would certainly sympathize with that excuse and cover for her at work. For the return trip, Khalil had researched the bus routes she could take that would head south on the highway through the valley, and was convinced she could cajole the driver to pull over somewhere near the dirt road that led to her house.

As for dealing with the mosque if and when she was offered the job, he suggested she utilize her fellow bouquet makers once again, this time as the source, claiming to hear about it through the scuttlebutt at the warehouse. To persuade the organization to allow her to take the job and move, he provided Marisol with a blueprint that focused on access to the upper echelons of society for Abraham, and by extension the cause, for the relatively small price of an extra half hour of commute time in each direction for his training.

In explaining to her new employers where Abraham was being driven to after school each day, Khalil thought that pinning it on some sort of intense Catholic catechism would explain it away. Based on his interactions with his classmate and conversations with the sister, Khalil gathered that the family was not the least bit religious, so while they may think it a bit much, they wouldn't have any knowledge-based suspicions. And due to their associations with liberal causes, they would probably take some measure of pride in not openly judging her, regardless of how they actually felt. Referencing Abraham's after-school activities as religious instruction meant that Marisol wasn't exactly lying to them, either, Khalil joked.

He then threw in another laugh line towards the conclusion of his letter about feeling very Tariq-like through the process of setting up the interview. He signed off by sending his love and wishing her good luck.

Now it was up to her.

Chapter Twelve: Across The Street

Khalil brought some of his textbooks and his laptop with him to bide the time, but was having trouble concentrating. He arrived very early, around seven a.m., to be sure he was able to get a window seat in the coffee house facing the bus station by the time she arrived, and to not miss her arrival in the first place. He figured she would want to enjoy some freedom before the interview. The rising sun was reflecting off the window, ensuring that she would not be able to see him. He did not want to interfere, and not strictly out of paranoia that Mohammed or someone like him may be watching. Marisol needed to focus.

After several buses that did not have the magic number on them, he finally saw the number 68 appear at around eight o'clock. Even though he knew he would not be visible through the glare, he instinctively leaned back a bit as passengers disembarked. His vantage point was a good thirty yards away from the rear of the bus on the diagonal created by being on the other side of the street, but he could still tell immediately which one was her by the way she carried herself. The small crowd dispersed to where they needed to go, leaving her alone under the old-fashioned looking clock perched on top of the likewise-looking lamp post. She checked the time and glanced around to get her bearings.

As she looked down the street towards his location, he was able to see her clearly for the first time in over four years. He did not try to snap a photograph. That struck him as the actions of a stalker, and besides it would not have turned out clearly through the sunshine-soaked window. Most of all, however, he did not need a picture. His eyes perceived the moment, but his emotions supplied the details. He felt it more than he saw it, and a photograph would have robbed his vision of its magic.

He watched her figure out which way would take her to the sea shore, as he knew she would. Marisol had not seen anything but the valley since they parted. Her instincts led her in the right direction. She headed for some of the beauty that had been taken from her. Khalil watched her walk away. He wanted so badly to follow, but realized the ocean was what she needed to clear her mind, not him.

Khalil considered hanging around for another hour to watch Chelsea pick her up for the interview, but did not think he could bear it. He finished his coffee and packed up his things.

Chapter Thirteen: By The Sea

She was a member of the Monterey County Historical Society, a volunteer for the Monterey Jazz Festival, a docent at the Carmel Mission, a Friend of the Monterey Bay Aquarium, a Friend of the Monterey Public Library, Friend of the Symphony, Friend of the Sea Otter, Friend of the Monarch Butterfly, and quite frankly felt more like a friend to her husband lately. The solution to this problem was obvious, but she couldn't help herself. She always felt as though she needed to somehow earn the leisure time she was eligible for as the spouse of a wildly successful entrepreneur. And in doing so, in joining charity after advocacy group after friendship, she was left with none of the leisure time she was ostensibly earning. She thought having a child would settle her down and inspire her resignation from many of her causes, but it had the opposite effect. On her first postpartum trip to the playground by the pond, she saw a Mexican mother with her three small kids sharing the last few slices of bread at the bottom of a Wonder bag that Chelsea had assumed they were going to use to feed the ducks. She felt guiltier than ever, and it was back to unpaid work and a nanny search.

The nannies she had procured through her connections had infuriated her, as all they were interested in doing with their time in a foreign country was going out and partying at night. She took a trip up to San Francisco with one of them to take her son Drake to some museums and do some sightseeing, but the girl never returned from her night out until the following afternoon past checkout time at the hotel. She brought subsequent nannies up to the city as well, but only on day trips, and they barely bothered to conceal their disappointment. She never berated them or allowed herself to get too huffy, though, as she considered it likely that she would have had some similar impulses had she found herself in an exciting new country as a teenager as well. But then that was her tendency: avoid conflict through modesty achieved by assuming the potential antagonist deserved her pity.

So with great excitement she went to pick up Marisol and her son Abraham on the day Marisol was finally available to start, as it allowed Chelsea to combine a promising long-term solution to the nanny conundrum with a huge pour into her glass of charity that never seemed full enough. Such a blend may finally allow her to be less of a Friend to her less vital causes, as she presumed taking on Marisol and her child was worth about three to four memberships, even though her new nanny would not be a product of an official charitable organization. The unofficial, dare she say under-the-table nature of the hiring made it all the more noble as far as she was concerned. The subject of Marisol's legal status never even came up during their conversation, as Chelsea thought that would be like bringing up someone's weight. Additionally satisfying about this prospect was that the Salinas Valley had been a blind spot in her community work. Aside from driving through it at seventy-five miles per hour on her way to Southern California, the only instances in which she would spend time there were for Historical Society functions at the National Steinbeck Society in downtown Salinas, and occasional non-profit fundraisers at a few of the wineries in the Santa Lucia foothills (as most benefits opted for the wineries in the swankier Carmel Valley closer to home on her side of the hill).

She had often wondered during her drives on the other side of the hill what life must be like for those who lived in those lonely old farm houses and outbuildings that seemed to have been dropped into some of the fields peppering the basin. She would briefly imagine how cold and damp it must be inside during winter, and during the spring and summer fleetingly speculate on whether the wind ever stopped pounding the walls and windows. Now she no longer had to wonder. She wasn't just raising money or toasting the work of someone trying to make life better for the less fortunate, she was right there in the valley personally helping someone cross over.

This was such a wonderful opportunity for Drake to learn some valuable lessons in the process, too. On their way out to pick them up, she had primed her son with a volley of dictums on how fortunate he was to have a mommy and a daddy and live in a nice house as she pointed out the symbols of hardscrabble existence that glided past their windows, and told him to do his best to make Abraham and his mommy feel welcome. Chelsea also hoped that Abraham would provide Drake with a sibling figure. She and her husband had realized early on in raising Drake that they were not fit for more than one child (with the one proving to be a bit of a stretch), and naturally felt guilty about it at times. But she would just remind herself that as needy as her son seemed to be when it came to playing with other kids and clamoring for his parents' attention, they were smart enough to know their limitations and didn't force each other into overcoming them by bearing any more.

Granted, there was still a chance that all of this goodness may not even happen. Marisol had told her to show up on this date, estimating the amount of time she would need to get her affairs in order without being able to keep Chelsea abreast of the situation thanks to the paucity of modern communications in her life. Chelsea was so impressed with her at the conclusion of their interview that she had offered to take Marisol into a wireless store not far from where they had chatted and buy her a phone, but the poor girl said that her church elders would forbid it. As soon as Chelsea heard that, she really wished they had gone someplace nicer than the coffee house across from the bus station. It was a nice place, but by that point she was convinced that Marisol deserved something sumptuous with a view of the bay. The thought of her spending the next few weeks after their morning together still stuck in that forsaken existence caused Chelsea much anxiety until the date in question. She should have trusted the recommendations of her brother's classmate concerning Marisol's character and done more in advance. She should have made reservations.

Chelsea drove slowly along the dirt road Marisol had directed her to in order to avoid kicking up any dust. She looked for signs that this was in fact the right place, and that they still had a deal. They passed what she assumed was the main house, and what she assumed was the landlord Abraham had dubbed "Auntie". She was stationed by the front door, scowling in Chelsea's direction. She took that as a good sign, for who wouldn't be upset at losing the company of such a remarkable young woman? Chelsea smiled and waved. Auntie spun and walked back into her house.

When Chelsea spotted Marisol and Abraham in front of the house they had been living in, her excitement at seeing them was thwarted by the heartbreak at seeing their conditions firsthand. She started to bawl.

Drake asked his mom why she was crying. Then as they pulled up to the valiant pair she saw how confused the two of them were at seeing her reaction, so she started to bawl harder out of guilt at bawling in the first place.

"I'm so sorry," she said as she got out of the car, trying to compose herself. She hugged Marisol. "I'm just so happy to see you." She bent over to give Abraham a hug, too. Then she looked at the house. "And I'm so happy for you. Oh my God," she started to cry again. "That sounds so arrogant. I meant that I'm so happy I can get you out of here. Oh Jesus, that still sounds bad. And I just said 'Jesus' and you're these good Catholics. Just...never mind."

Marisol laughed. "I understand. And we're grateful."

Chelsea simply nodded and pulled herself together with the help of a deep breath. Then she noticed they had one suitcase. "Is that all you have?"

"Yes," Abraham replied.

Chelsea started crying again.

"We packed quite a bit inside of it," Marisol assured her.

And Chelsea added laughter to her crying.

Such was the case for much of the early stages of their relationship: Marisol assuring Chelsea that things were fine, were okay, that she needn't worry, that she was doing a fine job of providing for them and that Marisol was the employee, after all. Let her take on more of the household worries.

And indeed the new arrangements did eventually relax into routine, as Marisol carried her responsibilities brilliantly. So much so, in fact, that Chelsea realized the most difficult part of having her around was making peace with the notion that Marisol was smarter than her, and that Abraham was smarter than her son. Not to mention they each possessed a stronger work ethic than her and Drake. Quite possibly her husband, too, but his fully formed sense of accomplishment insulated him from bothering to notice, much less worry about it.

Consequently she failed to slow down in her voluntary commitments, since the impressiveness of her self-styled charity cases instilled a sense of unworthiness in her. Now not only did she feel it necessary to earn her rarefied place in society, but she had the gnawing sensation that she did not deserve it in the first place. She used this to her advantage as best she could, consciously regarding Marisol as not only an extreme upgrade in childcare, but healthy motivation for both her and Drake. Her son was too young to notice much difference in skill level at this stage, but she knew he would eventually when he and Abraham started attending school together once summer ended and Kindergarten started.

Another encouraging product of school starting would be the relegation of Abraham's religious instruction to an after-school program. There was something cultish about the ladies who alternated picking him up in the mornings and dropping him off in the afternoons. They never got out of the car, never waved. Come autumn she would thankfully see them one less time each weekday, as they would be picking him up at school and only stopping by the house to drop him off.

As wary as she was about the level of religious intensity, she had to acknowledge that the instruction Abraham was receiving was impressive, and played no small part in the boy's remarkable development. It certainly ran rings around any pre-school program she had looked into for Drake, and made any of the "baby genius" products splattered all over the commercial airwaves of children's programming even more laughable than they already were. Chelsea was particularly taken with their emphasis on the study of other religions, as she had seen Abraham engaging Islam, and when she was out shopping with Marisol, she would make a point of asking Chelsea if they could stop by a book store to search for some Jewish, Hindu, or Eastern religious texts for Abraham's schooling. Chelsea imagined they were only teaching Abraham about these other faiths in the interest of finding their flaws and providing ammunition for future evangelizing, but nonetheless the boy was better versed in moral philosophy as a pre-schooler than most adults, not to mention gorgeously literate and articulate for said age. Plus Marisol seemed aware of the program's flaws and intent on making sure her son's point of view did not skew too excessively. They would read good old-fashioned children's books together, and she made sure that Abraham indulged in plenty of child's play, whether it was maniacally hurdling around the playground at full volume or drawing the splashy impressionist works of art kids are typically capable of before self-consciousness steals their creativity.

And the fact Drake was being incorporated into all of this delighted Chelsea. She may not have felt like she deserved what she had, but she was going to take advantage of it. Meanwhile any bouts of remorse she grappled with at the inkling she may be consuming

Marisol and her son for her own purposes were easily disposed of when she passed by their room and saw the two of them snuggled in bed reading in an environment roughly a century ahead of what they had been living in, or when she encountered Marisol standing at the window in the great room, contemplating the bay and the ocean beyond.

There was a trade-off. All things considered, she was doing some good in the world.

Chapter Fourteen: About Town

Marisol was very pleased that the boys would be able to attend school together. She had assumed when they moved in that Drake went to private school, but Chelsea maintained that in an area like Pacific Grove, there is no need to send your child to private school, as the zip code serves as an organic application and selection process. The only reasons to seek out a private school would be to satisfy a craving for name brand recognition that some also require of their handbags, or, of course, if one desires a religious education. "And heaven knows," Chelsea chuckled, "the boys are receiving plenty of that."

Per his mother's instructions, Abraham had been doing a fine job of keeping the true nature of his education from Drake, who didn't seem that interested, anyway, aside from the fact it prevented them from playing together as much as they would like. Each boy had spent a lot of time around adults in their lives so far, and relished this new world of having a peer within shouting distance. Within a few weeks of their arrival, the boys had begged their mothers to let them room together, to which the mothers gladly acquiesced.

She watched them hunt for sea life in the tide pools off the beach not far from the house and wondered how long Abraham would be able to maintain the ruse if Drake started to grow more curious, or more likely if her son grew more interested in sharing what he was learning with his best friend. She found it easy enough to make up an explanation for why they seemed to be the only people from Mexico who were Muslim (we had to leave for that very reason: we were being persecuted), and why they kept their affiliation a secret now that they were in the United States (persecution breeds paranoia), but now that he was developing a personal relationship with someone besides his mother, someone his own age, the tightrope she walked grew a bit more wobbly.

"Why can't I tell Drake about God?" he had asked her one day while Drake was at an allergist appointment.

"He has not had the kind of teaching you have had," Marisol told him. "It would be confusing to him."

"But I can help him understand."

"That is not your responsibility, Abraham. You are not qualified to teach anyone."

"But I'm afraid for him."

This struck her as odd. "Why?"

"People who do not know God's perfect words will not get into Heaven."

"Drake will not be eligible for Heaven for quite some time. He has a long life ahead of him."

"But what if something happens before he grows up?"

Marisol became a bit suspicious. "Why would anything happen to him before he grows up? Has anyone at the mosque said anything?"

"No, Mom. They don't even know about him there. I never talk about home with them."

That put her at ease. "Good boy."

"But they talk a lot about people who don't believe, and the Fire they will face. I don't want that to happen to Drake."

"Have they not told you that all children go to Heaven, no matter their religion?"

"No. Is that true?"

"We are born pure. You can look it up."

"So maybe when we are grown up I can talk to him about it."

Marisol laughed, relieved at having bought so much time on the issue. "Maybe."

"But until we grow up," Abraham continued to apply pressure, "Am I lying?"

"Well..." she felt like the curtain was being raised again after the show was over, and she had no encore prepared. Abraham, meanwhile, launched into a sermon on lying...

"Because liars are bad, too; lying is like not believing. And I don't want to be a liar."

Marisol found an opening. "You are not lying," she announced. "You are keeping a secret."

Abraham considered her words. She awaited his response nervously.

"Secrets can be fun," he cautiously acknowledged.

"Yes," she jumped in. "And they can keep us from hurting other people's feelings."

He arrived at his decision. "Okay, Mom," he concluded. "I think I can keep a secret."

Marisol hugged him and kissed him on his forehead. She smiled at the memory as the boys presented her with a small crab they had plucked from one of the pools. They took turns wiggling it in front of her face and she dutifully acted frightened before encouraging them to put the poor thing back in its home. She found it interesting that her daily conversations with Abraham and Drake were more challenging than the one she had with the representatives at the mosque when she had asked permission to move.

Not that it was really a conversation. More like passing notes. She mentioned the possibility to one of the ladies who picked up Abraham at the ranch one morning, being sure to include the arguments in favor of it that Khalil had proposed and she had articulated. That afternoon the same lady returned and before she said anything Marisol could tell that the answer was "yes" because she was already looking irritated at having to drive farther to pick up Abraham and drop him off. Without getting out of the car, the lady made it official by conveying Tariq's gratitude at finding a way to gain access to the wealthy and powerful while saving the investors' money.

Marisol thanked her, handed her the address of the new residence, and told her when she planned on moving. The lady took the paper, scowled, and drove away.

While that may have been the extent of their interaction when it came to this new phase, Marisol knew there was more to it on the organizational end. She assumed they had been scouting the house and the area periodically, and would be there, somewhere, when Abraham started school.

Then soon, perhaps it was starting already, there would be Mohammed. There would be more to it than discussions of the righteous and the non-believers. It would be time to plan on what to do to the non-believers. Things would get rather secular. And as Marisol watched the boys agitate another unsuspecting body of marine life with makeshift weapons they had made of sticks and shells, she speculated that the lessons learned from Mohammed would be a lot more difficult for Abraham to keep a secret from his close partner in crime.

She barked at them to leave the innocent creatures alone, and then cushioned her rebuke with the suggestion they go get a treat before heading home.

At the frozen yogurt shop they sat on barstools at the window watching the well-heeled foot traffic slowly drift past. Marisol had become adept at discriminating between tourist and local, and was playing that game to herself while the boys reminisced about imaginary friends.

"My favorite one was Blooga," said Drake.

Abraham almost lost his mouthful of yogurt from laughter. "Blooga?" he finally managed to say after somehow swallowing the yogurt.

Drake was laughing too. "I named him when I was little," he defended himself.

"Was he a whale?" Abraham asked.

"No," Drake giggled. "Why would he be a whale?"

"Because there are beluga whales."

"Oh yeah. Do you remember that song?" Drake started singing: "Baby beluga...baby beluga..."

"We didn't play music in our house," Abraham said, glancing over at Marisol. She looked back at him and shrugged. Drake continued signing the chorus...

"Baby beluga...baby beluga..."

"Is that all it says?" Abraham asked in exaggerated bafflement.

"No, but I can't remember the rest. I didn't even know it was about a whale."

"What did you think it was about?"

"A boy named Beluga."

"And that's how you invented Blooga?"

"Hey," Drake glowed with recognition. "Maybe it was."

They contemplated that possibility for a few moments, then Abraham picked up the thread once more. "My favorite was Bisher."

Now Drake could laugh at one of Abraham's figments. "Bisher?"

Abraham laughed along with him. "Bisher!"

"Both our favorite friends started with a 'B'," Drake observed through his giggles.

"Hey! Yeah!"

"Bisher and Blooga!"

Abraham launched into a biography of his imaginary friend. "Bisher would take off his shoes and when he was barefoot nobody could hear him and he could sneak up on anybody."

Drake found this delightful. And, of course, funny. "I wish I could do that."

The boys' conversation had Marisol smiling pretty broadly herself as she gazed out the window and started to attach some statistics to her estimates concerning tourists versus locals.

"My new imaginary friend is going to teach me how to do things like that," said Abraham. "How to sneak up on people and hear what they say, or surprise them."

"But you have me now," Drake said. "You don't need one of those guys."

"You're my playing friend," Abraham assured him. "This is my training friend."

Marisol still looked through the window but no longer saw what was on the other side. Her concentration was exclusively on what the boys were saying.

"A training friend," Drake considered the concept. "Hey, that's a good idea. I'm gonna make a training friend. What's yours called?"

"The Prophet."

"Wow! That's like a superhero name."

"I know. And he wants to give his powers to me."

Marisol had to hand it to Mohammed; the imaginary friend construct was pretty ingenious.

So it had begun. And he was thinking of ways to keep it a secret right along with her.

Chapter Fifteen: In Training

He would not let Abraham watch the throat being slit until he had spent some time with a live victim first. On their way to the holding area he explained the proper method: make sure you have identified the carotid artery and jugular veins, keep the knife concealed until the last possible moment, make sure the subject is relaxed, then make sure that your incision is deep enough to sever the veins, trachea, and esophagus, but does not sever the spinal cord.

A few of the sheep murmured as they approached. He did not even have to encourage Abraham to interact with the flock. The boy stuck his arm through the bars of the pen and connected with one of them, rubbing the top of its nose. The sheep responded in kind, rubbing along the bars and poking its head through the opening for more attention.

"She likes you," Mohammed said.

"She's sweet," Abraham said, seemingly as much to the sheep as in response to his teacher.

"One thing many people don't understand about being good at what we do, Abraham, is that being friendly helps make your job easier. You can't learn anything about anyone, you can't gain their trust, can't get close to them if you scare them. This is something you are already better at than me. I was too hardened by the time I started doing God's work. I have had to rely on intimidation, which only works in certain situations, and keeps me from doing more. You are destined for bigger things."

"Thank you, Prophet." Abraham had stopped calling him "The" Prophet since around the end of second grade. He had outgrown the superhero motif, had come to understand the purpose of his training and the value of keeping it a secret, and they both agreed that dropping the definite article of speech made it sound less like Mohammed was actually claiming to be "The" Muhammad, which was of course blasphemous. They bounced around with Abraham addressing him with variations on "teacher" and "sir", but agreed that their relationship was neither exclusively academic nor military; it was unique. So they went with the less-sacrilegious, more-diminutive "Prophet" nickname as a nod to their history together.

Around the same time is when they cut their training days down to twice a week since Mohammed didn't think every day was necessary, and he could tell that making Abraham wait in between sessions created a sense of anticipation in the boy, for the exercises were, as he promoted it to Abraham, "the stuff of video games made real". Needless to say, the ladies who shuttled him back and forth certainly appreciated the streamlined schedule. They never seemed to forgive Mohammed for allowing the move to Pacific Grove. The lighter load provided them with a less overwhelming sequence of spiritual lessons as well, which were still a part of the program, and for which they remained responsible.

As for what Mohammed and Abraham worked on, much of it was reminiscent of the kinds of things a rural father and son would do together: learning to fire a gun, though the variety of weapons in which Mohammed mentored him were well beyond the arsenal one might find on a farm; hunting small game and varmints, in order to instill patience and marksmanship; even fishing, again in the interest of understanding that stalking prey involved long periods of tedium.

Nothing that they did together was in the interest of enhancing Mohammed's role as a father figure; the agenda was strictly professional from his point of view. But he understood Abraham may see things from a different perspective, and by no means discouraged it. He just let it happen; knowing it was something the boy needed, and certainly wasn't going to get from that workaholic nonentity who paid the bills on the Monterey Peninsula estate he and his mom inhabited. The training exercises were a way to strengthen Abraham's attachment to him without having to consciously put forth any specific efforts, which was just as well, given that Mohammed's stony persona was decidedly non-paternal and would not lend itself to any blatant attempts.

Other tasks were more child-like and mischievous in their capacity to bond; the kinds of things a bachelor uncle would do with his nephew, or still-spry grandparent would with his grandson: going to the shopping mall in Salinas during the holiday rush and picking out a random person to stalk until said target left the premises; setting up a one-person scavenger hunt, in which Abraham had to find objects via clues and induction; deviously speculating as they sat together in a crowded public space how they could cause the greatest amount of alarm and chaos with the least amount of exertion so as to avoid attention.

Finding a relatively seamless way to make the transition from those fatherly and avuncular ventures into the grave matters for which those flights of fancy laid the groundwork was vexing, however. The visits to the halal slaughterhouse were Mohammed's initial nudge. They never really skinned or cleaned the small game they hunted; they fed it to some of the farm dogs in the area or left it to the coyotes. Even had they preserved their prey, such small animals would not provide an ample enough introduction to the amount of energy and viscous required of killing larger species.

"Death can be beautiful, Abraham," he told the boy as Abraham led the sheep from the barn to the slaughterhouse. "When in service to God, what can be more valuable than a life?"

"If it's so valuable, Prophet, why end it?"

Mohammed appreciated how easily Abraham questioned authority in the most reasonable terms. "Every life on earth has to end sometime. So the question is whether that ending will please Him."

"And this sheep is dying so that people can eat," Abraham jumped ahead to the next paragraph of today's lesson, much to Mohammed's delight.

"You got it, kid," Mohammed said as they reached the sheep's final destination. "Though maybe every once in a while you can just wait and let me finish my speech."

He meant it as a joke, but people could rarely tell when he was kidding given his severe air. Apparently even Abraham had a hard time despite the past few years of interaction, so Mohammed had to extend the punch line: "Luke Skywalker always let Yoda talk."

The boy eked out a smile for his teacher. Mohammed appreciated it, even if it was just out of courtesy. The owner of the ranch emerged and took the sheep from Abraham. They followed them in and watched the proceedings.

Mohammed was pleased with how well Abraham handled himself. It was clear the boy did not enjoy watching the sheep die; he turned away briefly when the knife separated the animal from its life. And he winced as the blood flowed out of the neck, clearly stunned not only at the sight of it, but how much came rushing out. Mohammed sensed that the only reason Abraham continued to face the slaughter was because of his trainer's presence, as should be the case. A child who delighted in the sight or exhibited an inordinate amount of curiosity would be unfit for any sort of duty. Abraham's reaction was perfect: an ability to follow orders and to act strong even if he wasn't feeling strong.

The boy wouldn't be allowed to slaughter any animals on his own until he passed puberty, as was custom. That deadline fairly well matched the timeline Mohammed had imagined for his process. Helping out at the slaughterhouse would not only help inure him to death by proxy, but the halal procedures provided a link to faith that he could exploit. That the methods were meant to kill in a humane manner provided innumerable opportunities to conflate death with devotion. By the time he was ready to wield the knife, Abraham would have no qualms about leading members of the flock to slaughter.

What came after that was something Mohammed continued to mull. He would have to find an easy target; "easy" in terms of the hatred that person would inspire. And there should probably be an additional phase of coaching to bridge the gap between beast and man.

Finding the right auxiliary victim for this intermediate stage would be challenging. He did not want Abraham to lose the innate goodness that was so apparent to the world around him. It made him so much more valuable to the cause.

Mohammed would have to tread more delicately than he was accustomed. He may even need assistance from those who would never deign to help him if they were asked.

Chapter Sixteen: Entering a Phase

Most parents would not be surprised if their son started to become guarded and quiet as middle school approached. Based on what Marisol was learning about parenting from being around so many parents who loved to talk about parenting so much, quite the contrary it would be an even bigger surprise, a pleasant one, if their son made it through the early double digits of their number of years on earth with a consistently sunny disposition.

But there was so much more to her son's situation that when it came to his "angry young man" stage, she wanted to make sure his anger did not lead to an international incident.

She had discussed their family background with him at an early age already, being forthright about everything other than their location. So he knew the circumstances of his conception, knew about her relationship with her parents. And having established those terms, it was fairly easy for him to understand why she capitalized on the movement's invitation to come to America. Perhaps due to hormones or some other pap the amateur child psychologists of Chelsea's circle liked to factor in to their children's development, Abraham was only now becoming maudlin over not having a father or any grandparents.

"It's not that, Mom," he said, mercifully without the eye rolls or belligerence that so often characterized his reactions to her these days. She had grown to resent having to talk to him as much as he seemed to resent talking to her. This current phase of his would have her momentarily wishing on occasion that they were back in her parents' hovel in Algiers, where she wouldn't be expected to talk to him about anything, other than to tell him to obey her and to shut up. But she was at the foot of his bed adorned with sheets that cost more than a year's pay in the old country, having just put away his laundry that consisted of more shirts than he would have owned in a lifetime had she given birth back home.

"You can tell me, Abraham," she said in a consoling fashion, imitating the tone of voice she heard Chelsea and her friends adopt with their children.

Abraham laughed at her. Ah, there it was. The attitude she had grown so accustomed to. She resisted an old-world impulse to backhand him across the face.

"What?" she asked him, sounding a lot like him in the process.

"Nice try, Mom," he condescended. "But the Chelsea-speak doesn't suit you."

She laughed heartily out of relief and thanked him for releasing her from the task of attempting it any further. It was a pleasure to share such an enjoyable moment with him again. She thought it was perhaps safe to negotiate the other elephant in the room.

"Is it something that happened in your training?"

It clearly was. She pressed him, sensing he wanted to talk about it.

"That's what I thought," she continued, very business-like now in an effort to flatter him. "I knew you were too strong to worry about being like the other kids."

He started to cry. She couldn't remember the last time she had seen him cry.

"It was a dog," he said. And he started to cry harder. She was confused by what he meant, but knew he would explain once he had a chance to settle himself down. She respected his space and waited for him to pick up where he left off.

"I had been helping slaughter sheep with Prophet and a friend of his who runs a halal meat business on his farm. I know why he was having me do it. I'm not stupid. But when it came time to kill something else..."

He broke down again. Marisol had rarely felt heartache when it came to her son. He was so strong and bright. But she felt it now. She thought she may ruin the moment if she tried to say something soothing so she just hugged him and let him be the confused, scared kid that he hardly ever allowed himself to be.

She didn't tell Abraham that she was going to do this, but she decided to have a talk with Mohammed for the first time in over a decade, and for more than thirty seconds. True, the mechanical voice that read Tariq's message to her and Khalil so many years ago had said talking is not what Mohammed does. But she would be the one doing the talking.

Designing the logistics of a meeting was strenuous. She briefly considered Khalil as a go-between. Chelsea had asked her several times if she would like them to invite that nice young law student who recommended her for the job over for dinner, but she had always come up with excuses for why she was not interested. Marisol wasn't so paranoid as to believe she was under constant surveillance by someone from the mosque, but all it would take is one coincidental sighting of Khalil at the house, and she could not take that risk, no matter how badly she wanted to see him. Chelsea eventually stopped asking. Marisol suspected her employer had only done it out of courtesy to begin with and was ultimately relieved that her singular attempt at matchmaking hit a dead end, as she never tried to set her up with anyone else or ever inquired as to whether Marisol was lonely. Addressing her loneliness ran the risk of losing her.

In spite of Chelsea's silence on the issue, Marisol still knew where Khalil was; Chelsea's brother came to the house on occasion and sometimes would give Marisol an update if he happened to notice her. Currently his old classmate worked at a law firm in the Oakland area specializing in immigration. Every time the brother would reference Khalil's specialization, he would shake his head with patronizing admiration and joke that maybe someday Khalil could secure diplomatic asylum for some fleeing dictator and make some real money. They weren't in touch very often, but apparently Khalil would happen to contact him whenever his business address changed.

For essentially the same reasons she refused the offers to invite him over for dinner, Marisol decided that contacting Khalil to set up a meeting, or mediate it, would be a bad idea, and was motivated by pure sentimentality. She would have to do this herself.

She walked to Abraham's school the next day that he was scheduled to be picked up for training and approached the lady in the car before the children were dismissed. She couldn't remember whether it was the same woman with whom she last interacted several years ago in getting their move out of the valley approved. The irritation this one exuded certainly had a familiar feel. She grudgingly rolled down the window only after Marisol had been standing there for several seconds, offered no greeting before listening to Marisol request a meeting with Mohammed, then remained silent as she rolled the window back up. The bell rang and kids started to abandon the premises. Marisol walked briskly away so that Abraham wouldn't see her talking to his chauffeur. As upset as he was about the turn that the training had taken, his junior version of male ego would still be mad at her for intervening on his behalf.

When Abraham was dropped off at the house a few hours later, Marisol went to the door after making sure her son was in his room and the lady beckoned her with the window already down.

"Mohammed will meet you at two o'clock before the next pick up. We will be waiting at the entrance to that beach you enjoy taking the boys to. The meeting will be no longer than ten minutes."

This time it was Marisol's turn to not say anything. She could only nod. As the car backed out of the driveway, she wasn't sure what was more nerve-wracking: the fact that she was going to speak with

Mohammed, or that apparently they had been keeping an even closer eye on her than she speculated. Thank God she had never agreed to invite Khalil to the house.

She arrived about fifteen minutes early on the scheduled day, and Mohammed was already there, sitting on a bench near her preferred path to the beach. As she drew within earshot, he said calmly, "Keep walking to the beach. I will be close enough behind you to hear what you are saying."

She obliged and continued down the path. "Can you hear me?" she said, obeying orders by not looking back.

"I said I would be able to."

The effect was of two people talking to themselves. She was glad so few people frequented the beach this time of year, and on a weekday, no less. She was about to start her spiel when an elderly couple came into view exiting the beach as they entered. Marisol smiled pleasantly at them, then glanced back to see when they were far enough away from Mohammed to speak again.

"Is this really necessary?" she asked.

"Would you want to be seen with me by people who know who I am?"

She calculated that it was really just a power play on his part, but she would do what was necessary to be heard. They continued their imitation schizophrenia as they reached the beach and headed toward the shore.

"Abraham will have a lot of opportunities coming up as he finishes middle school and starts high school," she said deliberately and clearly, "Teachers and administrators have already been approaching him about participating in student government and a program where the student body officers apprentice with members of the city council; they tell me he would be great for mock trial, which is when students simulate a trial by jury and they..."

"I know what mock trial is," he interrupted her.

"Of course you do." She was losing her breath from walking in the dry sand and from nerves. She turned before they got too close to the ocean and started to walk parallel to it so that she wouldn't have to raise her voice to be heard over the surf. "The point is, everyone notices how exceptional he is. There are so many options available to him. So many ways he can serve the cause that are more sustainable and valuable than using him as some sort of hit man. He can gather intelligence, work to change laws from the inside, and so much of this is thanks to you and the things..."

"You're right," he interrupted her again.

"Right about what?" she gasped as she trudged along. "The different ways he can serve? Or how much you have helped his education?"

"Both," he said, not sounding the least bit winded.

Her train of thought started to wobble along with her stride. She worked to regain it. "So I was wondering if maybe..."

"Yes," he said.

She wanted to say 'stop interrupting me, dammit,' but didn't want those to be her last words, so she played along. "Yes to what?"

"We can cease training for now. He is free to decide which path best suits his talents."

She stopped in her tracks and breathed deeply. "You're serious?"

"I don't think anyone has ever asked me that before," he said, sounding almost grateful.

"Thank you," she said, on the brink of tears. "This will mean so much to him."

Whatever humanity Mohammed betrayed in his voice a moment ago had disappeared as he modulated his tone back to business. "Abraham can contact us when he feels the time is right."

"Yes," she agreed. "Yes, of course." She turned to stare at the ocean, then wondered if he was still there.

He was.

"He knows where to find me," Mohammed said, looking right at her. He slowly spun about face and made his way back to the path.

She watched him for a few paces before deciding that she would rather look at the ocean. It looked as beautiful as ever. No surprise there.

Chapter Seventeen: On Top

Many claim to have been welcomed by any and all cliques in high school, and boast of the ability to move fluently between them. But Abraham really did. That included faculty, staff, and administrators. Nobody begrudged him his associations with other groups, as they were only too happy to have him spend time with theirs. And each member of each group always felt that the exchanges he had with them were sincere. There was a good reason for this: he was being sincere.

Years of keeping secrets throughout his childhood made him extremely grateful for not having to do so any longer, while he simultaneously maintained his gift of disarming charm that had served him so well back when he was forced to make the best of his duplicitous situation. This combination of natural and scripted talents made it difficult for anyone to resent his success. His main feather was academics, honed by his early years of intense study, which fed his dexterity when it came to student council and the community service his policies inspired. But he also made time to play a small role in the school play each semester, provide reliable defense for the soccer team, and some power at the bottom of the order for the baseball team. His patience made him an outstanding math tutor, and serenity under pressure the most valuable member of the chess team. In being so generous with his time, he at times had to miss the occasional practice, rehearsal, game, or match, but no one could imagine badgering him to make a commitment to one pursuit over another when all things were so extraordinarily equal.

Aside from his mother, no one loved him more than Drake. They had become twins by association. Every year they were asked if they would like to stop sharing a room, and their annual response was "Why?" Their inseparability was the primary reason they still lived at the house. Marisol was more of a housekeeper now, allowing

Chelsea to maintain her unpaid standing in the community with full confidence that her home was ready for entertaining at a moment's notice, and that perhaps her greatest contribution to her corner of the world was bringing Abraham into it.

If he still considered himself much of a Muslim at all, it was of a very moderate variety based more on intellect than emotion. He loved to discuss religion with people both casually and academically, adhering to the chestnut that all dialogue is at its core religious, and if you can negotiate an argument about faith, you can refine a point on any topic. So he relished in debating the existence of God, the role of human institutions in understanding our relationship to deities, and interpretations of scriptures from various doctrines of faith. He had not completely abandoned the emotional element of his spiritual training, though. It was his belief that everyone worships in some form or another, be it money, appearance, celebrity, order; that it was a standard feature of human sentiment; it's just a matter of what people worship and how healthy it is.

So he dated.

And someone without his appeal may have been accused of having commitment issues at best, and being a player at worst, but because he always had the right reason handy for why he could not go out with someone again after such a wonderful first date, and possessed an acute sensitivity for how comfortable any given girl was in any given scenario, he was never accused of being anything other than a young man who loved the company of young women.

"There is too much beauty in our lives," he said while overlooking the eighteenth fairway at Pebble Beach Golf Links. He was on a double date with Drake. A friend of theirs who worked in the lodge let them take the girls for a walk across the back nine after the last group had gone out. The sun was setting and the sharp light of winter now tinted slightly red.

"We are spoiled," he continued, "Spoiled brats."

The girls laughed. "So?" said the one with Drake, named Briana. They had been dating for a couple of months now, and accompanied Abraham this evening because they were setting him up with her friend, Samantha, who had apparently been waiting for this opportunity the whole time her friend had been seeing Drake.

"You're going to suggest a trip to the valley, aren't you?" Drake said.

"Hey!" Abraham said in artificial recognition. "What a great idea!"

His date curled her arm inside his and grabbed his hand. "Why don't we climb down to the beach instead?"

Abraham looked over at Drake and Briana. The two of them referenced her move with teasingly impressed looks. He stared back at them with an overly straight face. "I don't know," he said, turning his attention back to Samantha. "It's just going to be even more beautiful." He looked right into her eyes as he said it. He didn't dare look over at Drake while he did so.

"Abe likes remembering where he came from," Drake chimed in. "But only to a certain degree. He won't show me his old house, and I can't remember where it is. And he won't show me where he went to catechism, so we just go to this great burrito place that he only discovered like three years ago; online."

"Aw, man. Did you have to give away the online part, Dee?" Abraham said.

"I could actually go for a burrito," said Samantha.

"But do you want to drive, like, an hour for one?" Briana asked.

"You'll appreciate it more," Abraham assured them. "It's all about balance. There is no beauty without the banal."

"My God," Samantha shot back. "Does this work on other girls you've gone out with?"

Abraham chuckled and held tight to her hand. "Oh, you were right, kids," he addressed Drake and Briana. "This girl is something special."

Drake ran up behind Abraham and gave him a twisting, playful bear hug, breaking up his friend's hand-holding. "You know I've always got your back, Abe."

Abraham tried to shake Drake from his back, and they ended up on the ground wrestling. The girls formed an appreciative audience.

"That's one thing you should know about dating one of these guys," Briana said to Samantha. "You will always come second."

"Hey," Abraham said, unlocking himself from Drake's grasp. "I heard that." He and Drake stretched out on the fairway next to each other and settled down. "And it's only true in my case. I love him way more than he loves me."

"Wrong," Drake picked up on the idea. "I love you more."

"No," Abraham shot back, and they launched into an imitation of an overly lovey-dovey couple playfully one-upping each other with the "I love you more", "No I love you more", "No I love you", which then transitioned into "You hang up first", "No you hang up first", "We'll count to three and then hang up together".

"See?" Briana said to Samantha. "You didn't go to elementary school with them. It's been like this since they were kids."

The boys sat up with their forearms resting on their knees. "And the beauty of it is, as long as we're on the subject of beauty," Abraham said, "is that we grew up like brothers but aren't actually brothers, so when we finally decide to consummate our relationship, there won't be anything weird about it."

Drake gestured over to Abraham as if to signal the girls that he could not have put it any better himself.

"Well," Samantha said. "Every relationship has its issues. I guess I can deal with this one."

Abraham bounced to his feet and applauded. "You are a bright and an open-minded individual and I think I may be in love with you already." He kissed her briefly. "Now shut up and come get a burrito with me."

They held hands and walked towards the green. Abraham looked back at Drake and Briana, who were still in spectator mode. Drake was still on the ground. "Are you coming?" Abraham goaded them.

Drake and Abraham smiled at each other. Drake shook his head and extended his hand out to Briana for assistance. They caught up and the four of them strolled the eighteenth as though they held the lead at the U.S. Open and only needed to sink a tap-in putt to clinch the victory. Abraham could practically hear the sound of cheering as they walked the empty course.

He carefully studied Samantha's reactions to the taqueria. She handled the circumstances beautifully, which would not seem to be a big deal to most, for while it may have been a bit of a hole in the wall that smelled strongly of lard and faintly of raw meat, it was by no means a target of the health department. But Abraham had become highly sensitized to the subtle ways that disdain revealed itself in people from his years of hopping back and forth between affluence and scarcity, fundamentalist and secular. And while he understood preferences were a part of life, he could not abide by those biases born of not only a lack of understanding, but a lack of interest in understanding. He caught himself looking at her a little bit too long than would be considered cool as she talked with Briana, who sat across from her, while Drake and Abraham sat next to their dates.

"Briana," Abraham cut in. "I hate to interrupt, but does anyone call you 'Bree.'"

"Sometimes," she shrugged.

"Well I would like to, because then I can refer to you and Drake as Bree and Dee."

"Suit yourself," she smiled as Samantha meanwhile playfully rolled her eyes.

"Don't we get a say in that?" Drake asked.

"No," Abraham blew him off. "Because you two should have told me how wonderful Samantha is a long time ago."

Drake and Briana looked flabbergasted. Drake was the first one able to speak. "You're kidding, right?"

"We hyped her constantly," Briana added.

Abraham smiled. "You see," he said to Samantha while gesturing towards the protesting couple. "That's why it took me so long to ask you out. I was intimidated."

Samantha beamed. "I'm glad you got over your fears."

"Plus I thought you were going out with Darren Hoff."

The girls would have spit out their drinks had they been sipping them at that moment. "Oh my God," Briana said. "Whatever gave you that idea?"

"Aw, come on," Samantha said to her friend. "Go easy on poor Darren. I've known him since Kindergarten."

"And he's been following you around like a stray puppy since then," Briana piled on.

"He's all right," Samantha defended him some more, which actually pleased Abraham, as it demonstrated the kind of compassion he found so appealing in people.

"See that's the dark side of Samantha you don't know about yet," Briana said to Abraham, contributing a much different take on her friend's defense of Darren Hoff. "She likes having a lap dog at her disposal. Oh, Darren? Can you help me with my Trig homework? Darren? Do you have an extra dollar for the tip jar? I just spent my last one."

"What's the big deal?" Samantha now defended herself. "We're friends. Those are the kinds of things friends do for each other." She addressed Abraham and Drake. "It's like with you guys."

"But we were only kidding about the wanting to have sex with each other," Drake said.

"And poor Darren has been wanting you since before he knew what sex was," Briana added.

Samantha turned to Abraham. "Are you going to help me out here?"

Abraham was gloomily staring down at the table.

"What's wrong?" Samantha asked.

Still appearing distressed, he looked over at Drake. "You were only kidding about wanting to have sex with me?"

Their table shook with laughter, drawing stares from the weary patrons. Abraham then got around to defending Samantha. "I will just say this for my charming and beautiful date tonight: at least her weakness stems from not wanting to hurt someone, rather than not being able to stop from hurting someone."

"Aw," Samantha cooed, putting her head on Abraham's shoulder. "Thank you for explaining to them that I'm just weak."

Drake and Briana enjoyed Samantha's rejoinder. Abraham exhaled slowly. "We all have weaknesses. The question is whether we address them or pretend they're not there."

"Yeah, yeah," Drake teased him, preferring to keep things light.

Abraham decided to raise the stakes. "And in the spirit of that philosophy, I am going to put my money where my mouth is..." he paused for dramatic effect. "And show you the house."

Drake was genuinely surprised. "The house you grew up in?"

"Well, the one I grew up in until you and your mom dragged us over to that dump you call a house."

"Seriously..." Drake wanted confirmation.

"Seriously," Abraham responded. "Your house is a dump. I never told you that?"

"Come on, man..."

"Yes," Abraham gave him what he wanted. "It's a full moon tonight. Let's go visit some ghosts."

"Is it really haunted?" Briana asked.

Everyone started to clear the table and gather their belongings. "We're pretending you didn't really ask that," whispered Abraham loudly.

It was indeed a full moon, casting a harvest light, and the night was perfectly clear. The frosty winter air added an even greater sense of focus to the geometry of the valley; the rows, squares, rectangles, and ruts. As they drew closer to the dirt road that led to his past, Abraham instructed Drake to slow down. He then directed him where to turn.

"No wonder I couldn't remember this," Drake said as they rolled onto the dirt road. "There's no sign, no mailbox; are you sure this is it?"

"I go by the shape of the mountains on each side of the valley, and the tree line."

Drake and the girls looked around to see if they could discern the same landmarks. Abraham encouraged Drake to pull over so they could walk the rest of the way, in case there were still people living in the main house. He strongly suspected no one would be living in the small one in which he and his mother used to roost.

"So is some farmer gonna, like, come out with a shotgun if he hears us?" Briana asked as they strode lightly on the dirt road the rest of the way.

"Maybe," said Abraham. "Just let me do the talking."

"My hero," Samantha nuzzled up against his shoulder.

"See, Drake?" Abraham called softly over to the other couple, "Between the cold and the threat of violence, they're bound to rub up against us."

Drake was too interested in what lied ahead to engage his friend's banter. Abraham estimated it was about time to be quiet, anyway, so they walked in silence but for the sound of their footsteps on the hardened dirt. They reached the end of the skeletal tree line and saw no activity in the main house. There weren't even any cars or equipment parked around it any longer.

"Well we can relax," Abraham announced at normal volume. "Looks like our old landlords don't even live here anymore."

Samantha shivered, from the cold and, perhaps, the thought of living in such a house. "Good. Nobody should have to live in a house like that."

"Wait till you see ours," Abraham said.

"There it is," Drake proclaimed from behind them. "Am I right?"

Abraham turned around to look at it. "You are," he quietly confirmed.

They all faced the little house, their sight lines obscured sporadically by their breath steaming in the chill. The moonlight made it appear a bit larger, but even more empty than it clearly was.

Nobody said anything, much to Abraham's relief. He was not interested in anyone trying to modulate their voice into some sort of solemn tone as they conveyed their clichés. He decided to break the silence before anyone else dared to.

"Let's take a look around, Samantha," he guided her towards the side of the house they were closest to, hoping Drake and Briana would take a cue and head in the opposite direction. He thought the best way to keep everyone quiet was to turn the locale into a standard double-date finale in which each couple wanders into their own space to decide how much further their attraction will take them.

When Abraham and Samantha reached the back of the house abutting the acreage beyond, she hugged him tightly.

"I don't know what to say," she said as they continued their embrace.

"Good," he replied softly.

Her head was facing the fields as she rested it on his shoulder. He decided to face that direction too, rather than stare at the house. The fields had been picked recently, acres of leafy remnants scattered haphazardly, gleaming stark white with moisture that caught the light. They took in the eerie landscape for a short while.

"Would you consider that our first kiss on the golf course?" he asked her.

She thought about it before answering. "No," she finally replied. "It was too short, and part of a joke you were making."

So they kissed like a first kiss should be. It was new for them and classic at large. They breathed heavily yet were breathless for however long it took Drake and Briana to finally call from their end of the house that they were getting cold and it was time to go.

The drive home was quiet the entire length. Abraham realistically attributed it to everyone being tired, but luxuriated in a bit of self-righteousness by thinking that maybe the visit to the old house had augmented their empathy to some degree; that part of their hush was the sound of contemplation. Mostly what he thought about was the feeling of Samantha's hand in his, and how good her lips felt when every so often she would lightly brush his cheek with them.

Her house was the first stop. He walked her to the door and they kissed as briefly as they could bear, in case someone should be watching. There were no playful one-liners or teasing glances when he returned to the car. Their attraction was already taken for granted by Drake and Briana, as though he and Samantha had been a couple for a long time. They dropped off Briana, and then headed home.

Marisol was in the dining area reading when they walked in the door, and Abraham knew it was not out of concern, but because she wanted to read more than the few minutes it would take her to fall asleep if she read in bed.

"Did you have a good time?" she asked them as they stood in the entryway that looked through the large opening into the dining room.

"Sure did," answered Drake, giving Abraham the first sly look since the taqueria. Abraham smiled back. He really did have a good time, after all.

"I'll be in shortly, Dee," he said to Drake. "I want to talk to my mom."

Drake smiled and looked at Marisol. "Isn't that supposed to be your line when we walk in late?" he asked her.

She held up her palms briefly in resignation.

"Good night, Marisol," Drake said. "Don't wake me, Abe."

He disappeared down the hall. Once he heard the bedroom door shut, Abraham came over and sat in the chair next to Marisol.

"I stopped by the old house tonight," he told her.

Marisol was clearly surprised to hear this. She digested the news before responding. "You must have really liked the girl."

They exchanged perceptive smiles and Abraham leaned back as he considered his next contribution.

"We should go out," he said.

"Excuse me?"

"I can drive now. You've been alone for so long. We should hit some places. You still look young."

"I am young," she said. "Kind of."

"I can help you get on one of those singles websites…"

"I know how to do that if I wanted to."

"But then if you get some responses you can't do anything about it," he was becoming more enthusiastic about his proposal. "I mean, I'm sure Chelsea would drive you if you asked, but I know you don't want to ask. I'll give you a ride."

"Thank you, Abraham. I appreciate the offer…"

"I want to pay you back," he insisted. "I owe you."

They stared at each other for a few moments; he intently, she tenderly.

"Then you may have noticed I can take of myself," she gently reminded him.

"It's not about being taken care of. I'm talking about being happy."

"I will be happy when I see you off to college," she said, then leaned in closer, "in more ways than one."

Abraham nodded for a while and tried not to smile. He wanted to come up with the perfect line with which to end the evening, to express his joy and gratitude, but still zing her. He went with one he hadn't used in quite a while.

"I love you, Mom."

It seemed to work pretty well.

Chapter Eighteen: On The Air

Chelsea could not figure out that man. She had served on a couple of boards with him, engaged him in pleasant conversation during functions benefitting the schools that their kids attended together as they grew up, and had seen him at many a city council meeting providing public comments which tended to be respectful for the most part. But when Lane Hoff recorded his podcast, he was a completely different person.

She had heard comedians and actors mention during interviews that they were actually quite introverted people when the spotlight wasn't on them who just knew how to turn up the showmanship when it was, and apparently sitting in front of his computer had the same effect on Lane.

The relentless puns he wrapped around his name were the first clue that he must have felt destined to be heard. The show was called "The Fast Lane" and each segment adhered to his eponymous theme. His opening monologue was dubbed "The Sound Hoff"; the part in which he would easily shoot down a moronic example of an opposing viewpoint allegedly submitted to him by an angry listener was crowned "The Face Hoff"; the section where he commiserated with commenters who agreed with him and fanned their already-flaming sanctimony was referred to as "Hoff The Charts"; the best e-mail or comment sent to the website was brought to "Victory Lane" at the conclusion of the show, at which point listeners were encouraged to visit the site and order a "Hoff My Rocker" t-shirt, which had an inscription on the back reading "I Get Hoff in The Fast Lane" with the web address underneath accompanied by the assurance of "Common Sense for Monterey County".

Chelsea wasn't sure how many people listened to his show, which he linked to his website weekly. The site boasted that 81 people liked him on Facebook, and there were always several dozen comments attached to every screed that he posted, though most were submitted by the same bevy of fans hiding behind handles like RandMan79, USAlly, or RedOnBlue, and who regarded the threads as a members-only ideological circle jerk and would lash out at anyone who opened the door on them.

She could bring herself to listen every few weeks or so when she felt it was about time to adhere to her vow of understanding "the other side". She mostly marveled, however, at the breathtaking contrast between Lane Hoff, concerned citizen and PTO member, and Lane Hoff, podcast mini-mogul. She actually broached the subject with him once at a baseball game, as his son Darren played on the team with Drake and Abraham. They parried and dodged for a minute as she didn't want to offer her true opinion of the show, and he didn't want to offer the online version of himself in person, so she wrapped up the matter by asking him why he had decided to adopt such an angry persona. He looked at her as if she could not have asked a more stupid question.

"So that people pay attention to me," he said, trying his best not to let his tone of voice match the condescension he must have realized his expression belied.

"Of course," Chelsea replied, suddenly aware of how stupid her question really was now that she had heard the answer.

It was obvious Lane had dreams of breaking through to a nationwide audience, but he consciously tried to relate larger issues to local examples whenever possible so as not to alienate his regional fan base. An oppressive regulatory environment was illustrated by the installation of parking meters along a heretofore free avenue; signs warning people to keep their kids from hanging over the railing of the pier were evidence of a nanny state; if anyone associated with the City of Monterey suggested that building a roundabout may help the traffic flow at a certain intersection, they were guilty of turning America into Europe; and the unsuspecting cashier who wished Lane a "happy holidays" while he did his Christmas shopping was unwittingly unleashing a boycott and flood of phone calls to the store by his most charbroiled fans. Nothing was an anecdote, everything was a sign. And the latest chapter that Chelsea found herself listening to promised to be no different, based on the opening "Sound Hoff":

"As always, I am speaking to you from the belly of the beast," his voice announced, trying to sound deeper than it really was, "from the elite world of the Monterey Peninsula, where people care about your struggles as long as you stay away; where they praise the welfare state because that state is somewhere out there, a safe distance from their liberal fairyland. My friends, I am surrounded by people who hate you, and hate me too. They may say they are all about peace and love, but I assure you they hate the likes of us."

Chelsea had downloaded this latest episode onto her portable audio player that plugged into her car stereo, and was listening to it as she drove home from a Carmel Mission docents' meeting that had been attended by none other than Lane Hoff. He had contributed some well-received suggestions on how to provide an enhanced learning experience for visitors who may appear uninterested at first, but can be lured into hearing some history of the grounds through a variety of subtle techniques. She involuntarily snorted as she considered the irony of what he was saying in her speakers and what he had said in the meeting, then instinctively looked around to see if anyone heard her snort before remembering she was alone in the car.

"They hate everything about us; they hate that we don't play golf, that we work for a living and like a good hamburger, that we aren't afraid to shoot those who would do us harm either in our homes or overseas, they hate that we pray, and in general hate us because our lives represent reality, and they know it. We are the truth, fellow Fast Laners. I have seen more reality at Disneyland than I do here on the Peninsula. You live in the real world, my friends. I know most of my listeners hail from the Salinas Valley, and that is the real part of this county. I always feel like I'm sort of talking over the heads of the snobs out here to reach the true Americans out there, who feed us and keep this country strong. Of course when I say that, I know most people assume I'm just talking about the farmers and ranchers, the truckers, but today I want to address a key group of my audience that many will find surprising if they aren't thinking about things thoroughly, and most people don't; most people who don't listen to my show, they'd rather assume things about me and my listeners. Yes, today I want to address the fine men and women employed by those farmers and ranchers. What!? I can hear them now all around me. Lane, you're kidding! Mexican people don't listen to you! You're racist! Well of course I am. Freedom is racist! Christianity is racist! Self-sufficiency is racist! All the things I stand for...racist! But let's look at those principles I stand on, people, and decide who has more in common with the hard working men and women out in the fields: me, or these secular pseudo-intellectuals wasting their days in the coffee houses of the coast. Christian family values? Check. Strong work ethic? Check. The right to stand or fall on your own merits? Check. Check and mate, powder puffs! Those who keep the agriculture industry going don't need your environmental protections, your welfare checks, your holocaust on the unborn..."

"What about immigration reform, Lane?" Chelsea muttered out loud as she inched her way through downtown tourist traffic.

"...What they need is your respect, and contrary to what your touchy-feely vocabulary words may say, your actions speak louder, and your actions display not just disrespect for those who perform such backbreaking work, but contempt! Outright contempt! I know this not only because of the values I share with these people, but because they have been telling me. That's right, folks. The farm workers of the valley are starting to find me; they are seeking me out and contacting me. They are wising up to your verbal gymnastics and are rising up against the kind of soft bigotry you have sold them on for decades..."

"As opposed to the hard bigotry you sell?" Chelsea sneered a bit louder, then realized she was also starting to drive more aggressively and told herself to calm down.

"...See, they're starting to notice something about the elitists in this country, in this county. The comments and mail I receive on the website from you, my compadres, has been truly inspiring. And the gist of it is: farm work may be tough, but it's dignified, and beats the heck out of being an indentured servant. The only way for a Mexican to make a buck over here on this side of the hill is to wash the socks of the liberal elite, to scrub their toilets, to make sure their houses look good so they can throw parties you won't be invited to where they can talk about how enlightened they are, and how sorry they feel for you. And even if this work sounds better than anything the farming industry has to offer, señoras y señors..."

"Ooh, more Spanish. Nice touch, Hoff." Chelsea tried to make herself laugh about it.

"...you'd better have something more to offer than your dignity, because that ain't enough. A son or daughter who can help our school win a championship, or at least meet some quotas to earn it some more tax dollars, that would be great. Make us look good, el gente, help us show the world we're good people; camouflage the true nature of our hearts and do your utmost to help us convince ourselves we aren't the vile racists God knows we are."

Chelsea had to find a place to pull over. She found enough space in front of a fire hydrant and kept the engine running.

"...If we believed in God, of course. No wonder they don't believe in God; to do so would force them to admit they aren't who they think they are. They are using you, amigos, far more than any farmer ever could; and not only you, but like I said, your children too. You are no closer to citizenship thanks to their lip service, no more legal as they continue to pay you under the table, but your children? We'll take them, thank you very much. We'll strip all those values from them, the belief in God, the self-reliance; we'll make them one of us. We'll pit them against our own kids to inspire our little darlings to do better, since we're not half the parents you are. In fact, why don't you raise our kids, too, while you're at it? Sure, it's hard enough raising your own, but you're so good at it. You're such good parents. Maybe we'll help your kids become citizens if you keep washing our underwear for us. And if your kid's already a citizen? If you had him here on U.S. soil? Well, it would be a shame to have to go back to Mexico and lose out on all those benefits, wouldn't it? So here, take this sponge and this cleanser and be sure to get the kids to practice on time. We can't win without them. Ours aren't good enough. Our kids are soft. Without your little anchor babies, our little creampuffs will lose whatever edge they still have left..."

Chelsea put her hands over her face and leaned back in her seat.

"...Welcome to the twisted world of the Monterey Peninsula elite, my friends: a world where people have such little faith in their country, themselves, and their own children that they have to hijack the lives and children of those who mop their floors. We'll be back with 'The Face Hoff' after a few words about the good folks at Cody's Collision Repair..."

She turned it off and switched positions, resting her forehead on the steering wheel. It felt as though her home had been broken into and she was forced to watch it happen. She hoped that Lane would not continue this theme in the coming weeks, and that his listenership was as small as she suspected it was.

Chapter Nineteen: About Face

Neither Abraham nor Drake even knew Darren Hoff's father had a podcast until Chelsea warned them about it. Neither imagined many of their friends and classmates knew, either. They listened to the stream of episodes Chelsea most feared and read the website postings and figured that the content in general covered issues you become more lathered up about once your income grows and interactions with the outside world expands. And once you became a parent.

For apparently just enough parents were listening to The Fast Lane, and just enough of those listening had mentioned something in the presence of their kids, and since the latest content specifically referenced those kids in an oblique fashion, just enough of those kids took an interest and started to slowly tilt the disposition of the campus.

Knowing the likely source of inspiration did not make it any less weird to Drake's ears when someone first asked him if he felt like he had been riding Abraham's coattails all these years. It was first raised in one of the library study rooms during a group session attended by the members of a history project he was involved in as they prepared to make a class presentation the following class.

"No," he said to the boy who brought it up, whom he had spent little to no time with over the course of their years together in high school. "Why would I feel like that?"

"Well," the boy replied, clearly nervous but proud of himself for being the first to try and rupture the sway that Drake and Abraham held over so many, "a bunch of us were just thinking that, well, he's not your brother, and the only reason he's here is because your family took him in so his mother could, like, cook and clean, and it's like his job is to make you look good."

Drake needed a moment to process what just happened. The boy saw an opening and tried to fill it in some more.

"I mean, we were doing this thought experiment, and wondering what you would be like if Abraham had never come here. Would you be as popular as you are?"

"This 'bunch of us' you're talking about," Drake bounced back. "Let me guess, it's you, Darren Hoff, and some other idiot."

The other members of the group looked on anxiously, uncomfortable but titillated that they were watching minor history in the making. One of them laughed to try and ease the tension. The boy fed off of the small audience.

"You're avoiding the question, Drake. Come on, play the game with us. Would you be the same person you are today if not for Abraham?"

"And you're avoiding mine. Tell Darren Hoff that he needs to get over the fact Samantha Ulrich wouldn't fuck him if they were the last two people on earth."

The group laughed in unison at that one. Drake was ready to finish this. "And as long as we're bringing family into it, you can tell Darren his dad is an asshole, too."

"Why don't you tell him to his face, tough guy," the boy sneered.

"I will, right after I punch it," Drake stood up and made a move towards his study buddy, who was several inches shorter than Drake.

The boy jumped up and stood his ground. "I'm not afraid of you," he lied. "You're just Abraham's bitch."

Drake shoved him into the wall of the study room. "What about you? Would you be the same person if I crippled you?" Drake then grabbed him and spun him around into the window that provided a view into the library. The window rattled and caught the attention of everyone within sight. Drake saw everyone watching and saw the librarian approaching. He let go of the boy. The librarian entered and asked the boy if he was okay, and told Drake to go to the vice principal's office.

The vice principal, a long-time fan of Drake and Abraham, of course expressed his disappointment and reminded Drake what a role model he was for the other students. He asked what the boy could have possibly said to warrant such a display, but Drake didn't tell him the truth out of embarrassment, as he suddenly found himself wondering if what that boy said was true; if he truly was just a satellite in Abraham's orbit. He instead mumbled something about the boy making racist comments about Mexicans. The vice principal didn't seem convinced.

"Whatever the reason," he brought their meeting to a close, "don't let some punk jeopardize your future, Drake. You're not only a great example for students on this campus, but could be on your way to great things for yourself. Think about how your actions might affect that the next time some jackass gets in your face about something."

Drake appreciated that the vice principal referred to the boy as a punk and a jackass, but still found something hollow and unjust about the line of reasoning. Perhaps if he had confided in him the real reason for his outburst he would have been more understanding. He started to wonder, however, if a lot of people had been thinking likewise that he was a product of some sort of Abraham Effect, and didn't want to draw that out of anyone any further. At least it was over, he thought.

But it was far from over. As though everyone was aware of the administrative pressure being put on him to not retaliate, the chatter continued in tangential ways that seemed designed to test him, to dare him to do something about it. People asked him why he picked on someone smaller than him, and just as with the vice principal, he avoided the truth and shrugged it off as a mistake. He would notice Darren Hoff smirking at him from across the quad during lunch. Others would ask him if it was true that Abraham's mother was an illegal, and he would testily say he didn't know. Then they would adopt a knowing look as though his avoidance was affirmation. He got wind of a nickname for Abraham: Anchor-ham. When he would angrily ask people where they heard it, they would tell him to relax already, that it was all in fun. The atmosphere started to pollute his relationship with Briana.

"Do you think maybe Abraham has gotten too big for his own good?" she asked him one day after school as they sat in the yogurt shop he had frequented since he was a kid.

"I don't think Abraham is doing anything wrong," he said, dismayed that the subject had now come up between them.

"What about you fighting his battles for him?" she retorted. "Are you cool with that?"

"I'm not fighting any of his battles; I'm sticking up for him."

"So why did you have to bring Samantha into it?" she said.

"What are you talking about?"

"I heard from someone in the study group, that you were all, 'tell Darren that he can't fuck Samantha like Abraham can.'"

"Wait, what?"

"Is that the way you and Abraham talk about girls? About us? Why would you say something like that?"

"I didn't say anything like that. I said she wouldn't go out with him and so he should get over it and stop talking shit about Abe."

"He wasn't talking shit about Abraham. He was talking shit to you, from what I've heard. And what did Darren have to do with any of that, anyway?"

Drake looked around to see how the other few patrons in the shop were reacting to their argument. They were very quiet and obviously listening. He lowered his voice and responded to her. "He's instigating all of this."

"Darren? Oh, please."

"He and his Dad," Drake tried to maintain his low volume while his intensity increased. "Have you listened to his dad's podcast? Tell me that wasn't a direct attack on my family and my friend and his mom."

"You're nuts," she said, with an expression to match.

"You haven't listened to it."

"Nobody listens to it, Drake. And nobody pays attention to Darren, either. Honey, you're being paranoid." She reached out and ran her fingers through his hair. That calmed him down.

She continued her affectionate peace offering as she moved on to the next topic. "If Samantha breaks up with him," she said, "would that affect our relationship?"

He went from being soothed by her fingers to feeling like they were hollowing him out.

"Why?" he said. "Is she thinking of doing that?"

She nodded and continued to lightly massage his head. He knew what he should say. He knew what he should do. But there was a time not so long ago when he never would have thought he would ever be with such a beautiful girl. He used to ache when he saw girls like her, thinking that they would always be destined for someone else, that he would never be so lucky.

And again it occurred to him that maybe her presence in his life was only made possible by Abraham. Everyone liked him. And everyone liked Drake, too. But it was always in that order. He wondered if Briana liked Abe before she liked him. That thought experiment wrapped itself around him again. He may have refused to play it on the day Darren's lackey rubbed his face in it, but he had been thinking through an unstoppable range of scenarios since then. And whether or not Briana would be with him if he had not been associated with Abe was just one half of the projections he was making while she stared at him searchingly; the other half concerned his fortitude, and if he was really the kind of man who would forsake a friend out of self-interest. He had always been such a hero when he imagined the story of his life. The decisions he would have to make always struck him as so easy. But that was before he had actually been confronted with any.

He shook his head. She leaned in for a kiss. Her lips had the cool, sweet taste of vanilla frozen yogurt on them, a reminder of just how much she embodied his childhood fantasies of what love was going to be like.

This clash of the idealized future version of himself versus the actual realized version followed him home.

"I've been getting weird vibes at school lately," Abraham said as he played solitaire on the laptop computer they shared on the desk in their room. Drake was lying on his bed hiding behind a book he was somewhat reading. "Have you felt it at all?" Abraham asked him.

Drake shrugged. "I guess."

"Not enough to fight anyone about it, though, eh?" Abraham teased.

"What a mistake that was," Drake grunted.

"Sticking up for me was a mistake? For all the other Latinos that little jerk was denigrating?" Abraham praised him. "I know we're only supposed to start swinging as a last resort, Dee, but sometimes it's justified. You're a good man, bro."

The thought experiment slithered into Drake's consciousness again: if he had not served up that concoction about racial slurs to cover up what actually happened in the study room that day, and that kid really had made racial epithets, and Drake had never met Abraham, would he have done anything? Was he capable of any goodness without Abraham's timeline running parallel to his?

"Thanks, Abe." He hoped that was it. But Abraham continued.

"Even Samantha has been cold lately, really stand-offish."

"You're just used to girls fawning over you. You're not used to being rejected."

"Rejected?" Abraham said, spinning away from the computer to look in Drake's direction. "I didn't say anything about that. Has Briana said something to you?"

"Not really." Drake stopped short of telling a complete lie to his lifelong friend.

"Not really?" Abraham laughed as he repeated it. "Okay, then. What did she say?"

"Does it matter?" Drake suddenly barked as he popped up from behind his book. "Why can't you two work it out on your own? Aren't we getting a bit too old for 'ask your friend if she likes me'?"

"Dude..." Abraham let the outburst sink in. "Now you, too?"

Drake retreated behind the book again. Abraham stared at him until he realized no response was coming, then proceeded.

"What exactly is going on, Dee?"

"What do you mean?" he clung to his book.

"At school; am I missing something?"

Drake put the book on his nightstand while remaining on his back. He folded his arms across his chest and stared at the ceiling. "Nobody's asked you about your mom?"

"No."

"You haven't heard the nickname?"

"What nickname?"

"Anchor-ham."

Their room was more silent than it had ever been. Drake took advantage of a rare opportunity of late to have the upper hand in a conversation. He sat up and made eye contact.

"Nobody has been asking you to your face if maybe you're too big for your own good? That maybe you're a bit too cocky considering you were brought here?"

"I was brought here?" Abraham gasped. "Is that the kind of thing people are saying?"

"Yes, Abe, yes they are. And I have to field all of these questions and comments like I'm your publicity director or something."

"Well," Abraham jibbed, "poor you."

"Don't condescend to me. You don't think it hurts me, too?"

"Of course it must hurt, Dee. I get it. I mean, why should anyone who has earned their way into this community, like all of our classmates have, and you, why should someone who has worked so hard to get where they are have to bother with the plight of someone who has had everything handed to them, like me."

"You're turning this around, Abe."

"Turning this around? You really do think I'm the problem?"

"That's not what I meant. I mean, you're twisting my words around," Drake's frustrations got the better of him and he let them fly. "Yes! You're the victim here, Abe! And the hero, and the best thing that's ever happened to me, and the worst! You are everything, Abe! You are everything and I am nothing!"

They stared at each other for quite some time. Abraham finally looked off to the side. Drake put a hand to his forehead and looked down.

"Samantha is going to break up with you," Drake interrupted the stillness. He did not look at Abraham, but could hear him breathing heavily, as though coming to a decision as to whether or not he should cry.

"I'm sorry I can't do more," Drake added. "There are just too many battles to fight. I can't keep up. And everyone's watching."

Abraham continued to sound as though he just got off a treadmill. Drake managed to look over at him. He was still looking off to the side, away from Drake. "It's just a few more months, Abe. Just a few more months and we're out of here. Forget about her, and everyone else. Choose the college that's furthest away and don't look back. Money's no object. You're probably eligible for every scholarship and grant known to mankind."

"Ha!" Abraham caught his breath. "You're right. I probably am."

He stood up and headed for the door, pausing at the threshold. "You poor bastards who aren't," he glared at Drake. "How will you ever make it?"

Abraham continued out the door and announced that he was going to sleep on the floor in his mom's room.

Chapter Twenty: In a Corner

Marisol asked Chelsea to please answer the door because she was melting sugar in a saucepan and it was almost done, turning golden brown, and she wanted this dessert to turn out perfectly for everyone. The boys had been maintaining a tense space between them, and not confiding in anyone as to why, so as parents it was hard to feel completely comfortable with each other if the primary bond that kept the household together was not holding. She had no illusions that flan was the missing ingredient that would revitalize the adhesive properties lately weakening, but it could be a start. It could bring them all to the table together, perhaps. She hoped. The house had resembled a rest stop for years really, with meals taken individually at random hours from the assortment of dishes that Marisol prepared and immediately stored in Tupperware for whenever anyone needed them, but the boys had stuck together. If the two of them drifted apart, they all may as well be living in a furniture showroom.

She heard a male and female voice at the door. They spoke formally, giving each other a chance to introduce themselves and state their business, but what it was she could not tell. Chelsea was not responding to them. The male spoke in an effort to get her to respond. They took turns saying "ma'am" to her repeatedly. Chelsea still was not speaking, but apparently had let them in as Marisol could hear them walking methodically into the house.

A burly man and a mannish woman entered the kitchen with Chelsea, whose eyes were red-rimmed and glassy. The two guests wore matching windbreakers with badges affixed to them. Her first thought was that they were here about one of the boys. But then Chelsea quivered, "I didn't call them. I swear."

The woman approached Marisol and announced they were here from Immigration and Customs Enforcement. Marisol blacked out without passing out. Her eyes could see but she wasn't seeing anything. She heard the woman ask her questions about her name, her citizenship status, her country of origin. She probably answered the questions. She couldn't hear herself. She heard Chelsea's husband come in and say "Call your brother" to his wife. She expected the boys to come in but managed to remember they were at some sort of practice or study group or something that kept them out of the house right now, and she was grateful for that. She smelled the sugar burning and then was outside the house with the officers. She was in the backseat of a car. She saw the ocean out the window and then trees covering the hills they drove through to get to the freeway inland and then other cars and farmland and then houses and then buildings and more buildings and bigger ones and a skyline. What she mostly saw were scenes from Abraham's life, some important, some minor, all in great detail. She remembered things she had done and needed to do, and that she never would do. She had never thought that much about the future, as her life had been composed of so much routine since moving to Monterey, and now her lack of foresight seemed just as well, for there seemed to be nothing there.

There was a foreboding building as grey as the parking lot that surrounded it. There were people guiding her through doors and taking her picture and pressing her fingers onto inkpads and paper. There was a uniform she put on that had a number on it. There was a room that could have held janitorial supplies but held her instead. There were people who didn't introduce themselves and wanted her to sign something that had to do with "voluntary departure."

The word "departure" convinced her to wait as long as possible. She knew it was inevitable, she would be leaving. No case could be made. She did not exist in America, did not exist in Mexico. But she wanted to see somebody before she was sent away, hopefully Abraham.

She eventually went to sleep and when she woke up had lost her sense of time. She did not know how long she had slept, whether it was night or day, and she could not keep up with the speed at which her connection to everything that characterized her life up until several hours ago was evaporating. A bit more time in this bunker and she would start to question whether any of it really happened. All was on the verge. Nothing stood.

So when Abraham visited she spent some time early on convincing herself he wasn't going to suddenly disappear. And then when she did settle into reality it was no better because her fears of never seeing him again prevented her from saying as much as she wanted to. She didn't want to ruin this last moment together. And he was so angry. She wanted to say something profound to make him less so. But she felt like she was having one of those dreams of helplessness, where everything is going wrong and everything works against you as you try to reach the place you need to be.

All that she had been trying to guide him away from had caught up to him and smothered him. He was seething with hatred. He hated whomever turned her in, hated everyone at school, hated Drake for not sticking up for him more, hated Drake's family for not fighting harder to get her out of here, hated the internet for allowing Lane Hoff to have even the slightest audience, hated Samantha for only wanting to date him when he was popular, hated Darren Hoff for being Darren Hoff, hated every honor and achievement he had attained because they only seemed to have been awarded to make others feel better about themselves. He was not going to go to college. He was not going to allow anyone to use him as evidence of an American Dream they didn't really want him to have, but would applaud and pretend to be happy for him if he managed to pull it off. He hated America.

And though her name didn't come up, Marisol saw herself buried in his tirade, too. She had used him, perhaps worst of all.

Of course this is how it would end. How could it be any other way? Reality and fantasy were not just blurring because of her circumstances in the detention facility, they had been enmeshed from the day she set sail from Algeria. For two decades her reality had been tethered to lying about her very origins. And the biggest fantasy of all was that she thought she could get away with it.

A guard raised his voice from the other side of the room to tell them that their time together was coming to a close. The chair she sat in across from her son at once felt like her death bed. She thought she had as much chance of seeing him in heaven as she did on earth after today, so she decided to confess, in spite of the fact it would probably just deepen his anger. She did not want him to discover on his own the most important lie of all, to hear it from anyone other than her, the keeper of that lie.

So she told him that she was not really from Mexico, that they were not part of a small band of Muslims who were just determined to defend their faith from the tyranny of the majority; she told him that she was from the heart of the Arab world and had been employed by the members of a terror organization who were more interested in business opportunities than they were in God, that she came to North America from North Africa out of anger and frustration rather than a devotion to their cause, that everyone concerned agreed it was best that Abraham only know so much, that there were only so many lies he should be expected to conceal, that this would make it easier to keep the program running, that when it came down to it, everyone wanted what was best for themselves.

She apologized when she was done. She did not beg for forgiveness, as it seemed such an implausible request. She just said that she was sorry and that everything she did was to try and help him turn out to be a good person in defiance of the destiny she was paid to deliver, because she started to love him more the more she got to know him, and could not stand by and watch such a beautiful boy mature into such a handsome return on an evil investment.

She honestly felt like she was winning, too, up until that knock on the door. She felt as though she had found a loophole in her deal with the devil, in which hard work and dedication and a life living in fealty to clichés about a life well-lived could nullify the contract. But here he sat before her an angry young man, anyway. All of her efforts merely sent him on a different path and alternate series of motivations in getting there. He was not a religious fanatic, but instead a wounded member of a privileged class whose status was being taken from him.

He left the room as a man wronged, leaving Marisol alone at the table to wonder what her life had amounted to. She could have been held prisoner in her family's house in Algiers over the same time period and ended up in the same position: alone at a table watching her son go off to war with the world and nearly everyone in it.

She took to lying down most of the time, however much time that was, drifting in and out of consciousness. She was told that she would get a removal hearing soon, as she would not sign off on a voluntary departure. She was only buying time, though. She was not planning on fighting it. To do so would require her to reveal her true identity and open herself up to further investigations that would lead to her connections, and eventually incriminate Abraham. Perhaps that would be the wise thing to do, considering Abraham's state of agitation. Maybe he should be removed from society. But she held out hope that there had been enough goodness in his upbringing to lead him out of this turbulence and onto a productive path. She wanted to give him that chance. She wanted to give herself that chance. As she would hover somewhere near sleep she would reminisce about as many good times as she could recall in order to convince herself that her son deserved the benefit of the doubt, and that she had some moments when she felt like a pretty good parent.

At some point a voice startled her, telling her that her lawyer was here. Her lawyer?

As she was led to the visitation area she assumed it was going to be Chelsea's brother. She would thank him for the offer, but tell him that it was time for her to go. The idea that the family was putting in some effort to help her brought the first smile to her face since she had entered the facility. The smile was well-timed, she thought, as she wanted to be cordial in the process of declining his assistance. But when she entered the room she saw that it wasn't him.

It was Khalil.

He looked very much the same as he did eighteen years ago, a few pounds heavier with a rather lofty hairline, dressed in a suit that indicated he was doing well in his legal career. She realized her smile had given way to a gaping stare, as he looked unsure of whether she was glad to see him. She put her hand to her heart and took a deep breath, her lip quivering on the exhale.

"Hello, Marisol," he said formally, trying to sound every bit the lawyer.

She rushed towards him and embraced him. The guard lunged in their direction and snarled "No contact" while trying to separate them as if they were a couple of kids at a parochial school dance who had gotten closer than the length of their forearms.

But Marisol didn't want to let go.

"I'll just have to slip you that hacksaw under the table later," Khalil said gently into her ear. She was so happy to encounter some humor, and to pick up on the comfortable old rhythm they had shared during those wonderful months they had spent together.

"Please, sir, just five more hours," she said to the guard, still clutching Khalil.

The guard could not help but pick up on their easy affection for one another, and relented a bit with a tight smile of his own.

"Just don't get me into any trouble, eh?" he warned them lightly, gesturing to the windows in the door and the camera on the ceiling in the corner.

"Of course," Khalil said. They unraveled themselves from each other and sat down. The guard retreated easily to the back of the room.

Marisol and Khalil looked at each other contentedly for a little while.

"I know there's nothing you can do," she finally said.

"Legally, no," he agreed. "But I've made some arrangements."

"Don't tell me," she half joked. "You're coming with me."

"I would if I could," he said, half apologetically.

She deduced what the look on his face implied. "You're married, aren't you?"

He nodded.

"I understand," she said, disappointed but resigned. "I couldn't expect you to wait for a day I never even saw coming myself."

"I was so in awe of being in love with you," he said. "I couldn't believe such a thing could happen to me."

She put her hands up to her mouth as if in prayer. It felt so good to hear such things, even if it was part of being let down. Humanity was making its way back into her life, just when it appeared to have been lost. Khalil gathered his thoughts and continued.

"When it happened again many years later, when somehow another woman found some strange reason to love me, I thought that to turn my back on such a second chance would be an affront to God." He caught himself overselling it and they exchanged a knowing smile; always the over-romantic. "Not as much of an affront to God as joining Tariq's organization perhaps," he gracefully transitioned, "but an affront nonetheless."

"Is he still in charge?" she asked.

"No," he shook his head. "That's the good news. A big chunk of his investors left him. They felt he was stringing them along and wasn't really serious about wreaking havoc. The bad news is that Mohammed is off the leash now. He runs the operations here as an underground crime syndicate. They're more of a Muslim Mafia now than a terrorist organization. He convinced the profiteers overseas that if they want to make money, he could make them money; they just had to give up their dreams of watching Mount Rushmore blow up and get down to the kind of business that still eats at the heart of America, but without the dramatic footage. He sold them on the slow burn."

"Listen to you," Marisol teased him, "so lawyerly. Are you now going to tell me that you're his worst nightmare? That you won't rest until he's behind bars?"

"Actually," he said slowly in preparation for his next announcement, "he keeps me on retainer."

Her good humor plunged. She stared at him incredulously, not sure she could bear any more heartbreak at this point, not after she was starting to resemble a human being again. "Please tell me it's part of some plan of yours to bring him down."

He gave her a reassuring smile. "'Bring him down' might be overstating it, maybe 'slow him down' would be more appropriate."

She was not immediately persuaded. He apparently sensed this and changed course. "Or maybe I'm just a masochist," he added.

"That's what I was thinking," she snapped. "You hate yourself."

"I'm a self-hating Muslim."

She tried not to laugh at that one, but had smiled slightly by the time she could restrain herself. "It's your penance."

"My atonement."

"Your flagellation."

"You've gotten really good at pretending your Catholic."

She relented, if for no other reason than to find out what his grand scheme was. "Well?"

"Nope," he said. "I don't want you to know anything in case anyone asks. They'll see it in your eyes."

"That was Tariq's philosophy," she reminded him.

"It's a good one; kept me off the no-fly list." The reference to their past inspired a tug of dejection in her again. He picked up on it and moved on to the business at hand.

"And speaking of flying, and speaking of atonement, let me explain those arrangements I've made." He adopted a professional posture and spoke at a volume audible to her but not the guard across the room. "You need to listen very carefully because none of this can be written down. Are you with me?"

She focused on him and nodded.

"Good. Now the ICE assumes you're from Mexico. Go ahead and sign the voluntary departure. When they transport you down there, let them drop you off in Tijuana. Find your way to the airport and at the Air Mexico desk you'll find a ticket under your real name that will take you to Mexico City, from there you'll catch a flight on Lufthansa to Frankfurt, and then that flight will take you through to Algiers."

Marisol pursed her lips and contemplated a return home.

"I know," Khalil addressed her hesitancy. "I know you haven't exactly been yearning to go back there, but it's your only viable option considering the circumstances. And here's the good part: in Algiers I've lined up a job for you in a law office. You'll be making good money, more than enough to afford a place of your own. Someone will be waiting for you at the airport, and they will take you to a hotel that you're booked in for a week while you look for that place. Point being, you don't have to contact your family if you don't want to."

She was grateful but confused. "How did you...?"

"You're tri-lingual, a world traveler, and have been employed by a successful American entrepreneur for nearly two decades. I actually had to turn down a few offers for you."

She let the news cover her in warmth. She closed her eyes as if enjoying a massage. Then something occurred to her. "What I'm most proud of is my son."

"Of course," Khalil said. "I can make arrangements for him, too, and have him join you once you're settled in. I had heard he was doing really well so I assumed you'd want him to stay here and finish his education."

"I suppose he still might," she sighed. "But...however angry you were back when you joined the cause? Multiply that by about a million."

Khalil understood. "I'll contact Chelsea."

"Could you make up a story, please? I don't want her to know anything."

"Easy enough; I once had a goldfish that was more perceptive than she is."

Marisol laughed. "She means well." She then settled into an admiring look. "I can't thank you enough."

"It's the least I can do," he assured her. "You changed my life, and I couldn't do anything for you back then."

She tilted her head affectionately. "I know I only seem to say this when we are about to be separated for a very long time, but...I love you."

Khalil seemed to regard this as equal to any of the good news he had just given her. He looked like he wanted to say it back to her, but couldn't quite bring himself to do so. "I always felt good knowing you were nearby, even if I couldn't be with you," he said.

She understood why he did not reply in kind. "Come visit me in the old country. Maybe we'll go on a double date."

"I would love that," he said as he stood up. He then came over to her side of the table, bent over, and kissed the top of her head, burying his face in her hair. "And I love you, too."

He looked up and over at the guard. "I know," he called in his direction. "No contact."

The guard gave him a nod. Marisol stood up and she and Khalil hugged to the point where they were lightly rocking back and forth as though there was a slow song playing over the intercom.

Chapter Twenty-One: Through The Valley

Abraham felt so guilty about all of those times he had told people who were angry to "lighten up" because "life was good." He looked back in shock that nobody had punched him in the face. He certainly would have if someone said something similar to him now. But he couldn't imagine anyone would. He could feel how angry he must look. He had stopped for a late dinner on his way back from the detention center and noticed a few people monitoring him as though they wanted to make sure they were ready to dart under the table should he commence the rampage he apparently looked capable of.

Time alone in the car did not provide him with a chance to settle down. It only elicited more mental highlights of what made him fume. He talked to himself, assuming the nighttime darkness cloaked his quivering solo act from other passing motorists. He conducted angry conversations with people who weren't there and whom he put in their place. The monologues he delivered to his invisible nemeses had them cowering in shame. And even if they tried to come back with some defense of their venality, Abraham had an even more scathing rejoinder at the ready and a blunt object to their head to seal the victory.

He quieted down as he drew closer to the house. It felt as though the neighbors on such a sheltered street would somehow be able to hear him rant through his windows and theirs. He pulled the car into the driveway. He got out of the car and stood facing the house. The night air was cold, and he could just make out the sound of the ocean throwing its weight against the shore. The outdoor light by the front door was on, and inside he could see the entryway lit up, as well as the dining area in which his mother used to wait for him and Drake to return from a night out. He imagined it was Chelsea sitting in her place now. And if he went inside, he would have his mom's room all to himself. Drake's car was gone. He was probably out with Briana, holding forth on how terrible he felt about Abraham's mother being deported. She would feel so bad for Drake. She would make him feel better.

He took a deep breath and walked in the other direction, down the driveway and out into the street. There were no streetlights and no sidewalks, but the houses were so well-lit and the cars so few and far between that there was no need for public lighting. Each subsequent street he turned onto introduced a more aggressive flow of traffic and a harsher bank of lights. Eventually he arrived at the Transit Plaza. He studied a bus map and schedule that was protected by a plastic cover that had all manner of indecipherable etchings scrawled on it by people in love and in gangs. The bus he wanted wouldn't arrive at this late hour for some time, but he didn't mind. At first he was surprised that this didn't make him angry, and then he saw a contented middle-aged couple walk hand in hand out of the coffee house across the street and realized it was people that made him angry.

He paced around the plaza to keep warm, and keep calm. There were a few other people waiting for a bus. At last the 68 arrived, and he alone climbed aboard.

There were a few others on board headed from the peninsula back to the valley. They wore fast food uniforms and live-in nurses' scrubs. Abraham took a seat near the back and finally started to feel tired. The motion and hum of the bus put him to sleep.

He awoke lying on his side with the driver hovering over him.

"End of the line," he told Abraham. "Already took my break. You need to stay on and hit one of the stops you missed on the way back?"

Abraham sat up and gathered himself. "No," he stretched. "This is fine."

He got off and surveyed his location. A pink sliver of sunlight was just visible above the hills to the east. He recognized some buildings in the pre-dawn gray and started walking towards the frontage road. Once there he headed south and stayed on it as long as he could until he was forced to enter the freeway as town gave way to countryside. He walked along the far edge of the shoulder, the gusts created by the speeding vehicles keeping him off balance and sprinkling him with grit and dust. After several miles and the sun several degrees higher in the sky, a small town clustered around its one freeway exit loomed ahead. He wandered off the freeway before reaching the town, picking his way through the flimsy wires of a pasture fence and trudging past some cows who eyed him warily. He negotiated the fence on the other side of the range and crossed a street into an ultra-suburban housing tract one block long that had been built a few years back to lure a new breed of buyer into the valley, or provide an opportunity for current dwellers to upgrade. A few were abandoned, a few others for rent, and those still inhabited did not have enough money to install blinds or drapes on the windows and went with sheets and beach towels instead. He passed through another couple of blocks of homes that looked more typical of a farm town where only the labor lived, until he arrived at the edge of the small business district. The mosque was still there.

The parking lot was empty but for a couple of cars right next to the building. He went around back to the office and knocked on the door. One of the ladies who used to drive him to his lessons and teach him about the Quran answered, but did not recognize him. She asked if she could help him.

"Is Mohammed here?"

Now it all came back to her. She put her hand over her mouth and told him she'd be right back. She closed the door. About a minute later the door opened again. He was here.

"Hello, Abraham," he said, casually sizing him up. "You look tired."

"I walked from Salinas."

Mohammed tried not to smile too broadly. "Walked?"

Abraham nodded. "Can I come in?"

"You're always welcome here. You know that."

He held the door open for Abraham and put a consoling arm around him as he walked inside.

They all prayed together before Abraham took a nap that lasted until sundown, then prayed again before dinner, then prayed again before Abraham cleaned up, then again before bedtime. Abraham shared with them all that had happened. They thanked God for reuniting them. They asked God to take care of Abraham's mother. They asked God to help Abraham understand the glorious legacy of his heritage, which they had always wanted to reveal to him but were discouraged from doing so. Abraham asked God to judge harshly the people who had betrayed him. The ladies who had been his spiritual mentors as a child reminded him that was not an appropriate request to make of God. As they took turns explaining this to him, he glanced over at Mohammed, who grinned at him behind their backs.

And they kept on praying whenever they were all in the mosque together. But after the first day, that was rare.

The training that ensued was much more intense than when he had last participated as an adolescent. And Abraham loved every minute of it. It was an intoxicating rebound. Rather than sitting on a therapist's couch talking about how it felt to lose his mother, discover his true identity, and be uprooted from the home he was raised in, he instead worked out his frustrations through firing guns, building homemade explosives, learning to fight unfairly, and making the rounds of Mohammed's crime network. They would be treated to free meals, people would hand them rolls of cash, and if they did not, they would intimidate them and sometimes beat them.

At first Abraham wasn't sure he could go through with the beatings. He had enjoyed the intimidation thoroughly. Mohammed taught him that the upside of prejudice is the fear it instills, and to use that fear against those who would not bother to respect you otherwise. And that their particular background had the added advantage of being both the smallest and most feared minority, meaning they could have their way with all other populations. Beatings were just another form of intimidation, he assured him, physical rather than mental. He also coached him on how to disassociate yourself from violence as you committed it, to a point where it was even possible to enjoy it as one would a movie or video game.

The first step was using some type of simple weapon that was easy to wield, rather than using your bare hands, which was too intimate. Mohammed said he knew some guys who were actually into that, but didn't take Abraham as the type. A Little League bat was effective, as it was easy to conceal and did the job better than a big heavy one, as one of the biggest mistakes people would make in a bat attack was trying to swing for the fences, so to speak. "No," Mohammed told him as they drove to his first ambush, "you can hit a home run later. The first step is getting him down, so just take a quick shot to the knees and swing right through. Everyone wants to try and hit some guy's head out of the park, but that's an easy target to miss; he can duck or block that shot. Knees will always be there for you. Once he's down you go for the joints so he can't fight back: hands, wrists, feet, ankles. Precision counts here, since they're smaller targets, so it's best to flip your hands on the grip and turn the bat downward to use the top of it like a pestle grinding corn. Grind and churn away on the four corners, those joints. He's going to be screaming, so this is about the time you need to start imagining one of those people who turned on you, one of those people who decided to hate you and are glad you ran away from their little paradise. Think about how much you hate them, too, and just keep telling yourself that's who you've got beneath you now, that's who's screaming for mercy. They don't deserve it, Abraham." Mohammed stopped the car in front of a crackling stucco house with a brown lawn. He reached into the backseat and handed him a Little League bat. "And once they're on the ground and they can't grip anything and they can't stand up, that's when you can flip that bat back around into baseball mode and swing away. Do what you wanted to do in the first place. And to anyone you want. The meth head in this house here?" he gestured toward the sorry residence. "He's just a crash test dummy, a mannequin. He knows what he did, and that this day was coming. Those snotty punks who turned their backs on you? They have no idea. As far as they're concerned, they did nothing wrong. They think you're the bad guy. Take the most self-righteous one of all, Abraham. Imagine their face." He complied and thought of Darren Hoff. "Look at what that smarmy face thinks of you. How highly he thinks of himself. Now go in there and set him straight. Teach him a lesson."

He followed orders. He was proud of himself for not feeling the need to take too many swings once he had him down. A few high energy shots to the kidneys were all he required. He was a little frustrated with himself for calling the guy "Darren" as he delivered his message from The Prophet on the way out the door. Mohammed laughed about it when he told him, however, and said the important thing is that he got the sender's name right. He had put the "The" back in "Prophet" once he had taken over the organization and reimagined its business model. Abraham was allowed to call him just "Prophet" for old time's sake.

The assaults were fairly regular for a while. Abraham never reached the point of enjoying the work itself, but truly appreciated the feeling he would have afterwards. He was recapturing the sense of invincibility that he had enjoyed while at the height of his popularity in high school, the feeling that he was in complete control of his circumstances.

He rented an apartment in a mild-mannered complex, with playgrounds and large swatches of grass swirling around between the buildings. He didn't bother furnishing it with anything other than a futon. It struck him as not being much different than the dorm rooms his former friends must be living in. But when he stepped out of his door he was interacting with families and playing the role of cool younger adult to their kids. He was exchanging friendly insults with drywall contractors, cooks, hotel maids and tractor drivers. The irrigation supply store manager who lived a few doors down set him up with his daughter who had a place of her own and worked at the home improvement store. She and Abraham enjoyed each other's company but saw no future in their relationship, so they would hang out once in a while and try to provide insights into the opposite sex and agreed that if they couldn't find anyone else by age thirty, they would get married. There was no set type or age range of person with whom he socialized, no limits it seemed to the variety of businesses he was learning about in the process of trying to get in on their action. He couldn't imagine that college provided anything comparable to this as far as an education was concerned.

Eventually he was pulled from muscle duty as well. Mohammed told him it was merely part of his training, and not something he ever envisioned as part of his future with the organization. He told Abraham he was proud of him, though, for getting his hands dirty and for his willingness to learn all facets of the business. It was essentially a test as well, and Abraham had passed mightily.

This next phase involved being able to function in one of the legitimate branches of the network, and being able to contend with the monotony and routine that such duties often entail.

"It's important not to assume that what we do is always exciting or dangerous," Mohammed explained. "It is, at its core, still a business. And if you start to expect thrills at every turn, you will start to lose sight of the main mission, which is to make money. Drama is bad for business. We only crank up the soundtrack when necessary."

And so Abraham was given a job at a small trucking company that the organization worked with. He not only helped out with dispatching and maintenance, he earned his Class A driver's license and went out on hauls, some of them several days long, during which he not only would make deliveries and pick-ups, but explore ways that they could expand into these territories: the small town gambling of southern Nevada and recreational vehicle tourism of northern Arizona, the dueling opportunities within the pulsating towns on each side of the Mexican border, and any other points further south that caught his attention, deeper into the country he once thought held his family's roots. As with the more adrenalin-fueled phase of his apprenticeship, he found ways to enjoy the work, and was proud of his flexibility. It was indeed not as cinematic as the intimidation and the weapons training, but it implied a future for Abraham, which was obviously lacking in the kinds of jobs he had been previously performing for Prophet. Now he felt as though he had just as much of a future as those who would soon be earning degrees. During his meetings with Prophet he even started to get the sense that he was being groomed to take over some day, or at least serve in some sort of executive capacity.

It was easy to forget sometimes that it was a criminal enterprise he was engaged in. Most days he just felt like a hard-working young man trying to make his way up the ladder at his job, a good neighbor, a friend with benefits, and someone who had secrets just like anyone else.

Mohammed stopped by the truck yard one day and popped into the office to invite Abraham to lunch. Abraham suggested they go to an upscale bar and grill in the few blocks' worth of Salinas designed to appeal to the white collar lunch crowd. Upon arrival Mohammed teased his protégé about getting soft.

"When I told you to get acquainted with the dry side of the business I didn't think you'd take it this far," he said. "Next thing you know you'll be bald and wearing glasses and polo shirts."

"When was the last time you drove a truck fourteen straight hours?" Abraham fired back.

Mohammed nodded his appreciation. "Your commitment to the mundane is duly noted, habibi. Everyone wants be the holy warrior and no one wants to pay the bills; the manager's dilemma. You'll know what I mean some day."

Abraham tried to take his comment about the future in stride and not act too pleased. Fortunately their server came and he could direct his smile towards her. After they placed their order Mohammed continued to flatter him.

"I imagine being out there on the road for long periods of time, and getting to know some of our investments and interests, you've come up with some ideas on how we can keep our competitive edge."

"I have," Abraham sublimated his exuberance about where this was headed by adopting an overly serious tone and countenance. He furrowed his brow so snugly that it started to hurt.

"Well," Mohammed asked. "Are you going to tell me any of them?"

"Oh," Abraham said, massaging the lingering effects of the furrowing from his forehead. "Of course..."

And he piled on the ideas. He started with an overarching philosophy: sustainability; to make all subsidiaries appear as legitimate as possible, with the idea that slightly smaller payoffs over a longer period of time were ultimately more valuable than bigger payoffs that were more likely to get busted in a relatively short period of time. This would also help increase the distance between the activities of said affiliates and the executive board, namely The

Prophet. Then Abraham launched into explicit examples of what this sustainability and deniability would look like as applied to some of the specific holdings he had been studying. Their server would come around occasionally to deliver their food and check how they were doing, as would the busboy to keep their water and iced tea glasses filled, and it dawned on Abraham that there was no need to pause the conversation or speak in code, as everything he pitched to Prophet sounded like any other business conversation at any other table around them, which also helped illustrate how sound his innovations were.

Prophet listened to him burn with ideas and seemed to be silently feeding off the intensity Abraham exuded. The satisfaction that worked its way across Prophet's face had Abraham even more inspired about his prospects. When the check came Prophet grabbed it.

"I've got this," he said to Abraham with a hint of familial pride. "In the process of keeping our heads level, men in our position need to be able to think big, and act big." He laid some cash on the tray under the bill. "And you are showing me some of that, Abraham. You seem to have that gift of balance."

Abraham thanked him as the server came by to pick up the check. Prophet told her it was all there. She smiled, as it must have been about a fifty percent tip from what Abraham could tell.

"What do you say we blow off some steam tonight," Prophet grinned. "Squeeze off some rounds, maybe blow something up. You've earned it. Know of any fresh abandoned areas we haven't lit up yet?"

It suddenly occurred to Abraham, "My old house."

Prophet laughed. "Really?"

"I took a date out there a while back. I can't imagine it's any more in demand than it was then."

"You took a date out there?"

Abraham smiled sheepishly. "Whatever works, eh?"

"And did it?"

His smile faded. "For a while it did."

Memories of Samantha abruptly rendered him melancholy. He was surprised at the power these highlights held, but then he had tried very hard not to think of her since his walk back into the valley. Prophet let him brood for several moments before suggesting they leave.

As they walked outside amongst the agricultural gentry, Prophet followed up on Abraham's inward reminiscing. "Do you ever miss life on the peninsula?"

"What's there to miss? They didn't want me there."

"But do you ever wonder what life would be like if you were able to stay?"

"I try not to," Abraham said, then quickly realized a need to apologize. "Not that I'm not grateful for everything you've done for me, Prophet. I truly am grateful."

Prophet chuckled. "Don't worry," he said. "I understand. You had the world on a string, and they took the string from you. Now you have to fight for it. I'd certainly wonder if I were you."

They reached the intersection where the faux gas lamp streetlights ended and the uniform supply companies began. Prophet gave him a single pat on the back before going his separate way. "See you tonight, habibi. About nine?"

Abraham nodded and spent the rest of his afternoon at the dispatch office trying harder than usual not to think of what went wrong on the other side of the hill. When he got home he heated up a can of soup and quickly ate it before going outside to kick the soccer ball around with some of the kids in the complex. As the sun went down he regretted offering up his old house as their firing range for the night, but didn't want to call Prophet and change the location for fear of demonstrating regret (or indecisiveness).

Firing Glocks in the moonlight helped put his mind at ease. Prophet had arrived early and directed Abraham to park next to him by using the two shiny new handguns as traffic batons. They started by aiming at a large oak tree towards the back of the property past the homes. Abraham was relieved because he couldn't remember ever climbing it or carving anything into it, so he fired away free from any recollections and was able to enjoy the rhythm of the discharge and kickback, the feeling of power bursting from his hand. Then Prophet suggested they turn their sights onto the house. Abraham purposefully assumed he meant the main house rather than their little old rental, as he had few vivid memories of the foreman and his wife, other than the harsh smell of her drugstore perfume.

But he sold the bigger house to Prophet as "More to hit."

"Whatever," Prophet said, and unloaded a whole clip into the empty house, first filling the wood surrounding a window with bullets, then blowing away the glass.

When Abraham was finished with his barrage, which didn't adhere to a pattern like Prophet's, and instead arbitrarily hit random parts of the exterior, Prophet approached him with a new clip and a question. "Ever listen to that guy with the podcast, The Fast Lane?"

Abraham grabbed the clip and jammed it into the gun. "I did before I left."

Prophet loaded his weapon as well. "You went to school with his kid, right?"

"Sure did," Abraham said, and fired into one of the windows, watching the shards of glass catch the moonlight as they splashed about.

"He's on a kick about Muslims now," Prophet said, watching Abraham line up his next shot. "He's starting to piss me off."

Abraham fired into the next window and again paused to watch the cascade of moonlit glass. "He's always on about something, and pissing people off is the whole point."

"I know he's got a thing for illegal aliens. He went after your mother, didn't he?"

The question surprised Abraham. "Did I tell you that?"

"You were out of your mind when you showed up on our doorstep. You told us lots of things."

Abraham shuddered and started to seek out another target on the house. "He never mentioned her by name. So whenever I brought up the possibility, it was written off as overreacting." He became too agitated to continue scoping the house and lowered his gun. "But that's the loudmouth creed: their big mouths aren't the problem; it's how people react to them that's the problem." He turned to Prophet. "Are you trying to distract me? Is this a drill or something?"

Prophet laughed and walked over towards the little house that Abraham had shared with his mother.

"Where are you going?" Abraham called after him.

"I need a more challenging target."

Abraham caught up with him. "Those trees along the road are pretty skinny."

"What do you care?" Prophet stopped and looked right at Abraham, his eyes shining like the shattered glass from the windows they shot out.

Abraham shrugged, unable to come up with what he wanted to say.

"You don't like people defiling memories of your mother. Who would?" Prophet said. He changed course and started walking to his car. "Come here," he motioned.

Abraham followed him and they went around to the back, stopping in front of the trunk. Prophet took out his keys and unlocked it. The trunk door slowly rose. The automatic light kicked in and shined on a hog-tied man with duct tape pressed over his mouth. It took a couple of seconds for Abraham to make out his features.

It was Lane Hoff.

"Have you two ever met?" Prophet asked them, as though Lane was an unbound and ungagged member of the conversation.

Abraham and Lane shook their heads as they looked at each other.

"Imagine that," Prophet narrated. "The man who ruined your life never had the courtesy to introduce himself."

Lane's terrified eyes were locked onto Abraham, who was disappointed in himself for enjoying the sight, but enjoying it nonetheless.

"It may not look like it," Prophet continued. "But we're actually doing Lane a favor. We're proving him right. See, he thinks that Muslims are evil. Never mind what part of the world they're from. A Muslim is a Muslim, and we're evil."

Lane frantically shook his head with a grunt and widened his eyes as if to disagree. Prophet glanced over at Lane's gesticulating and swiftly cracked the butt of his gun into Lane's forehead. "See?" he said as his victim tried to shriek through the duct tape and writhe in pain despite the bound limbs and cramped quarters, "pure evil. And it's because we're Muslim."

Prophet bent down and turned Lane's head to face Abraham, who continued to stare at Lane and wonder if he was capable of forgiving him.

"You didn't even know that Abraham and his mother were Muslim, did you?"

Lane shook his head.

"Wow," Prophet said. "It was like a two-for-one deal right under your nose: Illegal and Islamic. If only you knew. You could have increased your audience by, like, five assholes."

Prophet stood up and took his place by Abraham's side. "Anything you want to say to the writer, producer, and star of 'The Fast Lane'?"

So many malformed questions and statements tried to arrive at an articulate place within the maelstrom battering Abraham's thoughts that he barely remembered to respond. He decided to keep it simple, as he could feel his voice was going to quiver whenever he finally settled on something.

"Were you trying to get people to turn on me because of your son?"

Lane shook his head. Prophet cracked it again. Lane nodded and moaned.

"Hey, look at that," Prophet mused. "We're proving another one of his pet points: torture works."

Lane shook his head again.

"What?" Prophet noted the head shake. "You don't believe that either? How much of what you spout off on that show do you actually believe?"

Lane shrugged.

"It's all about trying to make it big, then, isn't it?"

Lane nodded.

"More good news, then: we're going to make you famous after all, Lane. You get to be a martyr for a cause you didn't even believe in. And none of your followers will ever know. Congratulations."

Lane screamed as though screaming loudly enough might blow away the duct tape. Prophet closed the trunk. He leaned back on it and addressed Abraham, who still stared at where Lane had been in his field of vision.

"I knew the dog was a bad idea," said Prophet.

"What?" Abraham shook himself out of his head and into the conversation.

"I had a feeling that it was the wrong move, but was convinced we needed another type of animal, more human-like than sheep, before graduating to a person, and I couldn't see any better options: horses are too big, cats too small, all the other farm animals didn't seem to have any personality, I even looked into getting a used monkey from a science lab."

"Oh," Abraham at last made the connection to the incident from his youth, "that."

"The moment after it happened, I thought I had lost you. I was kicking myself for not listening to my gut."

"Well you did lose me for a while."

Prophet pressed on as though Abraham had not been contributing anything. "And then it occurred to me almost immediately after you went home that day exactly why it was a bad idea and what I should have done instead."

He stopped leaning on the trunk and stood upright, staring into the darkness beyond and talking to himself, it seemed, rather than Abraham. "Dogs are not like people. They're better than people. Dogs are good or bad through no choice of their own. But people can have the best of circumstances and still decide to be cruel. So it hit me: I should have just waited a while longer and gone right from the sheep to a human victim."

Now he turned his full attention to Abraham. "Killing a dog is like, an abuse of power. But if you can find the right person to kill, someone who deserves their fate, you're doing the world a favor."

He banged on the trunk a couple of times. "So here we are at last: Your final exam."

Abraham stared at Prophet and tried not to betray any emotion. Prophet darted merrily to the front of his car and called back, "Keep that gun and follow me."

He hopped in the driver's seat and started the car with a howl as though someone had just called him about a great party that they were now going to crash.

Abraham slowly climbed into his own driver's seat, not certain he wanted to kill Lane, but certain that if he didn't, then Prophet would kill them both.

The tail lights of Prophet's car pierced the dust that swirled up from under his tires, turning it red. Abraham followed the hazy beams and glanced in his rear view mirror. The image of his old house glowed for a few jittery moments before disappearing into the red cloud.

Chapter Twenty-Two: In Sacramento

Growing up in Monterey and having his big city experiences primarily associated with San Francisco and Los Angeles, Drake was not used to living in a city with a big river running through it. That was his favorite feature of the capital city, as he not only found it aesthetically pleasing, but a harbinger of his future. He saw himself living in a city of powerful rivers, like New York, Chicago, Boston, or Washington D.C., perhaps working his way up in the public sector first, and then transitioning into some bigger private money later on after he had built up plenty of good karma.

There was a point when he first entered law school that he wasn't sure if he was cut out to be much of a lawyer. He struggled as a student and didn't seem to grasp the coursework as fluidly as his classmates. But then his internship at the California Department of Justice provided him with the opportunity to discover his strengths as, essentially, a salesman. His ability to network and coerce showed him that he could do quite well if he just managed to make it through school and the bar.

It was a relief also to find himself in possession of some confidence again. Abraham's sudden disappearance at the end of high school, at the end of their childhood, had left Drake feeling as though he was constantly searching for the opening in an enormous set of stage curtains, perpetually sifting through and batting away at the swaying cloth and wondering what was on the other side: an answer to why he left, where he was, a reconciliation, and perhaps most of all a solution to the mystery of whether Drake could ever fulfill the promise he exhibited when Abraham had been around, but which seemed to vanish once Abraham did likewise. Last summer his stint at the DOJ had at least assured him he could fake his way through the lingering doubts, so he enthusiastically had signed on for another go round this summer.

Drake never saw anyone else from the office when he took his lunch by the river, as there was about a mile separating one from the other, and most of his colleagues preferred to stay close to work. When he would tell them where he had been after they asked why he didn't join them at a more localized haunt, they would make faces and disparage the presence of tourists. But the tourists in the Old Town section of Sacramento were about the closest thing to a reminder of home that Drake would experience during the summer. The traps were of course quite different up here: river boats and steam trains and old western facades on buildings meant to remind people of the days when the city was not just powerful, but cutting edge. The presence of vacationers loafing along a waterfront was a familiar pattern nonetheless, and Drake embraced them as an added bonus to his fixation with the river rather than a distraction.

So he was surprised when the hand that tapped him on the shoulder as he gazed down at the current did not belong to a tourist asking him to take a picture of him with his family, but to an attorney in the Criminal Law Division with whom he had been working.

"Ron," Drake quickly moved from surprise to schmooze. "I told you this was a great lunch spot."

Ron smiled but moved right into business. Another man in a suit, which is about as far as one could describe him, stood just behind Ron. His other defining characteristic was that he held a briefcase. "This is Federal Agent Garcia, from the Department of Homeland Security."

"Pleasure to meet you, sir," Drake reached out to shake Garcia's hand. "Which division do you work in?"

Garcia stepped forward and shook his hand, "A little of this, a little of that."

"Agent Garcia wanted to ask you some questions," Ron chimed in, "and we both figured it would be best not to do so in the office."

"It's difficult enough to get someone to effectively focus and cooperate without them being the subject of gossip and rumors," Garcia explained.

Drake tried to lighten the mood. "Well, if Ron knows, then that's a non-issue already. Everybody else will know by the time I get back."

His attempt failed. Ron forced a pallid smile as Garcia explained, "He has assured me that confidentiality will not be a problem."

Ron took that as his cue to leave. "See you back at the office, Drake. Don't worry about the time. Give Agent Garcia as much as he needs."

"Will do, Ron," Drake said as they gestured their good-byes.

Garcia got down to business. "Let's have a seat, shall we?"

They took over a picnic table with benches attached in the shade of a tree just off the river walk. Garcia placed his case on top of the table and opened it. "Do you know this person?"

He took out an 8 x 10 photograph and passed it over to Drake. His pulse rate soared as he took in the face blankly staring out at him from the picture. It was Abraham.

"Oh my God," Drake gasped. "Yes. Yes of course I do. You finally found him."

"What do you mean by that?" Garcia asked.

"My family filed a missing person report years ago. We didn't think we'd ever see him again."

"This has nothing to do with that."

"Oh," Drake said, re-examining the picture and looking at it in a new light. "Oh, wait. Oh no. I thought he looked a little weird. This is a mug shot, isn't it?"

"It's a driver's license photograph."

Drake breathed a sigh of relief. "That's good." Then he realized he was still being asked about his old friend by a federal agent, "Then again, maybe not?"

"What about this man?" Garcia passed him another photograph of a man who stared not blankly but angrily at the camera.

"No," Drake said. "I don't know him, fortunately."

"Well, unfortunately, your old friend knows him. In fact, he's known him since he was a child, and started working for him again a while back. Right after he disappeared from your life, I assume. He goes by the name of Mohammed, or more dramatically to those who work for him, 'The Prophet.'"

Drake looked hesitantly at Mohammed's picture, as if it was one of those spooky old portraits in a haunted house caper whose eyes follow you around the room. "He's known him since he was a child?" Drake wondered aloud. "How did I not know this?"

"We didn't know it either until recently. We had been tracking Mohammed before Abraham entered the picture. Only when we started to research Abraham's background did we realize he was actually re-entering the picture. Those after school sessions he attended?"

Drake turned his attention from Mohammed's picture to Garcia. "This guy?" he said as he jiggled the photograph. Garcia nodded. Drake exhaled. "And now you're going to tell me that this guy's not a Jesuit scholar, of course."

"He's an Islamic terrorist."

If they had still been standing by the railing along the river, Drake may have jumped over it. But sitting in the constricting space of the picnic table just left him feeling paralyzed. He tried to process the information, but nothing happened. All was still. He felt as though he may be fading from existence as he sat there.

Garcia broke the silence, perhaps imagining that was the only way out of it. Absent the ability to explain anything gently, he at least spoke slowly.

"Abraham's mother was contracted to have her baby on U.S. soil by a broker in the Middle East who has since gotten out of the business, pushed aside by Mohammed it seems. She posed as a Mexican immigrant, perhaps even arriving here via the southern border. When we learned she had been deported before our investigation started, we tried to track her down in Mexico and there was no record of her. We assume she was provided passage to return home under her real name, whatever that may be. It's as though she was never really here."

"She practically raised me," Drake said to no one in particular.

"Indeed. You had a lot of contact with her; and with him."

Now Drake snapped to attention. "Are you implying something?"

"I'm merely re-stating facts that you have helped to confirm."

"I didn't know anything," Drake spat.

"Based on your reactions I assume you didn't."

"You use that word a lot: assume."

"It's what people do when they don't know the whole story," Garcia said. "They fill in the blanks."

The agent let his words hang there. Drake contemplated where this meeting could lead once it was over. He heard the warning bells signal that the drawbridges on each side of them spanning the river were about to trigger. The automobile traffic was halted before the bridge to the south rose in the middle and the one to the north slowly spun.

"All right then," Drake sighed. "What do you want from me?"

"You're looking at this from the wrong perspective," Garcia said, maintaining his detached steady pace. "Think of the advantages this revelation provides you, the opportunities for advancement."

Drake nodded for a while before laughing mournfully at the prospect of once again catching a ride on Abraham's coattails. Garcia did not bother reading anything into Drake's reaction and got down to business.

"Mohammed is very good at obscuring his activities. He takes his cues from organized crime rather than a bunch of zealots driving vans filled with fertilizer into national monuments. But we have some promising leads that link him to a specific crime that carries with it the harshest of penalties."

"Murder?"

Garcia nodded. "We don't want to move on it until we have built up the strongest possible case. You're probably familiar with the disappearance of Lane Hoff a couple years ago."

"Yes. I went to school with his son." Drake then caught himself laughing again. "That's quite the reunion we're going to have someday."

Even Garcia grinned faintly. "Which brings me to my point: we would like you to reunite with Abraham and see what you can learn."

Drake shrunk slightly and turned his attention to the river. "I don't think I can help."

"We can tell you where he lives, the places he frequents."

"No, I mean he's not going to want to talk to me, at all, about anything." Drake watched the bridges reach their peak of pulling themselves apart. "Things didn't end well between us."

"What happened?"

"Everyone turned on him towards the end of high school. He went from king of the hill to bottom of the barrel, and I..." Drake had never said this out loud to anyone before, and now here he was stuck with a federal agent as his confessor. "I gave up trying to defend him. It was easier to just side with the crowd and tell him to get over it."

Garcia demonstrated about as much compassion as Drake expected. "Maybe your classmates could smell a rat."

Drake gave him a sharp look. "They were jealous. There wasn't anything he couldn't do. He was the smartest, most talented person on the peninsula, and there was a time when everyone loved him."

"And then what?"

"He was a housekeeper's son. And he was eating their lunch."

"Why didn't anyone think of that before?"

Drake slowly scanned the river as the bridges were putting themselves back together. He looked back at Garcia and shrugged and said he didn't know.

But of course he did know. And while the impulses were always simmering that led people to decide that anything they didn't like about themselves was caused by Abraham rather than their own scarcity, he also understood who first provided them with the excuse to act on those impulses:

Lane Hoff.

Chapter Twenty-Three: In Line

His old apartment complex was too dangerous, Abraham decided. Not for him, but for the good people who lived there. Now that he could no longer avoid the reality of what he was involved in, now that he was no longer the heir apparent to Prophet, no longer his most trusted confidant, he did not feel very secure about his future, and not just in terms of his career prospects. So he isolated himself in order to spare any innocent bystanders.

His new address was in a part of town that still seemed hazy on the clearest of days, on a wide street where the traffic was sparse, but very fast. There were still children in the building, but they stayed indoors and watched television or played video games while one parent slept with the bedroom door locked, and the other parent existed as the villain in the stories that were told during the waking hours.

He did not spend much time in his apartment, and battled feelings of hypocrisy in the process. For if the object of placing himself in desolate circumstances was to prevent collateral victims should his employment with Prophet be terminated, then hanging out in public, especially some of the more appealing areas of it, would seem to undermine that goal. But he had a hypothesis, or perhaps more of a rationalization, which stated that Prophet, and to some degree his enemies, were not stupid enough to come after him in a pleasant community setting where the police action would be swift and the witnesses plentiful and deemed worthy of protection. Therefore by avoiding his apartment building and inserting himself on social higher ground, he was protecting both ends of the economic spectrum.

Not that Prophet was making any overt threats. But it was obvious to Abraham that his star had been slowly fading since the Lane Hoff incident, or more specifically its aftermath. He apparently had not sufficiently reveled in it, or at least had failed to disguise how much it bothered him.

"If you can't handle that guy's death, how are you going to handle anyone's death?" Prophet had confronted him some weeks afterwards, as Abraham continued to quietly find a way out of the funk he, too, was surprised to find himself in, as he was frankly no less stunned than Prophet that he should give a damn about deleting that vile bastard.

"Maybe it's because I knew his son," Abraham offered, now that the subject had been brought out into the open. "Who was also a creep, incidentally; but because of those family associations I see him as a human being. If it had been someone I knew nothing about, then maybe I'd be fine."

Prophet appeared unmoved. Abraham wished he had simply said that he was handling it, he'd be fine, it was the first time, and it would get easier. He realized too late that analysis was not a valued trait when it came to certain features of their business. Scrutiny was fine for devising new revenue streams and considering how to avoid getting caught when committing the latest perfect crime, but the crime itself required a flinty amnesia. He tried to soothe his regret at expressing even a modicum of emotion by telling himself that there was nothing he could have said in response to Prophet calling him out, that the damage had already been done thanks to his moodiness throughout the preceding weeks.

He started to hear a lot less from Prophet. He was for the most part just a truck driver now, and not one that was sent out on Lewis and Clark missions designed to explore far-flung business opportunities. Instead he was running stolen or illegal goods that remained a mystery to him, as he always received explicit instructions from the new dispatcher not to look in the trailer. And when he did get a call from Prophet, or even more rarely a visit, it was to send him on the kinds of low-level errands that had characterized the early days of his training: rousting deadbeat meth heads, collecting payments from the most trembling of clients, and occasionally serving as a valet for some of the more intense operations, as if Prophet wanted him to know that his failure did not excuse him from being part of the business, only from being a vital member of it.

Abraham felt as though he had gone from being an executive in a powerful firm to cleaning toilets in the executive washroom. For a while he clung to the hope that this was just some sort of a hazing routine, that Prophet was observing how he responded to the demotion and would welcome him back to the major leagues if he liked what he saw, but Abraham was totally at a loss when it came to knowing what the correct response looked like. Should he call and ask for more responsibilities? Keep his head down and do what he was told? He decided to play it stoic, as he imagined desperation at this juncture would be about as appealing to Prophet as contemplation was during the days and weeks following the death of Lane Hoff.

And the deeper he sensed he was falling on the organizational pyramid, the deeper grew his sense of paranoia. Anyone on the lower levels of a company is going to feel expendable, he thought, but in his case and in this type of company, expendability took on a whole new meaning. So he moved out of his old apartment complex, motivated by his newly-crafted philosophy concerning protection of the rich and poor, and did little more in his new apartment other than sleep and shower, spending most of his private time in public.

He especially liked a particular coffee house that students from the local community college frequented. He would bring some hard copies of articles he had downloaded at work that sounded interesting and read them and eavesdrop on the conversations that surrounded him and join in when it seemed appropriate. He had developed a friendly relationship with some of the regulars in this fashion. When asked if he went to their school, Abraham would use himself as a cautionary tale to stay in school, making opaque references to his running away and committing crimes of some sort that led to his current narrow frame of opportunities. He was quite sincere, though, when he would emphasize how much he would like to be doing what they were doing, and his contributions to the discussions had them marveling at his breadth of knowledge and jovially berating him for not enrolling. Maybe someday, he would say, if circumstances allow.

After an especially satisfying talk amongst familiar faces concerning what a college degree is supposed to instill in someone, he settled into a copy of the local free newspaper to see if there was a low-rent concert at one of the bars he might want to attend if Prophet or one of his current wunderkinds had no work for him tonight.

Finding no inspiration in the listings, he unwrapped himself from this afternoon's debate and his reading by stretching out his arms and letting them drop as he cleared his mind by letting his eyes wander the room with no thoughts attached. He maintained enough awareness to notice someone staring at him a couple tables down to his left; a young woman smiling coyly at him while she lightly rubbed the screen she had placed on the table in front of her; and a lovely young woman at that.

And she was Samantha.

He was so surprised and she looked so beautiful that he instantly smiled back. And even when he momentarily reflected on the bitter end of his days in her presence and all those associated with her, he brushed it aside because she was a stunning woman who was smiling at him in one of his favorite hang outs. So he went over to her table. He knew what he wanted to say, but inwardly rehearsed it as he approached.

"Just when I thought I was over you," he said.

When she stood up and hugged him, he knew he had delivered his line with enough of the light touch he was aiming for.

"It's so good to see you," she said into his ear.

"What are you doing out here?" he asked.

"Avoiding the peninsula," she said as they separated but continued holding both hands.

"I can relate," he smiled, though it was harder to say that with the same lightness. Samantha in turn looked a bit sheepish, so Abraham turned the discussion to logistical matters such as if he could get her a refill or something else, and at which table they should sit. They decided on her table, and Abraham fetched a fresh cup for each of them.

"So," he said as he returned with their coffees and sat across from her, "I seem to recall you were set to go to UCLA."

She scrunched her mouth over to one side of her face before answering. "Well, I did go; for a year."

"No great shame," he assured her. "The freshman drop rate is pretty high in most universities. They don't broadcast that in their promotional literature."

Samantha looked at him affectionately. "That's sweet of you, Abe. You have every right to gloat after how I treated you. How a lot of us treated you."

"If I had run into you the year after, I probably would have."

"Where did you go?" she said, sincerely baffled.

"Here," he said, "Home."

"That's what Drake figured."

Abraham must have clenched up a bit upon hearing Drake's name, as Samantha mounted a quick defense. "His family organized a search for you. They notified the police, filed a report."

"I know," he said, trying to back down from whatever his body language may have communicated. "I saw some flyers around town."

"That must be weird," she speculated aloud, "to see yourself on a missing person flyer."

"Very," Abraham laughed.

Samantha lowered her voice and imitated a portentous service announcement. "Have you seen this person?"

"Why, yes I have," he played along. Then he confessed: "Whenever I saw one I would rip it down."

She took that as a cue that it was okay to ask a serious question. "So what have you been doing out here?"

"What everyone does; working hard, scraping by," he breezed through his answer. "What about you?"

"Not working very hard, not having to scrape by; you know, the nightmare scenario for every parent on the peninsula."

"Things a little tense in your house, then?"

"Not so bad," she said. "It's running into old friends who just graduated and have a jump on their lives that hurts. The holidays are the worst, especially working in a restaurant. 'Congratulations on getting into grad school, Briana...can I take your order?'"

"If she didn't get into grad school she'd probably be on the floor with you."

"Her rich fiancé would make sure that never happened."

"That rich fiancé isn't Drake, is it?"

Samantha shook her head. "They split up right after graduation; didn't want to try the long distance thing. I think he would have liked to try. He seemed more broken up over it than her."

"So you stayed in touch with both of them?"

"Everybody pretty much stays in touch with everyone online; well, as much as you can call social networking staying in touch."

Abraham briefly considered taking a vow to not ask about Drake, but couldn't resist. "What's Drake up to these days?"

"Law school."

Abraham laughed loudly enough that he felt like he should perhaps apologize to the other patrons who glared at him. He quickly settled himself down.

"I know, right?" Samantha said, grinning as well. "But apparently he's trying to be one of the good ones. He's pulled a couple of internships at the state Justice Department up in Sacramento."

"Well, good for Drake."

There was a lull in the conversation. They focused on drinking coffee for a while. Abraham re-introduced talk to the table.

"I assume you're going to school part time."

"Doesn't everyone under thirty working in the service industry?" she cracked.

"Not out here," he said, and then feared that he may have come across as too preachy. She rolled with it, though.

"Okay, well, everyone under thirty working in a tourist trap," she corrected herself.

He enthusiastically jumped at the chance to say something dull. "Any idea what you might want to major in?"

"No. It just keeps me from feeling like I'll be on the floor for the rest of my life. I take anything with a number '1' or an 'A' in the title. I hardly passed any of my UC courses."

"See, I don't get that," Abraham leaned into the space between them. "You were always so smart."

"But I wasn't a good student. And I couldn't fake it anymore." She became a bit maudlin at the recollection. "I didn't even have any fun. I tried. I figured as long as I was there I'd live the life. But it's hard to do that when you know you're spinning down the drain. I felt guilty for wasting my parents' money."

"Good for you," he said emphatically. "Seriously; I think that's great."

"Maybe that's why they've been pretty cool to me."

"Well, that and they love you."

Samantha hesitated before asking, "Do you keep in touch with your mom?"

Abraham hesitated in kind. "I don't know where she is." He was going to leave it at that, but decided she deserved some more explanation since she bothered to ask. "That was the stupidest part of running away. I bailed before she was deported. The friends I was staying with at the time contacted the detention facility for me, but she was already gone."

"Can't you look her up in Mexico?"

He leaned back. "Long story, but the short answer is no, I can't."

She leaned into the space between them that he had just abandoned. "If you're willing to tell me that story, I'm willing to listen."

Abraham searched for a way out of this line. "We've been back in touch for, what..." he looked at his phone screen, "ten minutes? Fifteen minutes?"

"I get it," she said, waving her hands as though signaling a missed field goal. "I'm sorry. I completely get it."

He had intended to blithely move them to another subject rather than with such a chill, so he tried to pile on some warmth to the ploy he had already committed to. "But if you give me some more details about what's been up all these years, get a burrito with me later, we'll be accumulating a lot more time together."

That seemed to help. She was clearly relieved at the chance to talk about less pointed items. They spoke comfortably about her adventures in failure and his in futility, their frustration bonding them without the anger that usually accompanies such feelings. They did not rant. They shared stories. Abraham thought that several years without reading her social networking threads was worth it to be able to catch up in person, in such a satisfying rush of reminiscence and commiseration, and told her so. She agreed and noted how distant she felt from most all of the people who had meant so much to her not so long ago, and meanwhile found his devotion to disappearing more intriguing than anything her friends had posted on their pages. She was always surrounded by representations of everyone with whom she had some measure of contact past or present, and if someone was missing, it was easy enough to find them. But a web search for Abraham was frozen in time from years before: high school baseball game box scores, Associated Student Body newsletters, local paper announcements concerning one accomplishment after another, then a blurb about his disappearance, then nothing. He danced around the authentic, illegal reasons for why he needed to remain absent by kidding that his ability to resist cultivating a virtual presence was a sign of confidence, but she was impressed and didn't disagree.

He asked her to call up the sites on her screen and dazzle him with what he had been missing, but of course he was also curious to see what some of his old classmates and childhood acquaintances were doing, or at least giving the impression of doing.

It hadn't been that long, so it would have been easy to identify them by their photos alone. Most had yet to put on much weight or age noticeably; facial hair and hairstyles were about the only variable. And the biographies were limited as well, adhering to a story arc familiar to those who grew up where they grew up: just out of college or almost done, starting grad school or settling into a job, no families of their own yet, a few weddings on the horizon, no major tragedies, except for Darren Hoff.

His profile picture was a photograph of his father, with the date he was last seen lining the bottom along with a caption in quotation marks proclaiming "The Day Free Speech Died."

Abraham found it easier to conceal his association with that date thanks to Darren's decision to mourn and grandstand at the same time. A more personal expression of grief may have elicited a more telling reaction. As it was, Abraham was able to genuinely roll his eyes. Samantha caught him doing it.

"Come on, Abe," she chided. "I know you didn't like him, but come on."

"If they find him alive, does that mean free speech comes back?" he ignored her reprimand. "Because I really miss it; who knew Lane Hoff held the keys? All this time I thought it was the Constitution."

"People grieve differently," Samantha put a little more edge in her voice.

"But if it rises from the grave, maybe it will be like zombie free speech," he continued to ignore her, "just wandering around saying whatever comes out of its rotten oozing mouth and taking no responsibility for its words. But then, that's pretty much what he did, anyway."

"Don't make me defend Darren," she said. "I don't like what he and his dad did, either. But for God's sake, Abe..."

"So here we go again, eh?" he settled down and met her gaze. "It's not them, it's me."

"I've said I'm sorry more than once today," she was now on the defensive.

He decided to back off, as he didn't want to chase her away. "I know," he said as soothingly as he could manage. "And as unbelievable as this may sound right now, I did feel bad when it happened, when I heard about it."

"Well, you know what it's like to lose a parent," she said, joining him in reconciliation mode.

"Thanks," he said unconvincingly. "But I'm pretty sure mine is still alive. His is probably dead." He pondered the score briefly before asking, "How connected are you to Darren these days?"

"Hardly at all," she answered. "He finally found a girlfriend in college; and of course it got very serious very quickly. When his dad disappeared I pretty much just followed it on the news like everyone else and wrote a consoling comment now and then on his page; again, like everyone else. He never wrote back specifically to me, just thanked everyone for the thoughts and prayers."

"Thoughts and prayers," Abraham mulled aloud. "I'm surprised that hasn't morphed into an online acronym: TAPS. It's a perfect fit; you can play Taps while sending your TAPS."

"See what a valuable member of the online community you would be?" Samantha kidded.

"You want to show me some more people neither of us give a crap about?" he nodded at her screen, "Or do you want to go get a burrito with me?"

She swiped it into sleep mode, picked it up, and started walking towards the door. He hustled after her.

"Is that a yes?" he called out. "Or did I deeply offend you again?"

She stopped and turned to let him in on her smile. "I hadn't really thought of the latter," she said. "But maybe I am, and if you buy, I'll get over it."

He led the way in his car since she had never gone back there after they broke up. Abraham, meanwhile, had become a mainstay, and was greeted with welcoming smiles and salutations by the staff and the cooks behind counter.

"All this time, all those flyers, and all those man hours," Samantha marveled as they sat down amidst the 'bienvenidos' coming at them from all directions. "All they had to do was hang out here and they would have found you."

Abraham laughed and assured her that he had laid low for quite some time before he figured the search was off and it was safe to re-emerge in public. He ventured into greater detail about some of his jobs, the legal ones naturally, and focused a lot on his trucking career, as it afforded him the opportunity to discuss the circumstances and lives of people in other areas and avoid questions about his life in the valley. She seemed to appreciate not having to talk about her life, either. And while broadening the conversation to points larger than themselves initially felt good due to relief at not having to hide anything, it eventually felt good due to a sense of comfort, as though they knew each other well enough already, and didn't have to verbalize their autobiographies any longer.

And when they closed the place down and were kicked out in good fun by the cat-calling staff, they spoke frankly about whether they should kiss or spend the night together or none of the above.

"The first two options are really just one," Abraham weighed in. "Because if we kiss, then we'll want to spend the night together."

"Oh, really?"

"Of course," he didn't miss a beat. "Now don't interrupt me. So it's really just a matter of yes or no."

"And...?"

"I'm leaning towards no."

"You are?" she was sincerely surprised. "A man in his early twenties who by his own admission hasn't dated much in the last four years; you're turning me down?"

"Yes, because there is no way I'm bringing you to my apartment. Someone might break in and kidnap you and have you working in a whorehouse in Chihuahua by tomorrow night." She laughed and he said he wasn't kidding, and he really wasn't kidding all that much, but of course he let it function purely as a joke. "And as for your place," he went on. "Well, do we really want to worry about getting caught by your parents? Aren't we humiliated enough about our current circumstances?"

"I suppose you're right," she said, and they kissed anyway.

After a few minutes, they separated and she said, "I guess we'll just have to keep seeing each other until our circumstances improve."

Abraham had certainly smiled a decent amount in the last few years, but it was either thanks to a rush of excitement over money or advancement in the company, or designed to intimidate someone.

This smile felt warm, however; the kind of warmth he had not felt since the last time he said good night to Samantha knowing that he would see her again.

He shut her car door for her and waved as he watched her drive away.

Chapter Twenty-Four: Online

Hey Drake—

Love the pic you posted of the chick in the stretch pants waiting to get on the river boat. Who knew skinny people could look just as bad in those things? LOL. Just wanted to let you know I'm not sure I can do this thing with Abe. We hung out and had a great time. I don't think he did it and I don't want to be a narc. I know you told me where to find him and I know this means a lot to you, but maybe you can find another way to get what you need, if it's even there, which like I said, I don't think there is anything there. OK. I'm starting to babble. Thanks again and sorry again.

—Sam

Samantha—

This doesn't just mean a lot to me. This means a lot to the DHS. You would be doing your country a great service by finding out if Abe had anything to do with Hoff. And if he didn't, then you would be doing Abe a big favor by clearing his name. It's not too late for him. If he hasn't done anything bad yet, you can help us stop him. Please reconsider. BTW, I finally noticed it was your birthday a few days ago. Sorry I didn't post anything. It's been crazy at the DOJ. Happy Belated Birthday!

—Drake

Come on, Drake...

What's with all the "we" and "us"? This means a lot to YOU. The amount of money you're waving under my nose is no doubt half (or less) of what you're keeping for yourself. I love you and all, but don't treat me like an idiot just because I don't have a degree on my wall. Yet. Which reminds me, are you going to the alumni game this Friday?

—Sam

Honest to God, Sam, I am forwarding every penny your way if my bosses decide the information is worth a reward. I admit that the jump start this could provide my career will more than make up for it in the long run, but think of what it could do for you. Two years of tuition, a place of your own, whatever. And again, even if you find nothing, you still get the satisfaction of knowing you were right, and then you and Abe can live happily ever after. And no, I can't make it to the alumni game. Have a good time. Say hi to everyone for me.

—D

Pump the brakes, Drake! I didn't say Abe and I were falling in love again or anything. We're having a good time, yes. He came into my work the other day and sat in my station and chatted up the customers around him and convinced them all to leave me these huge tips without actually telling them to. Does that sound like someone afraid of showing his face? Someone on the run from the law? He's like the old Abe we knew and loved. But we're a long way from walking off into the sunset together. Still couldn't get him to come to the game with me. I don't blame him. After about five minutes I wished I hadn't gone. I told everyone at half time I was tired and was going home, but went over to the hill and met Abe at this cool little roadhouse bar on the way to the valley. Glad to see your mother won that Volunteer of the Year award. She deserves it.

Thanks, Sam. I'll tell Mom you noticed. I'm not sure she'd do any of it unless people noticed. As for Abe, I'm glad you two are having such a good time. Truly, I am. He deserves some good times after what he's been through. But you need to be realistic about what a future with him looks like, even just as a friend. When I first sent you the message about getting back in touch with him, did you not read the part about the kinds of people he's been spending time with? Even if Abe hasn't done anything, do you understand that his "co-workers" have done things? Lots of things? Really awful things? And that it's hard not to spend time with those sorts of people and not be sucked into that lifestyle as well? I could tell you some more things about who these people are, and more about Abe's background, but I hope it doesn't come to that. I'm curious, have you even brought up anything about Darren or his dad? If so, what was his reaction?

Sorry it took a while to get back to you, Drake. I've been in the hospital recovering from wounds suffered when I got caught in the crossfire of a gun fight between Abe and his buddies. JK! But seriously, what have you gotten me into? Is it really that bad? Should I be worried? I've been freaking out a bit since your last message. And what's this deep dark secret about Abe's background. Are you holding out on me until I give you something? If so, I can tell you the Hoffs did come up on our first "date", if that's the right word. You know, the one where we "just happened" to run into each other? We looked at some of the pages of the old crew and Darren's profile came up with that cheesy caption on his dad's picture. Abe had a strong reaction, but it seemed to me more about him being disgusted with Darren holding up his dad as this free speech icon. And can you blame him? It's a lame enough picture without knowing he helped ruin your life. He even mentioned that he felt bad when it happened. There. Satisfied? Have I earned the right to know more?

Thanks for giving me something, Samantha. And no, you're not in any danger. Whatever Abe's been up to, I can't imagine he would subject you to anything associated with it. He may have fallen in with some bad people, but he's still Abe. As far as his past is concerned, I'll leave that up to him to tell you if he wants. I was just getting a bit crazy thinking about everything. Sorry if I went overboard. His past will only be as dark as he lets it be, I'll just leave it at that. About Hoff's dad, did he really say he felt bad "when it happened"? As in he was there? It may not mean anything, but my bosses could find that interesting. Thanks again. Hope all is well with you two. I don't want to come between whatever may be developing, or re-developing. Having you back in his life may save Abe from whatever he may have gotten himself into. I found some old pictures of you two in my files the other day, and have attached a few. Briana and I were in a couple of them and I cropped us out. LOL. Enjoy.

Oh, thanks Drake. No pressure or anything, right? Just be sure to save Abraham's life, either by digging up some dirt on him or being his friend. Oh, and watch out for those thugs and felons he's been hanging out with! WTF!? Fine, let's just get this over with. I'll pass on anything that sounds suspicious to you and your "bosses" and hopefully we can clear this up and either you can get your promotion or whatever while I get some money, or I can get an innocent Abe. Sounds like a win-win to me. Once this whole thing is over, I am seriously going to un-friend you. If I never hear from you again, it will be too soon. BTW, yes he did say "when it happened" I'm pretty sure, and then said "when I heard about it", meaning when HE heard about it, of course. Nothing to see here, folks. Just keep walking. Then again, it sounds like you're about ready to read anything into anything he does. I'll see what other tasty treats I can toss your way. Oh, and nice try with the pictures. I have plenty of my own of all of us. But thanks for the tip on cropping you and Briana out of them. I hadn't really thought of that before.

Thank you, Samantha. And I'm sorry you feel that way. I am praying right along with you that as far as Abe is concerned, there is nothing there but a bright future. When this is all over, if you ever need a reference or a letter of recommendation for anything, let me know.

Chapter Twenty-Five: Under Review

Abraham wondered whether that truck stop he liked was really worth recommending to Samantha and a promise to take her there, or if that was just him playing the role of working-class hero and mentor to her emerging awareness of the indifference of the universe. So he was determined to stop there on his way back from a run down to Mexico and try to see the atmosphere and taste the food from her perspective. It wasn't exactly right outside of town, it was way in the southern end of the valley, just past the Monterey County line in fact, so he wanted to be sure it was worth turning it into a destination rather than a stop.

He was a few minutes away from the crossroad that hosted it when he noticed a luxury car playing peek-a-boo with him in his rear-view mirror. This was nothing new, it was a standard move for cars that wanted to pass but had to wait for traffic in the left lane to dissipate first, but there were no cars in the left lane. Abraham attributed it to either age or corrective lens prescription, but it went on long enough for him to think it may be due to some other kind of prescription. Once the honking and rude gestures started, he realized it was Prophet, who finally pulled up next to him smiling with his phone in hand.

Abraham's phone rang, and Prophet asked him where they could stop around here for some good food and conversation. He said it as a joke, given the relatively wide open spaces, but Abraham was pulling over soon anyway and thought his favorite truck stop would serve as a pleasant surprise for Prophet. He of course would have preferred to attend his stop alone so that he could focus on the question "What would Samantha think?", but Prophet was still his boss, and impressing the boss is a difficult tradition to resist.

With Prophet falling back onto his tail, Abraham merged into the left-turn lane and swung onto the sparse country cross street where the truck stop sat a few dozen yards from the freeway. Prophet rose from his vehicle and Abraham descended from his, as they met in the triple digit heat that appeared to buckle the parking lot pavement.

"Ouch," said Prophet. "You couldn't wait another half hour till we got into the cooler part of the valley?"

"The food is good," Abraham quipped, feeling oddly unaffected by Prophet. It was unexpectedly liberating, as though he had resigned himself to his modest station in the organization and had started to embrace the benefits of being unremarkable.

"Better be," Prophet teased, who meanwhile was being more affable than Abraham could ever recall.

This reconstructed warmth continued as they made their way indoors and sat in a booth while Prophet kept up the friendly chatter. Abraham meanwhile started to focus more on surveying the scene for Samantha's sake, and wished Prophet hadn't intruded on his research. Prophet seemed to sense his disinterest and became even more aggressively chummy.

"What's up, habibi?" he asked, trying to peel Abraham's attention from the menu he studied carefully with Samantha in mind. "I haven't seen you for months and you're all blowing me off."

Abraham was starting to feel like a girl being hit on by an ex-boyfriend. "Sorry, Prophet," he said, "Long haul."

"I hear you," Prophet assured him. "Tired people are fun to mess with."

Abraham politely smiled and nodded but couldn't quite follow through with a laugh. A large grizzled server paradoxically dressed in an old-fashioned pink waitress uniform arrived and they ordered iced tea. She then suggested they order their food as well. Her demands prompted Abraham and Prophet to exchange suppressed smiles. They each came to a snap decision, Abraham not actually ordering what he wanted but instead trying something that

Samantha would likely order. She thanked them by rote and taxied away.

"I think I went to boot camp with her," Prophet remarked once she was safely out of earshot. Abraham chuckled sincerely and the ice he had constructed between him and his boss appeared to be melting.

"So what were you hauling?" Prophet asked.

Abraham shrugged. "Beats me; you know the rules: don't look in the back."

"Where did you drop it?"

"Mexico, in Tecate; you're the head of this operation, for God's sake. Don't you know anything?"

"Plausible deniability," Prophet laughed. "Besides, nobody likes to work for a micro-manager."

Abraham nodded and straightened up for the return of the server with their drinks. He thanked her out of curiosity and as expected did not receive a "you're welcome." He pondered whether Samantha would find the ambience as funny as he did, or if it would be a turn off.

Prophet jokingly raised a glass to Abraham's efforts and they appreciated the cool of their drinks for a while as a respite from the heat they were temporarily avoiding.

"People," Prophet exhaled after he had inhaled about half the glass.

Abraham figured that was a prelude to a larger statement. "Go on," he said.

Prophet took his cue. "Sometimes I wish I was in a business where I could use more robots."

"More robots," Abraham said, "As if you're using any now."

"I guess I'd still have to hire some people to look after the robots," Prophet ventured aloud. "Ah, well. I suppose I'm stuck with people for employees no matter what."

"You were born a few generations too soon, Prophet."

"I'm ahead of my time."

"You're a young soul."

Prophet raised his eyebrows. "That doesn't sound like a compliment."

"I'm just playing along with your introduction until you get to your point," Abraham said. "Did one of your new prodigal sons bail on you or something?"

Prophet glared at him. Abraham wondered tensely for a moment if he had pushed his nonchalance too far.

"No," Prophet finally said. "I should be so lucky."

"That bad?" Abraham was as relieved as he was interested.

"Morons," he barked, "So at least there's a good chance they'll get themselves shot or arrested. They've got that going for them. Or, I've got that going for me, I should say."

Abraham chuckled and used his iced tea to think for a short while. "They don't listen very well, do they?" he didn't ask Prophet so much as tell him.

Prophet nodded rhythmically and stared out the window. "And they think it impresses me," he said at last as he kept his gaze on the shimmering pavement and golden hills baking in the sun. "They do all sorts of crap I don't ask for and then drop it at my feet like some cat leaving a dead mole on your doorstep. Did I ask you to do that? Did I ask you to carjack that deadbeat pharmacist? How's he gonna pay us if he can't get to work? Did I ask you to get your cousin to start turning tricks? There's no money in whores, you imbecile. Pimps were dead once cell phone companies started offering unlimited texting and photo uploads. Bah," he waved his hands in exasperation and turned to face Abraham again. "But then what should I expect? I'm not exactly recruiting from the deepest talent pool. It's not like I can set up a booth at career day."

"Right between the San Jose State University booth and the Coast Guard booth," Abraham piled on.

Prophet seemed not to hear Abraham and instead seemed to be looking at him for answers. Abraham enjoyed the feeling momentarily before offering one.

"They need devotion," he said.

Prophet was taken aback. "Weren't you listening? They're too damn devoted. They're humping my leg."

"God," Abraham laughed, "The Almighty, he of the peace and blessings; that kind of devotion."

"You know that's not the kind of operation I run now, Abe."

"I know you're not trying to set up a caliphate, but that doesn't mean you have to abandon the greatest motivator in the history of mankind. What operation couldn't use that kind of authority?"

Prophet looked pensively into his glass and then back at Abraham. "I think I'm too far down the road in the opposite direction to be much good at that nowadays."

"What about the mosque ladies," Abraham asked. "Isn't that what they're there for?"

"They don't like what I've done with the cause," Prophet explained. "Once the mission statement focused on money and stripped away most of the religion, they were pretty much out. I still conduct some business there, but that's all it is: business. It's like corporate headquarters now rather than a spiritual center."

"I can talk to them," Abraham offered, "either bring them back into the fold, or take over the training myself and use the space. You need a sanctuary if you're gonna do this."

"Wait," Prophet waved him off, "that's a good point: *if* I'm gonna do this. How did we get here, anyway?"

"You mentioned you're having problems with your inner circle, so I assumed you wanted some help or at least some advice, and that's what I'm offering."

Abraham leaned slightly forward and crossed his hands on the table. Prophet leaned back and took a deep breath. "I wanted it all, Abraham."

Abraham didn't know what he was talking about. He kept quiet and waited for Prophet to continue.

"My business was blessed by a unique talent, one that any legitimate company would be lucky to have, much less a company like mine. Smart, both book smart and street savvy, charming, willing to work on any floor of the building so to speak. But I wanted him to be a killer on top of all that. I wanted everything."

Abraham figured this was as close to an apology that Prophet was capable of. Even dancing around one was clearly difficult for him.

"I'm good with the bat," he tried to put him at ease.

"Even that was pushing it," Prophet said. "I should know what I have and play to people's strengths. I was looking so hard for that one thing, that killer instinct, that now all I've got is a bunch of killers without a clue between them."

"You think any of them might turn on you?" Abraham decided Prophet would be most impressed by sticking doggedly to business in the face of his unprecedented humility.

"All of them," he answered immediately. "It's just a matter of which one makes the first move."

"This is where God could come in handy."

"These guys are impenetrable."

"You just finished praising my charm and salesmanship," Abraham reminded him.

"And so what if you did sell them on it? Him? Whatever."

"Come on, Prophet. There was a time when you were fighting in God's name, yes?"

Prophet smiled. "Yes."

"And how did that feel?"

"A lot simpler," he replied, and then considered why. "The sense, the purpose, it was all so straightforward."

"So let's bring it back," Abraham urged him. "Bring back that feeling, and introduce these guys to it. You've gotten away from the thing that makes any extreme or risky enterprise work: moral certainty. It makes your enemies appear much more evil and keeps your followers in line. And the more prone to overindulgence your followers are, the easier they are to convince, because they appreciate having an excuse for their tendencies; a divine one at that."

Prophet seemed unsure of how ready he was to commit to a reawakening. "And what if they decide to take out those tendencies on me?"

"They won't," Abraham said confidently, "Because they will love you for giving them the excuse."

"What about you?" now Prophet was reasserting himself. "If you're holding the bag with God in it, how do I know you won't turn on me?"

"Because I don't have the slightest interest in running this operation anymore, and you know it."

They sized each other up for a while, long enough for their orders to arrive and the food slinger to not ask them if they wanted any more iced tea. Her steadfastness when it came to providing rude service once again had them suppressing laughter.

"I've honestly never seen her here before," Abraham said. "I'm sorry. But the food is good. You'll see."

"I'm the one who should be apologizing," Prophet said.

Abraham was just about to take his first bite and froze.

Prophet noticed his reaction. "That's right. I'm sorry. I'm very sorry. I mean, let's be honest about the real reason you would never turn on me: you're too good a person. You had every right to take a shot at me over the past couple of years and didn't; what I put you through not only wasn't fair, but extremely stupid on my part. I tried to say as much earlier, but there, I'm saying it now."

"Wow," Abraham put down his food, "First my old girlfriend, now you."

Prophet suddenly put up his guard again. "What old girlfriend?"

"From high school; I ran into her a little while back and she apologized for everything that went down towards the end of my days out on the peninsula."

"Where did you run into her? Were you hanging out in Monterey?"

"No," Abraham answered warily, wondering why he was so interested. "She was at this place in Salinas I like to hang out at."

Prophet grew more sullen.

"What?" Abraham asked him.

"There are no chance encounters in this business," he announced. "At least, that's the way you have to treat them."

"Oh, please," Abraham dismissed him. "I haven't told her anything."

"Has she asked?"

Abraham decided it was time to take his meal after all. "Why yes, she has. Oddly enough, she was curious what I'd been up to these past several years."

"But just how curious is she?"

"You're kidding, right?" he said as he started eating. "Is this what happens over time? Paranoia sinks in this deeply?"

"Precaution," Prophet corrected him. "There is a difference."

"Call it what you want, Prophet. But I can't live like that."

"Then you can't work for me," he said sharply.

Abraham was once again temporarily stunned. He searched for a way back to articulation. "Well...okay."

"No," Prophet was growing more intense. "Not okay. Killer instinct? Whatever; like I said, I can take or leave that at this point.

But sloppiness? No. No way. Even if you walk away, you have to show me your old flame hasn't compromised us."

"And what am I supposed to do, torture her?"

"We're going to test her," Prophet had reached peak intensity and was now maintaining a steady keel. "We're going to come up with some sort of scheme that she will need to report to whoever she may be working for."

"If she's even working for anyone," Abraham interjected.

"That's right. And if she isn't, then no problem. Our fake little transaction will go down without a hitch, and you will have my blessing. I'll be the best man at your wedding if you ask me."

"And if it doesn't?"

"Then she's been deceiving you and you won't ever want to see her again, anyway."

Abraham looked around the room and thought that he would wait and take Samantha here later, after she had proven her innocence. He didn't want to think that way, but it was a fairly long drive just for dinner, and his head was quickly congesting with doubt.

"I've got some ideas for the test," Prophet interrupted his thoughts.

"I think I'll come up with my own," Abraham replied.

"What for?"

"Because this is important to me, and I'm not sure I can trust you to keep it fair."

Prophet smiled at him. "You always were a quick study." He started digging into his lunch. "I can't believe I almost let you get away. What was I thinking?"

He immersed himself in enjoying the meal, which he raved about to Abraham, and thanked him for the recommendation. Prophet even called over the server to ask her to give his compliments to the chef. Abraham meanwhile grinned loyally and contributed just enough to the discussion to keep the food disappearing and the check arriving, but was already thinking of ways he could clear Samantha's name. A couple of ideas were germinating, but until Prophet merrily paid the check and sped ahead of him onto the highway, he didn't have a chance to refine any of them.

Once on the road and faced only with a single lane back home and the sound of the engine, he settled on what he felt was the most promising plan and worked out the details. He would make a date with Samantha and then cancel it, claiming he had to take a trip someplace overseas to hand deliver some materials. He would be deliberately opaque and suspicious about what those materials were. As was tradition with airline travel small talk in their area, she would at some point ask if he needed a ride and what airport he would be leaving from: San Francisco, San Jose, or Oakland. He would tell her that he was going to catch a flight down in Mexico, claiming it was cheaper and that he had forgotten to renew his U.S. passport and had a Mexican one that a friend made for him that he was going to use instead. He would promise to make it up to her in a big way, and give her an actual flight number and date of departure and return so that she could track his whereabouts and plan ahead, since he would be making a lot of money from this trip, and was going to spend a bunch of it on her when he got back.

Once the plane was boarding, he would hang back and get a sense if he was being watched by some agency or other, Mexican or American, or a joint effort. If it was difficult to tell, he would make a last second dash to board once everyone was on, and see if that flushed them out. He was hoping it wouldn't come to that, as then he would be taken into custody. And even though they would have nothing on him, the hassle of confirming his innocence would be made all the more excruciating in knowing that Samantha had failed her test, that he would never be able to see her again, and that yet another person who was close to him, who professed love for him, had lied to him.

Chapter Twenty-Six: At Last

The experiences that made Khalil's life difficult as an adolescent and teenager were rather nebulous; none stood out as a specific illustration of what he hated about that phase of his life. It was like an abstract work of art that elicited a bitter emotional response. So it was somewhat curious that his otherwise very satisfying adult life should be colored so steadily by one vivid memory that made him quiver with shame each of the thousands of times he replayed it in his mind: the morning that Mohammed sent him away from Marisol like a disobedient dog, cowering shoeless from her house to his car. It was the reason he tried so hard to make things right for Marisol once it was time for her to become Najah again and fly home, the reason he sought to become Mohammed's lawyer once he became known more widely as The Prophet, and the reason he was now looking forward to finally exacting his revenge on his most notorious client and lifelong tormentor.

Mohammed brandished the fact that he had permitted Marisol to pull her son from the training with a certain conclusion in mind, deliberately allowing Abraham to feel like he was ingratiating himself into gentrified society only to have the crown knocked viciously from his head. He bragged to Khalil that he had engineered Abraham's fall from grace with the pampered class by corresponding with Lane Hoff under a Mexican pseudonym and inspiring the tirades that made the ripples that became the wave that swept his most valuable asset off the beach and back into the valley, knowing full well that Abraham would feel as though he needed to be with familiar folk once he realized he was being orphaned by his adopted community. And just to insure that Abraham would feel sufficiently bereft to head in his direction, Mohammed confessed that he had sealed the young man's fate by reporting Marisol to the immigration authorities. Mohammed told him this not because he wanted to get it off his chest, but because he loved to antagonize Khalil and wordlessly dare him to do something about it.

And indeed Khalil had not done anything about any of the exact slights that Mohammed lobbed at him; he instead allowed Mohammed to pay him handsomely and consider him the same nebbish he was two decades ago, all while concocting a plan of his own, a plan that he could now unbridle thanks to Abraham being in custody.

He had never been so thrilled to receive a call from Mohammed. "Your godson that you've never met just got picked up," he reported to Khalil in typically spiteful form.

Khalil took advantage of being on the phone rather than in person by pumping his fist in exultation. He composed himself and calmly asked, "What for?"

"Nothing," Mohammed laughed on the other end of the line. "Unless finding out your girlfriend is snitching on you is a crime."

He then explained the situation. Khalil listened to Mohammed's mocking interpretation of events and actually enjoyed it, knowing that this would be the last time Mohammed would be able to bat someone's life around so carelessly. After wrapping up the story as if it was the punch line of a lengthy joke rather than yet another soul-sucking disappointment absorbed by Abraham, he told Khalil where Abraham was being held and ordered him to go and take care of it. As was customary, he hung up without any sort of a sign-off, and before Khalil could insert one of his own, either.

"Good bye, habibi," Khalil muttered to an imaginary version of Mohammed as he sat back in his empty office. "Since you've never said it to me, let me say it to you: Good. Bye."

Khalil had seen Abraham in a few photographs that had accompanied articles concerning his accomplishments, as he liked to keep tabs on him as he grew up, occasionally checking the Monterey local news online and the schools' websites. So he knew roughly what he looked like, but was curious how the last several years had worn on him. It was only within those last several years that he had decided Abraham would be the perfect conduit through which he could ultimately dispose of Mohammed. None of the other members of the organization he had represented at Mohammed's behest struck him as suitable; they did not have enough knowledge of the system or came across as unreliable. And based on what Mohammed had been telling him of late concerning his current blend of right-hand confidants, they were terrific dullards.

Thus Abraham it was, as it probably always should have been. But there was that question of how he had weathered his time in the organization, about which Khalil had only heard second-hand via Mohammed. He would be angry, certainly, especially in light of recent events; Khalil had always assumed a certain level of anger in him when they finally got the chance to meet, since by necessity it could only happen when Abraham got caught for something that required a lawyer. But Khalil wondered whether Abraham's anger would blanket his entire perspective, or if he could convince him to center it squarely onto Mohammed.

He had been following Abraham's life so closely from a distance that the opportunity to see him in person felt a bit like a fan meeting their favorite celebrity, as though he had won a date with Abraham. The chance to take down Mohammed provided an even greater sense of sweepstakes to the conference room as he awaited his arrival.

Plus when Abraham entered, he was shorter than Khalil expected, which struck him as such a standard reaction to meeting someone who had, up until the personal encounter, existed solely in media and second-hand legends.

"Hello, Abraham. My name is Khalil. I'm Mohammed's attorney."

Abraham nodded a hello from within his morose haze.

"I understand there is really no case here, just some release forms to sign."

Abraham nodded again.

"I also know why. Mohammed explained the situation."

Abraham glared, but still didn't say anything.

"I'm sorry. I understand how disappointing it must be."

"Do you?" he scoffed.

"Maybe not your exact circumstances," Khalil explained. "But I certainly know what it's like to have love taken from you by forces beyond your control."

"Are you my lawyer or a shrink?"

Khalil chuckled and apologized as Abraham continued.

"I wasn't aware that I had to undergo a psychiatric evaluation before being released."

Khalil stopped him cold: "I was in love with your mother."

He let it breathe for a few moments before pursuing the issue. "By order of the leadership of the cause I thought I was devoted to, I picked her up in Mexico when she was pregnant with you and brought her across the border. In violation of orders, I shared her first sunset over the Pacific, found her to be the most incredible young woman I had ever met, fell in love with her, helped her out for the first few weeks after you were born, fell even more in love with her, then was forbidden from seeing her by the anchor baby terrorist board of directors."

Abraham was genuinely intrigued.

"And to make sure I stayed away," Khalil went on, "they unleashed their attack dog: Mohammed."

Abraham processed the information. "And now you work for him?"

Khalil smiled. "Your mother found that rather shocking, too, when it came up during the arrangements for her release from the detention facility."

"Do you know where she is?" Abraham asked wide-eyed.

"She's back home in Algiers, working for a law firm, living in a nice place with a view of the harbor. I hear she's dating a nice man these days as well."

Abraham tried to mask his emotions, but the glistening of his eyes and tightening of his mouth gave him away. He composed himself as best he could before speaking.

"The people at the mosque," he lowered his voice to compensate for its quiver, "the ladies, Prophet...I mean, Mohammed, they said they checked with immigration and that she was released into Mexico."

"She was. Then I took it from there."

Abraham seemed about ready to give up trying to pretend he didn't want to cry. Khalil added on to the build-up. "I was going to send you along right behind her, but you ran away...to Mohammed."

Abraham surrendered and sobbed openly.

"And," Khalil forged ahead, "thanks to that man's high-minded willingness to take you under his wing, I had to scrap those plans, because the moment you and 'The Prophet' became an item, it not only put you on the no-fly list, but pretty much on the no-fly list all-star team."

He let Abraham purge some more of his regret, his frustration, his grief, and sat quietly by until exhaustion turned the volume down. The young man continued to hold his head in his hands and stare at the floor as the only sound he had left was heavy breathing. When Abraham's breathing finally normalized and the room was practically silent, Khalil made his move.

"Now what if I told you there was a way you could still get to Algiers," he announced, "start a new life, get in touch with your roots, be close to your mother, and out from under the thumb of Mohammed."

Abraham held his gaze towards the floor to the point where Khalil was about to ask if he heard what he had said. But then Abraham finally sat up straight in the chair and responded. "I think I know where this is going."

Khalil smiled. "So what do you say I leave the room and turn things over to a friend of mine from the State Department?"

Abraham went from looking at him to staring at him. He held him in his sights long enough for Khalil to grow uncomfortable.

"Would you like some time to think about it?" Khalil asked.

Abraham stared a little while longer before answering.

"No."

Khalil proceeded cautiously. "So you're ready for me to turn it over?"

"This is your plan?" Abraham blurted out, a scornful smile forming.

Khalil could feel his foundation starting to weaken, but did not want to come across as panicked. He took a deep breath. "If you're concerned about Mohammed sending someone after you, I can assure you that your location would be completely confidential..."

"Yes, he would never suspect that I'd go where my mom is from..."

"And," Khalil insisted over the interruption, "we're quite certain his current operation is almost entirely based in America, and that any Middle Eastern or North African contacts he may have are strictly investors and would not have access to the kind of people..."

Abraham shook his head the whole time Khalil spoke, so finally Khalil stopped himself and changed course.

"Oh I get it," he said. "You're not a snitch; how noble."

"That's the wrong word," Abraham shot back. "I'm not a liar. My entire life has been consumed by liars, and I've obviously done my fair share. I want to break the cycle."

"I understand how..."

"No," Abraham cut in, "you don't. If you understood, your plan would not involve sneaking around behind the scenes cutting deals to incriminate your client."

"Have you really been mentored by my client long enough to forget what kind of person he is?"

"So have him picked up," Abraham became more animated. "He's been involved in terrorist activities; doesn't that mean he can be detained indefinitely? Stop screwing around."

"We don't want him to become some sort of symbol, a martyr for the cause. When we get him, I want his ass in court right away for a slam dunk case that I won't even have to try to throw. I want him on display and in a cell for eternity." Khalil's intensity now matched Abraham's. "I want people to know the truth about that man, and say his name with the same level of disdain and hatred that they reserve for all the great monsters of our time."

Abraham seemed taken aback by Khalil's virtuosity. "He really must have humiliated you terribly," he said with a surprising amount of empathy.

Khalil was caught more off guard by this than his earlier intransigence. "So what," he retorted, feeling a bit juvenile about his tone. "I'm not the only one."

"I know that, Khalil," Abraham appeared to be trying to reverse their roles. "I know who he is. I get it."

"Do you?" Khalil decided it was time to regain the upper hand. "Because I could tell you some things you don't know."

"So like I said before," Abraham rolled his eyes. "Resign. Report him. Pick him up. If you've got so much dirt on him, strap him to the waterboard already."

"I'm not talking about criminal dirt, Abraham." Khalil shifted in his chair to find a more comfortable position, but also to build tension.

"Oh, let me guess," Abraham said. "He's talked trash about me behind my back. Well, I guess I just won't pick him next time I'm a team captain for kickball at recess."

Khalil let him feel superior for a moment before pulling the pin. "He turned your mother in to the ICE. He made the call."

He let the announcement hover in front of Abraham's silence before proceeding. "But in my client's defense, he only did it just in case his manipulation of Lane Hoff's podcast wasn't enough to inspire the good people who took you in to light their torches and grab their pitchforks and drive you back over the hill."

The air was thickening with each revelation, and Khalil decided to add to its density. "Yeah, he was pretty much the extent of The Fast Lane's supposedly Mexican fan base. And speaking of manipulation, the only reason you were allowed on the peninsula in the first place was to give you a false sense of belonging so that he could take it all away from you, so that you could become the same resentful, violent man that he is."

Abraham remained stoic. Khalil applied more pressure. "But there was one person in your life who knew what you were up against, and who did her best to fight back and keep you from total immersion in his bile. And she would love nothing more than to see you again."

Abraham's stillness endured for a little while longer until he finally exhaled for several seconds. "I guess you didn't think you were going to have to use any of that," he said calmly to Khalil, "That I would recognize the greater good in turning him in; which means that apparently deep down inside you do understand that a personal vendetta is no way to pursue justice."

Khalil burned. "I'll do whatever I have to do."

"No you won't," Abraham explained. "You'll do whatever provides you with the greatest amount of cover."

Khalil was starting to feel desperate. "I haven't tried threatening you."

"But I didn't do anything. We've established that."

"Not in this particular instance; but all that training, though, with a known terrorist."

"Oh, come on, Khalil. If you think Mohammed would be a destructive symbol of indefinite detention, think of the stir I could cause."

"Mohammed is a high profile suspect. Nobody knows who you are."

"I don't think Mom would really appreciate that."

Khalil almost had to laugh at how easily Abraham swatted away that strategy. He leaned back, all options seemingly exhausted.

"He would never do the same for you."

"It's not about him."

"Clearly; it's all about you."

"That's right, Khalil. I'm the selfish one."

"You're letting one of the worst people on the planet continue to walk free."

Abraham put his head back and sighed. "You obviously went to college; you're an educated man." He lowered his head and set his sights on Khalil. "You ever read *Notes from Underground* by Dostoevsky?"

"No," he said. "I read *Crime and Punishment*, though."

"Anyway," Abraham continued, "there's this guy, I can't remember his name, but his actions, or lack of action, really stuck with me. He's humiliated, shown up by some hot shot that he can't stand in his town, and it just kills him; the very thought of this guy makes him fume. So he stalks him and learns his daily routine, where this jerk walks to and from every day and at what time, and it's easy for him to study his movements because of course the hot shot never even notices him, but this ineffectual, angry little cuss is going to have his revenge. He maps out a situation where he's going to bump into this jerk, the object of his obsession, at a moment where he can get maximum exposure, on a busy street, and he's going let him have it in front of all these people. He's got the speech all worked out, the choreography down cold, and he makes a few practice runs to insure the timing is right. But then when it's show time, he can't do it, he can't follow through. He walks by that son of a bitch every day for like, months, and can't bring himself to get close enough for the bump to happen. And naturally the pompous ass continues to not notice him in the process, which drives him even crazier; he realizes that the day that cad humiliated him was just another day in that guy's life, it meant nothing to him; but to this poor character it was everything, it defined his life; and so he brushes by him every day and falls short every time, until he's just about driven himself completely insane. I've always thought it was hilarious. I knew it was supposed to be tragic as well. But as far as the feeling it gave me, it was all about the comedy."

Abraham paused and focused a bit more sharply on Khalil. "Now I finally understand how sad it really is."

Khalil sat quietly, letting his last ounce of motivation slowly evaporate. Purely out of curiosity he asked, "Since you're turning over this new leaf, and making honesty your core value, is there anything you could tell me about the disappearance of Lane Hoff?"

"He's dead."

A jolt of inspiration shot through Khalil. "You know that for sure?"

"As sure as I know I didn't kill him."

"Did Mohammed have anything to do with it?"

Abraham smiled. "You'll have to ask him."

"Do you know where the body is?"

"No. Can I go now? I believe you said there were some papers to sign."

Khalil paused for a moment. If he was working for the state, he would have held him based on this information. But he was stuck working for Mohammed, and Abraham knew it. "They're on the front desk. The guard outside the door will take you there."

"Thanks," Abraham said casually and stood up to leave.

"You know," Khalil called after him as he headed for the door, "someday your past will catch up with you."

Abraham turned and looked at him in disbelief. "Catch up with me?" he chuckled. "The past has been out in front of me blazing a trail my whole life; I'm the one that needs to catch up."

He knocked on the door for the guard and said, perhaps to himself, but loud enough for Khalil to hear, "Honestly, I don't know how that expression stuck around long enough to become a cliché."

The door opened and Abraham was escorted out.

Khalil was left alone. He sat there for quite some time and wondered how a person could devote decades of their life to a mistake that everyone else could tell was a mistake at a glance.

Chapter Twenty-Seven: Everywhere

Drake had been having dreams where he found himself stuck in various points throughout history with hindsight firmly on his side, fully aware of the right thing to do, as he was not a product of each time but transported there in his dream. And each time he still chose the wrong thing to do. The cowardice and disappointment would cause him to wake up stressed, and if he woke up very early in the morning he found it difficult to get back to sleep thanks to the anxiety.

He dreamed he lived in South Carolina at the dawn of the 19th century and inherited a dozen slaves comprised of a couple different families, and instead of setting them free as he had promised them, he got wind of the invention of the cotton gin and the vast sums of money now made possible in cotton production and decided to sell half of them so he could buy a plantation and keep the other half to work it, separating the families in the process. He dreamed he was a Western frontier bureaucrat in the Jackson administration called to testify in a land dispute involving members of the Cherokee Nation and some settlers who were attempting an unjust land grab in newly annexed territory, and the settlers bought him off by floating him some of the land in question. He dreamed he was hosting a dinner party in his house outside of Weimar in the heyday of the Nazi party, and his terrified Jewish neighbors with whom he had enjoyed good relations showed up at his door pleading for shelter, and he turned them away because he could not afford to interrupt the party since his boss was one of the guests and Drake was thoroughly convinced that he was close to earning a promotion by the end of the night.

He dreamed such dreams regularly. He would have to choose between justice and self-interest, and his self-interest prevailed every time. It was no coincidence, according to the psychiatric self-diagnosis he performed on himself, that these dreams started around the time that media coverage of Abraham's life enjoyed its run as a reliable presence on every electronic device in the country. The course of his relationship with Abraham was no longer just an internal battle he fought, but was now part of the narrative being broadcast breathlessly on what seemed to be every outlet on every screen in the nation. And even when their childhood was not included in whatever dynamic was being explored in the episode he happened to catch out of the corner of his eye while in a gym, lounge, or airport lobby, there were always photographs of his old friend driving the proceedings, the expression on Abe's face either extremely menacing or extremely innocent, as though he had never simply looked at a camera in his entire life. Initially Drake read or viewed some of the reports by choice, but he stopped doing so relatively early in the cycle, the inaccuracies and sensationalism far too prevalent and too frustrating to witness.

And even if he had been able to come to some sort of peace with the stories that never stopped begging for his attention (with titles like *The Terrorist Next Door*, *The Evil Among Us*, *After School Extremist*, *Valedictorian of Terror*, and *Born in the USA/Raised on Jihad*) the commentary that accompanied each successive crash in the pile-up was utterly unabashed and uninterested in any reconciliation anyway. It was delivered by women and men who wore layers of makeup and delivered monologues or sat on panel discussion groups, by readers of websites who identified themselves with nicknames and profile photos that no doubt would reveal something about them if anyone bothered to archive and analyze their contributions, by people Drake overheard at coffee houses and delicatessens and while waiting in various lines who weren't aware of his presence, and wouldn't have recognized him anyway, because they didn't know him, didn't know his family, didn't know Abraham, didn't know Marisol, but had plenty to say about all of them. And there was Darren Hoff, basking in the heat like a lizard sunning himself on a rock, positioning himself as an inside source since he attended school with them, breathing life into the theory that Abraham, or at the very least Mohammed, killed his father. He took over his dad's podcast and had more of a following than his dad ever dreamed of. And there were others who were willing to talk: classmates, teammates, Briana, Samantha, all with no insight to offer other than they went to school with him or were friends with him or dated him, and their stories merely revealed experiences typical of most any child, teenager, or young adult, only now they would add to the description that they either had no idea what was going on, or always sensed that there was something going on.

None of the lead characters in the story dared subject themselves to the scrutiny of an interview. And disclosing the denial of an interview naturally became a staple of any broadcast on the subject. Drake had almost sat down for one when Anchor Baby Terrorist Fever exhibited its first symptoms, as his frustration with the opinions being tossed back and forth over his head like a game of keep-away led him to think that a chance to grab the ball and set the record straight would actually set the record straight. But upon agreeing, as the day approached, he kept his eye on the pre-interview analysis in which people who know everything started to include what they expected to see from him as the latest thing they knew. They primed their audience on what to look for with regard to his body language, tone of voice, and the words used during his responses to certain questions they expected to be asked. Drake started to imagine how intense his deconstruction would become once the interview was actually recorded and everyone started studying it like the Kennedy assassination home movie. So he backed out the night before, which still gave the machine plenty to build on, but at least it died out about as quickly as any other shocking new revelation that was dropped into their bowl.

His parents didn't agree to any interviews because they had left town almost immediately after the storm broke and were attempting to re-establish themselves in a new area which could only be accomplished, if it was at all possible, by making sure they remained marginal players in the many retellings.

Marisol was far enough away that she could simply turn off her phone or change her contact information and keep it all at bay electronically for the most part; occasionally some outfit would spend the money to send a reporter to Algiers or tap a Middle Eastern correspondent to chase her down the street with a microphone on her way to work.

Everyone was afraid of Mohammed, so while his image and his legend were often the center piece of a given account, the footage of him tended to be from surreptitious angles as he entered his lawyer's office or one of his business contacts, looking as though the cameraman was positioned behind a bush or in the back of a van.

Mohammed's lawyer, Khalil, granted interviews on occasion, during which he would recite prepared statements and give the impression of someone being held hostage and forced to repeat flattering propaganda on behalf of his captor. Whichever on-air personality happened to be broadcasting the current interview would inevitably announce that Khalil was part of the same terror network as Mohammed and had allegedly driven Marisol across the border to give birth to Abraham after she arrived in Mexico by ship. Khalil would be asked about this, and in refusing comment would betray some emotion, so Drake figured it was true.

Of course Abraham had it worst of all, as he was the star of the show. His name became a part of every de facto title that evolved for any proposal to tighten border security, racially profile, rewrite the 14th amendment, protest halal foods in grocery stores, the construction of a mosque, the wearing of a hijab. All of these acts became "The Abraham Act", "The Descendant of Abraham", "The

Rule of Abraham", and as the spring of Biblical references to his name started to dry up, versions grew from Abraham Lincoln allusions as they invoked truth marching on, grapes of wrath being stored, and assassinations. In addition to death threats, some of which were thinly-veiled contributions by members of the coiffed media complex who seemed oblivious to the microphone fastened to their lapel, there were calls for his arrest, detention, deportation, torture (though it was only called torture by those typing in all capital letters on website comment threads; those who were paid to offer their opinions tended to use some sort of euphemism). Occasionally someone in a given mob would remind the others that Abraham had yet to be accused of anything criminal, which was met with bellowed variations of "it doesn't matter."

For weeks there were camera crews, religious fundamentalists, and people dressed as American flags and colonists milling around the front of Abraham's apartment building. Drake would stop by to check out the scene every so often. The lane closest to the driveway was closed off to accommodate the crowds and allow the continued flow of traffic, which locals claimed had never been so heavy and so slow on that boulevard. The dazed tenants would initially be interviewed whenever they would emerge, normally having a hard enough time adjusting to the light of day and now suddenly having to incorporate camera lights into the equation as well. Whether speaking English or Spanish, their responses were predictably incoherent and would never air.

Abraham meanwhile remained mute, and never once said even a passing word into a microphone, much less sat down for an interview. Traversing the ten yards between his car and his apartment took several minutes. Questions and invectives would be shouted from the brew of reporters and activists. The frenzy that would erupt at the sight of Abraham appearing in his doorway sounded like several blocks' worth of neighbors rushing from their houses in unison to bray at each other over years' worth of pent up grievances and to snap photographs of each other's misdemeanors. Drake held his breath every time he watched Abraham take that walk, convinced someone was going to take a shot at him, either by gun, blunt object, or fist. Protection came unintentionally via the circle of cameras and the people attached to them that formed a fairly impenetrable perimeter around him that went where he went, keeping the most crazed-looking of the protestors in the margins. The exhibitionists would satiate their need to leave a mark by pelting his car with food items and paint products as he pulled away.

Drake continued to stop by every few days and monitor the size of the pack. It finally started to dwindle as weeks turned into a month. The camera crews and video journalists were the first to give up, as they had to find new monsters to tap on the windows of their audience. Their disappearance caused some consternation for Drake, as his old friend now no longer had his movable bunker to escort him between his car door and his apartment door, and the stragglers who remained from the ranks of the protestors looked like they had very little to lose by taking a chance at infamy. Drake comforted himself in knowing that Abe could protect himself just fine, and that the unnerving creatures who stalked him were more afraid of him than he was of them. Nonetheless he braced himself for news of Abe's murder in between his visits to the site.

All lanes were open once more, the traffic regaining its speed and scarcity, so in order to remain inconspicuous Drake had to stay in his car and park a few units down the block across the street.

At least he thought he was being inconspicuous. Since there was much less to see than previously, he was compelled to provide himself other reasons for making the drive from Sacramento. One Sunday morning while checking the Monterey real estate listings online to see if his parents' house had sold, he noticed that the realtor was conducting an open house. Drake decided to take a tour and visit some of their favorite childhood hangouts, then swing by Abe's building on the way back.

He teetered around the tide pools not far from their old home, the sea life looking the same as always, in spite of being dozens if not hundreds of generations removed from the life they had teased and captured as children while Abraham's mother would look on. The house, by contrast, seemed so different thanks to its lifelessness. It was like finding the tide pools empty of species, just water between rocks. The room he shared with Abe was indeed a room, and nothing more. Their presence had left no physical reminders anywhere in the house. It had been repainted, the carpet steam cleaned, the floors shined, the light fixtures replaced, anything that had leaned in a distinct direction in terms of taste had been replaced with something neutral. It was designed to portray a blank canvas onto which prospective buyers could project their fantasies, and it worked. It was future-oriented, its past hidden under a layer of accommodation.

Even the smells had been cleansed from the air. He could not detect the slightest hint of Marisol's cooking, the chili verde, poblano, and tomatillo sauces which were part of any meal at any time of day and kept the house fragrant and their sinuses clear. He stood in the kitchen and wondered if her style had been so aggressive to overcompensate for the fact she wasn't really Mexican, or if she had been putting her own cultural flair into the dishes to create something unique. There were all kinds of things he would never know about two of the most important people in his life, which is what bothered him the most when he pondered all that had been hidden during his upbringing. The stunning revelation that the whole country was convulsing over had really only stung him briefly, upon first learning about it, and since then Drake had found it fascinating. He discovered that he still loved them as much as he ever had, and now wanted to understand them.

So as much it pained him to see them pilloried into caricatures by the givers and receivers of a voracious news and entertainment cycle, he did appreciate the initial point of fact that the fury revolved around: that there was more to Abe and his mother than he knew about, a life of their own apart from Drake and his family that was as absorbing as a secret could be. He therefore found himself feeling oddly grateful to whomever leaked the story.

As he sat in his car and watched the dregs of the once-mighty throng mill about the front of Abe's building, he wondered if the word had been spread by any of the agents with whom he had been communicating, if their embarrassment at having been duped by Abe had inspired Agent Garcia or one of his cronies to lash out. Drake had never heard from them again after delivering the news from Samantha regarding the phantom flight from Mexico. It was as if they felt they had one shot, like luring a stray cat into a cage, and if the trap door wasn't shut in time and the cat got out, that option was done. Drake assumed the other options would be much more severe, which is why he felt the need to check in on Abe as often as he could.

There was a stirring amongst the remnants. Abe had opened his door and was on his way outside. But rather than head towards his car, he walked across the driveway to the sidewalk. The protestors were thrown for a loop, their shouts cut off in mid-sentence and their signs lowered as they recalibrated where they needed to move to surround him with their slogans. Abe stood on the curb and let a couple of cars fly by at highway speeds before crossing, leaving the frustrated gathering behind to pace frantically and howl like dogs stuck on shore watching their owner take a swim. Drake laughed at the sight, but soon tensed up when he realized that Abe was veering in his direction.

He thought of driving away, but lately had spent too much time feeling spineless and wanted to regain a sense of dignity. His goal ultimately was to re-connect with Abraham anyway, he just hadn't expected it to be now, so soon, and he hadn't prepared anything to say. He straightened up and tried to create some body language that would inspire some fortitude. He ran through some options for an opening line as Abraham, meanwhile, appeared more determined with each step and fully aware of what he wanted to say, at least until he reached the center line of the street, at which point he seemed to go from ascending to descending, his steps becoming more measured and the steel melting from his expression as his squint turned from intimidating to inquisitive.

"Drake?" he said when he reached the car, as though trying to convince himself.

Abe's shift into timidity took Drake by surprise, leaving them equally stunned. "I thought you saw me."

"I saw your car," Abe said. "You start to notice people sitting in parked cars when you're in my position."

They sized each other up while having a hard time making eye contact. Drake looked across the street at the motley pack. They seemed ready to wade in and catch up. And though they appeared to be more loud than dangerous, it was still worth fleeing them in the interest of having a conversation.

"You want to go someplace quiet?" Drake suggested.

Abraham looked over his shoulder. "Sure, why not? The cameras are all gone." He went around to the passenger side and climbed in. "Just think what the photos of our reunion would be worth."

Drake started the car. "If any of them had any patience they would have gotten their stories straight."

"Oh, I don't know," Abe contemplated. "I've found some of the versions to be much more interesting than the real thing."

"Of course you do," said Drake as he pulled away from the curb and left the desperate herd behind. "You get to come across as the evil genius. I'm always the naïve dunce."

Abe chuckled. "So where are we going?"

"No idea. I wasn't expecting to hang out. Hungry?"

"Sure. Wherever is fine with me. As long as you run in and pick it up."

"People recognize me too, you know."

"But do they stalk you?"

"Fair enough; I'll buy."

"Thanks. I left my wallet in my apartment."

"I figured."

"Let's get some burritos and bring them to that spot on the riverbank."

"I guess it's early enough that we won't run into any drunken teenagers."

"Perfect. That way we can make out afterwards."

"Nah; I'll have onion breath."

Abe shrugged. "I don't mind, but if it bothers you that much, your loss."

They drove in silence for a while. Drake started to feel uncomfortable now that the verbal towel-snapping was over and he was bound to focus on the weightier issues he was determined to raise.

"It's good to see you, Abe."

"Thanks, Dee. Good to see you, too."

Drake took a mental deep breath and girded himself for his next maneuver. "I know this sounds weird, what with all the fanatics lurking in front of your apartment, and you being the most hated man in America..."

"I think Mohammed is more hated than me..."

"Possibly; is it true that you guys called him The Prophet?"

"The peons called him The Prophet. We were tight so I just called him Prophet."

"Dude..."

"There's a history there, all right? Not a healthy one, but there was a time when I felt like he was all I had."

"Well, that kind of leads me to what I was going to say," Drake turned off of the wide industrial boulevard that Abe lived on and onto the more narrow and crowded street that ran through the business district. "Again, as goofy as it may sound, you seem to be in a better place than when I last saw you. Does that make any sense?"

"Actually, it does." Abe smiled. "Thank you for noticing."

"You just seem so calm in the middle of all this, so easygoing and at peace. Which is why I'm hoping you'll be able to forgive me." Drake was relieved that he was driving while confessing. It provided a distraction that kept him from getting too caught up in a moment he would have preferred not to face.

"That was years ago, Dee," Abe consoled him. "We were teenagers. What teenager doesn't screw up?"

"I'm not talking about that," Drake said, his voice thinning out slightly. He paused as he pulled into the cramped parking lot in front of the restaurant and maneuvered his way into a spot. He turned off the engine and looked over at Abe, who had remained silent, apparently sensing that Drake was not looking forward to saying what he wanted to say next, and deciding it was best to let him say it at his own pace. Drake took a deep breath and exhaled. "I sent Samantha your way to try and get some information from you. And once she started to spend time with you, she didn't want to do that; she was convinced you were innocent. She was really enjoying being with you again. But I pushed her."

He tried to read Abraham for any outward signs of his thoughts on the issue, but found nothing. Abe just looked at him serenely. Drake continued.

"I've been working for the Department of Justice, well, interning there, maybe you heard..."

Abe nodded. Drake forged ahead.

"And I was approached by this guy from the DHS. He told me about your background, and knew about our friendship, or, you know, how we grew up together..."

"Our friendship," Abe confirmed.

"Thanks," Drake smiled self-consciously, "Yes, our friendship. And anyway he promised me some money and even more importantly, some career advancement if I cooperated. He also implied that my career would stall if I didn't play along. At least, that's the impression I got. Maybe I was reading too much into it. I don't even know anymore. And I didn't feel like I was up for lying to your face, or that you would even want to see me again, so that's when I got the bright idea to use Samantha. Oh God, Abe..."

"It's okay, Drake," Abe reached over and put a hand on his shoulder. "I hardly have room to judge. Who was the first one to keep secrets?"

Drake looked over at him and was almost certain that whatever affection he had for Abe when they were growing up together was now surpassed by the love he felt for him at this moment. Especially considering how incomparable their deceptions were.

"But you weren't spying on me," Drake reminded him. "You just didn't tell me some things. Some big things, yes, but you weren't out to get me."

"But I never offered you the truth," Abe sat back and took his hand off of Drake's shoulder so he could gesture as he spoke. "In fact, you finally heard it from someone else. You, on the other hand, approached me about what you did. You told me yourself. Not long after it happened, too. I had years to tell you and I never did."

Drake stared out the front windshield for a moment and blew a soft laugh through his nose. "You're right. I guess I am pretty great."

"The greatest," Abe followed his lead. "Out of all the snitches out there, you have the most integrity, by far."

"And if that bust down in Mexico was real, and you had gone to jail, I totally would have visited you at some point, probably."

"See? That's the difference between you and other informants: you only narc on people you care about."

"It's why I got into the business."

"Feels good, though, doesn't it?" Abe kept the tone light while re-directing it towards a sincere item, "Having things out in the open, being honest."

"Are you saying we're 'keeping it real'?"

"We are keeping it so real."

"And you're right," Drake finally joined him in sincerity. "It feels good."

"I had my realization when Mom's old flame Khalil offered me a deal to roll over on Mohammed."

"I knew it!" Drake exclaimed. "So he did drive her over the border."

"Well...yes." Abe was slightly perplexed.

"And he did love her. I could tell in those interviews."

"Did you even hear the rest of what I said about him?"

"Of course," Drake's enthusiasm vanished. "I'm just pretending I didn't."

"You just experienced the glory of unburdening yourself of secrets and dishonesty and now you're going to get high and mighty on me over my decision to do likewise?"

"But he's a horrible person."

"Indeed he is," Abe agreed immediately. "Not only that, the offer was to fly me to Algiers to be with Mom once I gave the feds enough to build a case."

"Is this supposed to impress me? All that you left on the table for the sake of honesty?"

"Maybe I'm just extremely loathe to being one of those grown men who live with their mother."

"Come on, Abe," Drake was not ready to follow Abe's lead into lightness. "How can you pass up the chance to put that man away?"

Abraham sighed and stared straight ahead. "How about we get those burritos?"

Drake reluctantly gave up his interrogation. "Sure. You want carnitas?"

"Al pastor if they have it."

"Be right back."

Drake returned several minutes later with the food and two bottles of what he seemed to recall was Abe's favorite brand of horchata. Abe acknowledged that he remembered correctly, and the peace offering softened the edges of the silence that filled the car as they drove to the riverbank.

They headed west past the city limits and onto Highway 68, as though driving back to Monterey, but turned off before exiting the valley, catching the river as it curved to make its way to the ocean. The riverbed was a sandy collection of spacious puddles with wispy trails of water flowing between them, most of the water running underground, making its way to the sea out of sight.

Small talk ensued as they sat in the car with the doors open on the solid ground where the water would crest after a couple days' worth of heavy rain. Abraham shared stories of his initiations and travels in the name of Prophet, Drake poked fun at the minutiae and tedium of his studies and internship, as there was really no way to make them exciting. They finished their food with a ceremonial crumbling of the bags, straightening themselves out from the car and wandering into the dry bank with their half-drunk bottles in hand. Abe spoke of his last meeting with his mother, how he was agitated and crass the whole time and never mentioned that he loved her. They talked about whether learning of his true ethnic identity had much bearing on his self-perception, or if the obscuring of it had the greater impact. Drake piggy-backed on that theme and discussed his reactions to the truth: his initial shock, and eventual captivation. They compared what it was like to hear it from someone you love, as opposed to a DHS agent.

"Was there anything in particular they wanted you to get information about?" Abe asked, "A specific case?"

Drake took a sip from his bottle and adjusted his perspective from the sharing of emotions to the sharing of events. "Yes."

That's all he could say, as he was both intrigued and fearful of knowing whether Abe had really been involved in a murder.

Abe waited for the follow through. And he waited.

"Are you kidding?" he said.

"No," Drake kept his eyes on the shallow patches of water swirling faintly between the grit and the weeds. "They wanted to know if you had anything to do with Lane Hoff's disappearance. They said they had some promising leads linking you to his murder, and wanted help sealing the deal."

He glanced over to get a peek at Abe's reaction. None was forthcoming, as Abe joined him in staring at the mottled riverbed.

"Obviously I hadn't been able to give them anything about that," Drake carried on, trying to seduce Abe into speaking, "As your conversations with Samantha testify to. So they got antsy, and I did too, I suppose, since I thought my career was depending on it; and so when I relayed the Mexico plans I guess they figured it was better than nothing, and a chance to get you into custody for something, and they could take it from there."

He left it at that and waited to see if Abe was interested in pursuing the point. As the time went tensely by, he thought about how nice it would be to have the sound of a strong current from the river to sublimate the silence. Abraham finally broke it.

"The night Lane Hoff died was pretty much the end of my relationship with Mohammed."

He paused, and Drake wondered if that was going to be the extent of it. But then Abe pressed on.

"We were real tight for a while. Like I said before, I felt like he was all I had, and that he was providing me with a future of some sort. A lot of those experiences I was telling you about, they were all part of grooming me to take over the operation. It was pretty exciting at the time, I have to admit. One night he invited me out to fire off some rounds, something we did on occasion for fun. We went out to the homestead where Mom's old rental house was, I figured it was still deserted, and sure enough it was."

Abe appeared to be losing himself in the memory, gazing out across the river and at the mountains beyond as though Drake was no longer there.

"So we proceed to light up the foreman's old house and some of the surrounding trees, must have squeezed out several dozen rounds between us. Then he starts rehashing the time back when I was around ten or eleven and he was trying to get me used to the sight of blood, and killing, by bringing me to this slaughterhouse, and how he tried to help me make the move into people and blew it by using a dog as like a transitional step. He was sort of apologizing, it seemed, but then he brought me over to his car and made this little speech about how it's actually easier to kill the right person than a dog. So he pops open the trunk and there's Lane Hoff bound and gagged and squirming and screaming for his life."

Drake tried to remain expressionless in case Abe turned to face him.

"Or maybe he made the speech about the dog after he closed the trunk. I think he brought up the podcast first, tried to get me all riled up about Mr. Hoff before revealing the big surprise in the trunk. Anyway, he tells me to follow him and we head out to the coast, up through Castroville to Highway One. I assume the plan is to kill him and ditch the body in the ocean somehow. Sure enough, we drive out to a spot a bit south of Moss Landing. We drive off road for a while till we're close to shore. We get out and he makes the official announcement: yes, we're going to kill him, or more to the point I am going to kill him, as some sort of final rite of passage or something. Then I'm supposed to wait there with Lane's corpse while Mohammed drives up to the harbor at Moss Landing and grabs a boat one of his associates lets him borrow. The water is practically as calm as a lake, so he's clearly had this thing mapped out for a while now, waiting for the tides to be right so he can pull the boat easily to shore and pick me up, or pick us up, if you want to count a dead body as a member of your boarding party."

Drake almost laughed at Abe's line, thinking perhaps that was the intent, or that it would help motivate Abe to continue. But he decided to keep quiet, and watch Abe as people watch a death-defying stunt or circus trick, breathlessly awaiting the outcome.

"But when Mohammed opened the trunk, Mr. Hoff was already dead. Must have suffocated or banged his head one too many times on the way there. Maybe had a heart attack or something, died of fear. And Mohammed is furious. All that work for nothing. He rants and raves for a minute or so like some guy whose team just lost the Super Bowl on a bad call or a missed field goal. Then he seems to find a silver lining. He settles down and tells me to drag the body down to the shore and he'll be there soon with the boat. He drives away and I do what he says, a little freaked out by having to pull Mr. Hoff by his ankles over the dirt, and even more freaked out by having to carry him over the rocks down to the beach, but still relieved more than anything that I didn't have to kill him. We get out on that boat, though, and things get real disgusting."

Abe stopped staring out into the space in front of him and turned to face Drake, no longer recalling events, but wanting to say something about them.

"I'll spare you too many details. But what I learned that night is the best way to dispose of a body is to bring it way offshore where the big fish hunt, then open it up like you're cleaning a fish, from crotch to throat, and let everything hang out to attract the marine life. They'll do the rest."

Drake felt as though he now had permission to speak. "And I take it he made you do all that stuff?"

Abe nodded. "It saved the night from being a total loss, I guess."

He looked at Drake as if to see how his punch line, or perhaps his confession as a whole, went over. All Drake could say is "I'm sorry."

Abe added a postscript. "I got a bit moody for a while afterwards. I don't know what the accepted time limit is to brood over such a thing, but apparently I exceeded it, and Mohammed demoted me, I guess that's how you'd describe it. He actually wanted to make amends not long ago, and he seemed genuine enough. He talked about utilizing my strengths instead of trying to mold me into something I wasn't. So his intent was still to use me, but that's life." He stopped as if intending to make that philosophical resignation his conclusion.

But he wasn't quite done after all. "Then I mentioned Samantha and his radar went up."

Drake didn't know how to take that late addition. He looked quizzically at Abe, who returned his look with a reassuring one of his own.

"It was for the best, Drake," he said soothingly. "He almost pulled me back in, just when I was starting to realize maybe I had other options. Of course, that was before I got famous."

"I've been wondering who did that," Drake said, finishing his bottle now that he felt like he was breathing again.

"Could be anyone," Abe shrugged, also tilting back the rest of his drink, as though wrestling with his past made him just as thirsty as an actual wrestling match.

"I was thinking it was one of my guys," Drake said. "They seemed pretty frustrated towards the end of our partnership. I never even got any money or job interviews, which serves me right."

"Or Khalil, since I ruined his grand design; or Mohammed, in order to get rid of me once and for all...the list goes on." Abe was about to throw his bottle into the distance, but stopped himself. "What's the use?" he said. "It won't even break. Just make a thud on the dirt somewhere. No fun in that."

They stood and watched as the sun drew closer to the mountains on the western horizon and started to dim.

"So what are you going to do?" Drake asked.

"Not sure," Abe said. "Mohammed doesn't want me working for him; too much attention. And I can't imagine anything else I could do or anyplace I could go where I wouldn't be driven away." He paused and held up his bottle, as though raising a toast, but instead simply studied the way the sun shined through the glass, "Maybe when all of this fades."

They walked back to the car and started their return to Abe's apartment. Drake thought it was going to be another quiet one, but Abe spoke up as they re-entered the city limits.

"Remember when you and I took Mrs. Judson out for coffee after school one day because we wanted to talk more about that class discussion we had about the dialogue between Socrates and Crito? That reading she assigned us?"

"I remember tagging along because I wanted to look smart and maybe get some extra credit from her," Drake said.

"So I don't suppose you remember what that was about, then?"

"I couldn't even keep up at the time, Abe. I just narrowed my eyebrows and nodded a lot."

"It was about Socrates' wealthy friend Crito offering to spring him from prison; he had financed some fool-proof breakout. And Socrates refused."

"Oh, I see," Drake feigned a glow of recognition. "You're going to make me understand why you didn't turn on Mohammed."

"You don't answer injustice with injustice," Abe ignored Drake's sarcasm. "That was his point. And you seemed to agree with that idea back then."

"I just told you, Abe, I was there to kiss ass and drink coffee."

Drake thought for sure that he was going to reply with something dry and witty, but Abe just smiled and leaned back in his seat.

He didn't say anything else until they were within view of the lurkers keeping each other company in front of his apartment.

"Drop me off here so they don't rush the car."

Drake complied, pulling over about a block from the building on the same side of the street. He was about to turn off the engine, but Abe was already making moves towards leaving. He gestured toward their bags and bottles on the floor by his feet.

"Could you take care of our garbage?" he asked Drake.

"Um, sure."

"Thanks. It was good to see you, Dee." Abe reached for the door.

"Wait a second," Drake barked, temporarily halting Abe. "I'm sorry I don't understand your decision. Forgive me for having some problems with you allowing that beast to roam free."

"It's okay," Abe replied calmly. "I didn't really expect you to. I wouldn't expect anyone to if it ever got out, which may very well happen if they ever want to re-ignite this story." Abe then laughed a little, "Whoever 'they' are."

Abe proceeded once more to get out of the car.

"Do you want to hang out again sometime?" Drake leaned over to ask him before Abe shut the door.

Abe bent over to respond. "I can't."

"Why?"

"I've got my own plans for Mohammed."

And with that Abraham shut the door and gave the hood of Drake's car a friendly couple of pats as he walked down the sidewalk towards his building. His hate club that awaited him noticed his approach and rushed to jeer him. Abraham glanced over his shoulder at Drake and gave him an exaggerated look of despair meant to make him laugh.

But instead Drake felt like crying. He sat there helplessly as the crowd surrounded Abraham and spluttered abuse at him. This is the part where I get out of the car and catch up to him, Drake thought. This is the part where I punch a couple of those freaks and vow to fight by his side, no matter what happens. This is the part where I tell him he's the best friend I ever had.

Really, though, it was the part where he watched his friend peacefully walk through the venom that surrounded him and disappear into his apartment. It was the part where the crowd then turned their attention to Drake and started to sprint in his direction, and he sped away before they could reach him or recognize him. It was the part where he would never see Abraham again.

Once on the freeway he wished he never had to stop. He wanted to keep driving and never have to set foot on the ground again. He wanted to float just above it with complete control over what he heard and where he went. The thought of having to get out of the car at some point filled him with sadness.

Chapter Twenty-Eight: Anywhere

I see him here about one night every three months. The timing is that precise, too: every three months within about a day or two of the last visit. As the years went by and the pattern became apparent, I did some math involving the average walking speed of a man roughly his age, looked at a map, referenced some towns he had mentioned visiting, and estimated what his route might be. It turns out to be a rather impressive distance, if my calculations are even remotely close. He claims he has to keep moving, that people are after him.

Which is just the kind of talk I often encounter from those we feed here; many of them are mentally ill by birth, others are driven mad by their circumstances. They either can't take care of themselves, or can, but are working harder than ever before to do so. Therefore the paranoia runs pretty consistently down the line they stand in to wait for their meal, and around the tables of the church fellowship hall we use for our nightly servings.

But his talk always strikes me as legitimate. He keeps himself relatively clean. The beard is standard-issue homeless but somewhat groomed; his clothes are worn but faintly fresh smelling; and his own scent is mild as well, supporting his claim that he has a network of Laundromats and locker rooms that he utilizes along his route.

He credits his training for the ability to establish patterns and the discipline to maintain them. And apparently the people who paid for his training are the ones who are after him. Not that he constantly mumbles about these people, as the illegitimately paranoid are prone to do. He can entertain most any timeless subject—faith, morality, purpose, love—with a stunning array of references to augment his point: the sacred texts of each great religion and the theologians who studied them, the most pivotal spiritual and economic philosophers, artists from every medium who contemplated the human condition. Current events tend to elude him, given his perpetual mobility, but part of why I appreciate seeing him come through the door and stand in line is knowing I can run some recent items by him and get his take on how they fit in to the eternal framework. Once he finishes his dinner, of course.

I gave up being self-conscious about bothering him and me slacking on my duties for the night pretty soon after discovering his wealth of knowledge. It's only about four times per year, after all, a visit for each season essentially, and he doesn't seem to mind, and I'm a volunteer. (I can't stand when my fellow volunteers use that same excuse for doing lousy work, but I rationalize my usage of it by noting that they invoke it constantly, whereas I only raise it every ninety days.)

The exact nature of his training became more apparent during his winter visit last year. He commented that a beard came in handy when it was cold, living the way he lives, and how ironic it was that he had grown one now as opposed to when he was supposedly in service to God and should not have been shaving, but it was necessary to shave back then to fit in with the population at large, as it was the kind of religious order that craved attention on a large scale while avoiding it on a daily basis.

"And trying to convert people through the spectacular, through fear, rather than living an exemplary life wasn't even the biggest paradox," he told me over his tater-tots and meatloaf that evening.

"Are you telling me you were a terrorist?" I said, feeling like a contestant on a game show.

He acted like he didn't hear me and proceeded to take a couple more bites of the canned green beans that made the night's offering a well-rounded meal. Then he propped up his posture, as though his lower half could be in the lotus position, and adopted the heavy accent of a sage in the Middle Eastern desert. "Most everyone wants to see the face of God. Some try to get there by loving others, some by killing and maiming them. Who's to say who's right?"

His smile was only apparent thanks to his beard rising at the edges, but I was still digesting the information and wasn't ready to join in. We left it at that, and I had some time to ponder his revelation and consider ways to pry more out of him come spring.

He anticipated my curiosity, however, when that night arrived, and even came across as somewhat eager to talk about it; to a point, at least. I'm still flattered to think he remembered where our previous conversation had left off, and that he saw me as worthy of his declaration. Of course he may have had confessors sprinkled along his path to whom he unburdened himself regularly as far as I knew.

His sagacity faded a bit when the discussion became more personal; deflection and deferment started to characterize his thinking as opposed to when he was holding court on more abstract topics. For example, he offered me something of an assurance, I guess you could call it, that he had only killed one person, and it was the man who taught him to kill, as though it was therefore justifiable.

"In fact," he recalled, "when I was about to pull the trigger, he urged me on, imploring me to do it, claiming it was about time I vindicated his training. When I hesitated he started calling me every synonym imaginable for the word 'weak'. After I shot him, he may have even said 'my work here is done,' but sometimes I feel like I may be projecting that line in there for effect. I can't remember exactly."

I gathered it was time to back off, as it was clear at this point he did not have others along his passage who had heard this as well. We each seemed to figure such an admission was enough for one visit. We shifted focus to examples of historical and literary violence, and when it was perhaps permissible. In the meantime I was already anxiously awaiting his summer stopover, hoping I had not scared him away in search of an alternate route.

I ruminated on his name, or at least what he told me it was, and what he told me had happened. Something sounded familiar, but

I couldn't make any connections on my own. So, tired of spinning around in my chair at work one afternoon, I typed in some various key words until I came upon a combination that hit me with that old case of the anchor baby terrorist which I had long forgotten about. I re-visited the headlines, read some articles, watched some videos, and remembered the panic it had created amongst my parents and their friends (my friends and I being too young at the time to succumb). The photos of Abraham seemed to resemble that of our tri-monthly visitor at the Good Samaritan dining hall; he was of course younger and beardless in the pictures. I printed one of them and with a black Sharpie fine point drew a beard and some age lines to produce my amateur update, and while looking more like a defaced poster at a bus stop than a police sketch, it did confirm my suspicions.

I had never even known about the cliffhanger conclusion of his news cycle domination; all I knew is that our parents stopped talking about him. Perhaps they were disappointed that it didn't end in some sort of conviction, or better yet, a dramatic shoot-out or tense stand-off. They must have been so dissatisfied that it all culminated in an abandoned car found a few hundred yards off the Pacific Coast Highway south of Moss Landing, California. The car was registered in Abraham's name and had been spotted leaving a business believed to be a front for his boss, Mohammed, with Mohammed in the passenger seat. A large dog, a German Shepherd, was rescued from the trunk. It was exhausted but alive, with some bruising from its earlier struggles to try and get out. There was outrage expressed about the dog abuse, so much outrage that the disappearance of the two men became secondary to a large segment of the public. The dog was nursed back to health and adopted, people hanging on updates of its recovery and the adoption process, in which hundreds of people applied to take him in and were whittled down by virtue of a quasi-reality show, with the final episode garnering huge ratings. I actually remember that show pretty vividly, but hadn't realized the connection to the case that weeks earlier had held the nation in the grip of panic.

Mohammed's blood, meanwhile, had been found in and around the car, and a boat that belonged to one of Mohammed's associates was missing right along with the two of them. Mohammed's lawyer, Khalil-something, claimed that they had escaped overseas, that they met up with a larger boat further out in the ocean and sunk the motorboat they had taken from Moss Landing. The lawyer, who seemed to be about the only person anyone bothered to interview about the case, came across on video as genuinely excited about it, which would have led me to believe it was true at the time, but now strikes me as odd knowing that he was losing such a lucrative client.

The dearth of comments left below the stories suggested that, as had been the case in my neighborhood, the public at large was simply not as interested in hearing about them vanishing as they had been in hearing about how they were going to instigate the end of Western civilization. Those who did offer their thoughts on the message boards were quite engaged, though, and formed something of a close-knit society of theorists on the subject, sharing their reconstructions of what happened that night and where everyone ended up. The cultish devotion of the Abraham chasers even led to their own website, which still appears to be fairly active based on the date tags of the comments.

The ideas on what happened tend to fall into four camps, with the specifics of each version varying between members of each camp: the dog-as-hostage group (the German Shepherd belonged to one of their enemies and the exchange went horribly wrong somehow), the dog-bites-Mohammed group (Abraham set the dog in the trunk as a trap), the guard dog group (it was protecting something valuable that the two of them then took with them when they made their escape), and the one I find most promising, the dog-as-decoy group (Abraham told Mohammed that the noise in the back was someone he was going to kill, and once they reached the spot, Abraham killed Mohammed instead and dumped the body at sea).

As for the "Where Are They Now?" portion, while most in the online community agree Mohammed is probably dead, a small but vocal segment believe he survived and is in fact living in another country, and they share second-hand accounts consisting of someone they know seeing someone who appeared to be Mohammed in a hookah bar in Amsterdam or driving a shark tour boat in Cape Town. And since all of them agree Abraham is still alive, the accounts of his at-largeness are myriad and disparate and bizarre, at times going so far as to posit plastic surgery and hiding in plain sight as a city councilman in Dearborn, Michigan, or living above a falafel café in Queens owned and frequented by people who cover for him.

I've had a few people at the dining hall over the years tell me that they were various figures who are believed by many to have gone into hiding—an Elvis Presley here, a Jesus Christ there—but it makes sense that the one time I apparently truly met one, he was cagey about his identity; they're trying to hide, after all. I consider posting my encounter on the Abraham chasers' website every so often, not that anyone would believe my account any more than the others, but I always decide not to when I think of my last conversation with him.

Summer came and much to my relief he adhered to his schedule and showed up. He was definitely more guarded upon seeing me, however, and I was fully aware of the need for finesse, which was difficult because of how insatiable my curiosity had become by that point. We spoke of nothing beyond weather and road conditions, and the notion started to creep up on me that he was sufficiently wary to consider changing his path anyway and avoid me in the future, so I may as well cast caution aside and go for it while I had the chance.

I asked him if he is the Abraham of past hype and present lore.

He stared down at his tray for a while, as though the mashed potatoes may have been communicating an answer through the contours of its lumps.

"I was an investment," he said at last. "People had high hopes for me; different people, different hopes. And instead of satisfying one, I disappointed all."

I thought he was done, and was about to get up and leave him alone, but he added one more time: "I was an investment."

Before leaving I measured things I might say, questions I might ask, but estimated my best chance at ever seeing him again was to let it go, and demonstrate my resignation on the issue via silence, and perhaps an understanding glance when he looked my way. I practiced that glance as I worked behind the line serving the others. But he never did look. He ate, he left, and three months later there was no autumn visit, and none in the several months since.

I still volunteer, but no longer at just the one dining hall. I spend time at a variety of charities throughout the city, and even a few in the suburbs and in the somewhat rural areas beyond. I tend to look very carefully at the faces of the people shuffling along the side of the freeway as I drive past them, and of those slouched over picnic benches in the park and looking out the windows of Laundromats.

I want to be certain of what I think I know.

Also by Sean Boling

The Current Mr. Orr
Devin's Best Afterlife
Once in Two Lifetimes
Revenge and Wellness in the Sweet Hereafter

Standalone
Cut Flowers
Abraham the Anchor Baby Terrorist
Pigs and Other Living Things
The Summer of Our Foreclosure
Satellite Campus
A Charter to That Other Place
The Latest Version of My Love Story
Show Them What They Won
The Name Field
Should
Moral Adjacent
Over Here We Have

About the Author

Sean lives with his family in Templeton, California. He teaches English at Cuesta College.